What is Hidden

Praise for
WHAT IS HIDDEN

"*What Is Hidden* is a fresh, unique tale full of romance, intrigue, excitement, and a woman torn from the life she's always known. Skidmore paints exquisitely detailed masks and a vivid world that's nothing like you've imagined. She's created a world I'd like to see, and characters I'd like to know in this tale reminiscent of Cinderella."

—CINDY C BENNETT
author of *Rapunzel Untangled*

"Intrigue, vengeance, love—all hidden beneath the shadows of the masks Evie is forced to wear. *What Is Hidden* will get your heart pumping and your mind racing."

—STEVE WESTOVER
author of *A Nothing Named Silas*

What is Hidden

LAUREN SKIDMORE

SWEETWATER
BOOKS
An imprint of Cedar Fort, Inc.
Springville, Utah

This is a work of fiction. The characters, names, incidents, places, and dialogue are products of the author's imagination, and are not to be construed as real. The opinions and views expressed herein belong solely to the author and do not necessarily represent the opinions or views of Cedar Fort, Inc. Permission for the use of sources, graphics, and photos is also solely the responsibility of the author.

ISBN 13: 978-1-4621-1429-0

Published by Sweetwater Books, an imprint of Cedar Fort, Inc.
2373 W. 700 S., Springville, UT 84663
Distributed by Cedar Fort, Inc., www.cedarfort.com

LIBRARY OF CONGRESS CATALOGING-IN-PUBLICATION DATA

Skidmore, Lauren, 1986- author.
 What is hidden / Lauren Skidmore.
     pages cm
  Summary: In the island nation of Venesia, where going barefaced into society is scandalous, mask-maker Evie's life is changed forever when the bandit Chameleon kills her father, destroys her home, and brands her face with his own dangerous criminal mark.
 ISBN 978-1-4621-1429-0 (pbk.)
 [1. Revenge--Fiction. 2. Masks--Fiction. 3. Kings, queens, rulers, etc.--Fiction 4. Social classes--Fiction 5. Love--Fiction.] I. Title.
 PZ7.S62634Wh 2014
 [Fic]--dc23
                                    2013050898

Cover design by Kristen Reeves
Cover design © 2014 by Lyle Mortimer
Edited and typeset by Melissa J. Caldwell

Printed in the United States of America

10 9 8 7 6 5 4 3 2 1

For anyone who has worn a mask

ONE

"*I* CAN FEEL YOU STARING AT ME," I SAID, NOT bothering to look up from my work. I was putting the finishing flourishes on a particularly complex design and didn't want to lose my place. I'd been up since dawn working on this mask. The early morning sun provided the perfect lighting through my window, and hearing the soft cadence of the canal waters greeting its walls and the distant calls of the seagulls relaxed me. The mask—a doctor's—was extremely intricate, and it wasn't often that my father trusted me to do this kind of work, even if I *was* out of my apprenticeship. My father might be a well-respected artisan, but I still needed to prove myself. Our family didn't have generations behind its name to rely on as other mask makers did.

I needed all the calm the early morning could afford to give me.

"You can't feel a stare, Evie," my intruder said. Aiden.

"I can feel yours," I retorted.

My friend laughed, his voice filling the room. I sighed and put down the paintbrush, casting a forlorn look at the mask in front of me. I wasn't going to get any more work done now. Although, as far as intruders went, they couldn't get much better than Aiden. I felt like I'd known him forever, though it had been only a few years. After one fateful day by the canals when I'd saved him from being hopelessly lost, he wormed his way into becoming my best friend without me realizing it until it was too late. The scoundrel.

"Can I help you with something?" I asked, turning to him.

"It's the first of the month," he said.

"Why, yes it is. Congratulations," I teased. "I'm glad to know some of you nobles are able to keep track of what day it is."

"You said you would take me to the market," he pleaded, ignoring my gibe and shifting from foot to foot like an excited puppy.

"What are you, twelve? You've been to the market before."

"Yes, but I've been in so many never-ending lectures and meetings lately I feel like I'm going to die of boredom."

"Are these educational lectures or have you been caught sneaking out at night again?"

His face was the picture of indignant innocence for only a few seconds before it split into a wide grin. "I might have stolen a few pies from the kitchen."

"A few?"

"Fine. A half dozen and then eaten myself sick. That doesn't really matter." He waited patiently for me to finish laughing before continuing. "They were really good pies."

"I should hope so." I pushed away from my desk to hang up the mask to dry and clean my brushes. "Let me finish here and then we can go."

A short while later, Aiden led the way to the part of town where the one-manned stall boats of the markets lined the canal waters on one side and the more permanent shops on the other, each one fighting to be more brightly colored than the last. Space was limited, and the narrow storefronts did what they could to get noticed. My favorite sweets shop had a giant dog statue I'd loved to climb on when I was a child, and it smelled like sugar and fried dough.

My own Akita dog, Hachi, trotted alongside us, tail wagging, seemingly glad we weren't taking a water taxi. The little beast always cowered under my skirts anytime we set foot on a boat of any size. It was a bit inconvenient since Venesia was known for two things: the masks we were never seen without and its canals. The canals crisscrossed in a grid pattern across the city, and boats were the primary mode of transportation.

"Come on, Evie. Let's cut through the Naked Square." He tugged my arm, and I made a disgusted face at his nickname for the place where the criminals were punished. "What?" he asked. "That's what it is. Why call it anything else?"

"I don't know. I just don't like that name." It was a fitting enough name, true, but something about it always rubbed me the wrong way.

The official name was the Square of the Accused and the Punished, but most people just called it the Square or, like Aiden, the Naked Square. Its nickname came from the most common form of punishment: a criminal would have his mask and clothes stripped from him and be chained to a wall or placed in the stocks in the middle of the square. Depending on the severity of the crime, he would also be Marked. For petty crimes, the scar from the hot iron brand could be easily covered with a mask or piece of clothing, but the especially serious cases were more painful in the branding method and more difficult to keep concealed by the masks we wear.

"So are we going or not?" Aiden prompted when he saw I wasn't following him.

"You know I don't like going that way."

"I heard the prince is supposed to make an appearance," he said slyly, as if that would tempt me at all.

"So? He'll be covered from head to foot, as always."

Aiden's shoulders slumped. "Normally I'd be happy that you weren't like the girls that fawn over him, but of course the one time it'd be easier for me if you were average, you have to be as contrary and stubborn as always."

I flashed him a wide grin. "I do what I can. Why do you want to go so badly, anyway?"

He groaned. "I just want to make sure no one I know is on the block."

"Really? Is that a common concern of yours?" I asked, a little alarmed.

"No, but you never know who you'll find. Maybe that idiot who keeps shortchanging my man on boots finally got caught."

I sighed. "Fine. Have it your way. Just don't let any recent release grab me or anything, okay?"

He snaked an arm around my waist, pulled me obnoxiously close, squared his shoulders, and winked at me. "Nobody would dare."

I laughed and rolled my eyes as I pushed him a respectable distance away. "Get off me. Everyone knows your bark is worse than your bite. I'd be better off with just Hachi."

The dog whined and looked up at me with big brown eyes. I dropped a kiss to his head and scratched behind his ears. "You're a big, strong dog. You could protect me, couldn't you?"

He wagged his plush tail and barked, appeased. I looked back at Aiden, my chin raised expectantly. He simply rolled his eyes.

"Fine," he said, sighing. "I can see when my services aren't wanted."

As we crossed a canal on the bright red bridge leading to the Square, I could hear shouts and cheers amid the sounds of trumpets and the beat of taiko drums. The prince was about to arrive.

We quickly scrambled closer to get a look; for all I protested and teased Aiden, I did want to catch a glimpse. I stood on my tiptoes when the crowd prevented us from moving any further, and I used Aiden's shoulder to keep my balance. I knew exactly when he spotted the prince, because I felt his muscles tense.

"There he is," he said through clenched teeth, pointing.

I wondered at his sudden change of attitude but was sidetracked by the display before us.

The prince was covered in white from head to toe. White was the symbol of royalty—no one else could afford to bleach the masks so pale or keep their clothes so spotless. His face was completely obscured by the snow-white mask and a piece of fabric was draped over the back of his head. The rest of his clothes were extravagant and covered every inch of his skin—it was forbidden for anyone outside of the royal family to see him. His name (as well as the names of the other members of the royal family) was kept secret. They were simply known as the king, queen, prince, or princess. If their names were ever revealed, I wasn't privy to such an occasion.

To even make a public appearance like this was unusual.

His mask, though, was beautiful. I couldn't call myself an artisan if I didn't notice the workmanship. It was a wonderfully delicate porcelain, with the purest white swan feathers at each eye, and lined with diamonds and pearls. I would give my right hand to watch something like that be created.

The royal family's masks were made in the palace by the finest artisans and with the finest materials. Even though I was a mask maker myself, it was extremely unlikely that I'd ever witness such a process.

I couldn't tell much about the prince himself. He carried himself aggressively and was tall and wiry, but I couldn't even tell the color of his eyes or hair because they were both covered. I wouldn't be able to pick him out of a crowd if he wore normal clothing.

"You think he ever dresses like a regular person and just walks around town?" I asked, my mind still admiring the workmanship of the mask.

"Don't be ridiculous," Aiden scoffed. "As if he'd have the time or the inclination. Would you ever want to leave that palace?" Venesia wasn't a poor nation by any means, but nothing of the city matched the luxury of the palace.

"I guess not," I murmured, trying to get a better look. I wished I had a chance to wear masks like that. My own mask was predominately green, to match my trade and rank as an artisan, and made of simple mâché. Its intricate designs marketed my skills and flattered the oval shape of my face. It covered a modest amount, from my hairline to below my cheekbones.

Suddenly the crowd began shushing each other, and people shifted in front of me until I could see the prince as he raised his hands for silence. He didn't speak, of course. The only ones to hear a member of the royal family speak were the royal family members themselves and one designated Speaker appointed from court.

The Speaker stood next to the prince. She wore a full mask as well, but her eyes were not shrouded like the prince's. Pearls and crushed crystal formed a winding design around her dark eyes, and the sheer lavender fabric that secured her mask created a lovely contrast against her inky curls and brown skin.

As the crowd fell silent, the Speaker's voice rang out strong and clear. This was a voice that possessed the commanding quality that demanded you drop everything and listen—and obey, if you knew what was good for you.

"As you have gathered"—she spoke without introductions, as they were completely unnecessary—"the Crown feels it must make the public aware of a precarious situation. They have chosen this location to announce it, because they feel it will travel quickest by the mouths and ears that pay attention to the execution of our laws, be it for moral reasons or other." She gave no inflection to indicate that she meant the gossips and busybodies that had nothing better to do than hang about the Square in search of a scandal, but the whispers and giggles that coursed through the crowd made it quite clear that they caught the underlying message.

"The situation is thus: a criminal named the Chameleon

is on the loose," she continued, despite the whispers that sprung up again. "He has many masks to his name and uses them to assume the identities of victims or simple fraudulent characters. I am sure you can imagine the dangers in that alone, but there is more. He is not a mask maker gone rogue—he burns the houses of his victims and steals the masks and anything else of value. His preference leans toward full masks of respected ranks and positions. He then uses the stolen mask long enough to escape and then destroys it or uses it to plan his next attack.

"And so it is our duty to warn you and to urge you to warn everyone you know. Do not trust the masks alone. If you have any information, please take it to the authorities at once. You will know it is him by the Mark on his face." She nodded toward the obsidian-faced militia that accompanied her. One man hung a poster on a wall on the east side of the Square filled with other posters and announcements, presumably with a drawing of the Mark and other details for those who could read. The poster was so large that it covered three others. "That is all. Long live the Crown."

With that, she turned to the prince, ready to leave. The prince looked out at the crowd, nodded in our direction, and then disappeared from my view.

"Wow," I said, turning to Aiden. "I'm glad I listened to you for once. What do you make of all that?"

His shoulders were still remarkably tense as he stared after the retreating forms of the prince and his party. "I suppose I'll have to keep you even closer," he finally said, the tension between us vanishing as he grinned down at me. "Can't have someone trying to imitate my lady here."

TWO

*T*HE CARAVAN MARKET OF VENESIA WAS A KALEI-doscope of color. Bright banners, sails, and flags burst from the large ships in the usually scarcely populated harbor set aside for trade, each doing its best to draw attention to itself and pull in the wandering eyes and purses. Each boat became a store and each dock a storefront as the merchants and townspeople descended upon the fresh merchandise. To advertise its wares, each boat used a flag—emerald green for the commercial goods and artistry, crimson red for farmed food from other islands, and cerulean blue for anything out of the sea. Our small island was famous for this market.

Each individual boat was decorated from front to back and top to bottom with more specific signs of what the seller had to offer. As I navigated through the canals and walked along the piers with Hachi trotting at my heels, we passed ships dedicated to foreign books, pets, fruits, and other delicacies. Unlike the smaller boats farther in the city that only sold a particular item or two, such as food or the odd trinket, these ships were stocked close to bursting with everything imaginable.

"So," Aiden asked, sounding more upbeat. He seemed to have shaken off whatever had put him in a sour mood when he saw the prince. "What's on the list today?"

"You're not going to talk about the announcement?" Gossip was already washing over the crowd around us like a tsunami. I could hear snippets of conversation as we walked, each more paranoid than the last.

"No. There's nothing we can do, and I came here to enjoy myself today," he said, squaring his shoulders. "What's on the list?" he repeated.

"Mostly pieces for the balls next month. You know, the usual—peacock feathers, ribbons, maybe some swan feathers. Anything sparkly. That sort of thing."

He nodded. "My sister is all about the swan feathers right now. Makes the mask appear lighter than it is and all of that."

"And we both know how people will do anything to make the color lighter." The lighter the color, the more expensive the dye and, consequently, the higher the wearer's rank.

"Yeah, she's funny like that." I thought he was about to go into a bit of a rant about her, but he didn't say anything more. He found a stick alongside the road to throw for Hachi. He had one younger sister, who was only a few years his junior, but I'd never met her. It was clear he cared a lot about her, though; I could hear it in his voice. She might annoy him to death, but he'd do anything for her.

If I thought about it, that could describe our relationship as well. Not that we had a *relationship*, per se.

"All right, let's get to shopping, then." I led the way into the cluster of green-flagged shops dedicated to the fineries

I was interested in seeing, to distract both myself and my eager companion.

Aiden hovered like he always did, watching me like a hawk as we entered the hull of a ship filled with spools upon spools of ribbon. Once the ships arrived in port, all the cargo was unloaded inside of the ship itself and displayed for customers there. The cargo hold was small and musky, but every inch was covered in fine ribbons from a city in the north famous for its fine weaving.

I took my time, picking out a lovely shimmering pale blue ribbon that was sure to be popular among the older girls looking to catch a suitor's eye. Aiden laughed when I explained my purchase and promptly found a similarly eye-catching spool of emerald green.

I tried not to look too excited as I accepted it and wondered, not for the first time, why he was hanging around. He told me once that he was going to take over his father's business, though he never really got into specifics of what that business was exactly. Most sons followed their father's trade. Even I followed my father's, though I wasn't a son. I also didn't know why Aiden wasn't already in that business; he had to be roughly eighteen, the same age as me, if not a little older. While his mask was predominately the purple of the nobility, it had green trim, so I knew his trade had to be artistry of some sort, but he always claimed talking about it bored him and would quickly change the subject. I could tell he was keeping something from me, but I felt awkward pestering him about it, so I let him keep his secrets. He was nobility—he was born with secrets.

Regardless of who he was, I knew he enjoyed watching me barter for trinkets and materials and bemoaned the fact that he wouldn't have my "feminine wiles" to assist him when it was his turn to do the shopping.

"You're ridiculous," I told him as we left another boat shop with my purchases in my basket, which Aiden politely carried. His lips were pressed tightly together in a poor attempt not to laugh.

He surrendered and laughed loudly. "*I'm* ridiculous? You're the one who's all 'Please, sir, I'd really appreciate it,' and 'You'd do that for *me*, sir?' with your big green eyes, and being too pretty for your own good."

"I'm going to use every tool I have if it means getting a good deal!" I defended myself, feeling my face redden in embarrassment. "If you're just tailing me for a show, I'm not going to tell you when I'm going next time. You can go learn from someone else. Or not all, for all I care," I threatened.

He laughed again. "Right. Like you could ever hide from me."

I shoved his shoulder with mine and quickened my pace. That was another annoying thing about Aiden—he had this uncanny knack of being able to find anyone or anything. I once lost my favorite necklace—a small circular locket that I wore nearly every day—and searched for it for days before I enlisted his help. He turned up with it the very next day. A similar thing happened when the little boy down the street went missing; as soon as Aiden was alerted and joined in the search, the boy was found in a matter of hours.

"One of these days I'll elude you," I said. "And who'll be laughing then?"

"You'd do that? Hide from me and then laugh at me?"

His dark eyes went into a full puppy-dog pout, and I shoved him away from me, giggling.

"I laugh at you every day. What makes you think I'd do anything else?" I grinned, and he couldn't help but chuckle.

"Fair enough," he conceded and draped an arm over my shoulder to steer me toward the fishing docks. "Now let's get some food. It's time for me to toughen up and get all this shopping out of my system."

"Yes, because nothing says 'toughen up' like shopping."

"Hush up. For that, *you* can pay. *And* carry everything. This basket isn't light, you know."

I rolled my eyes and took the basket from him. "It isn't that heavy—you're just pampered." He made a sound of protest and immediately snatched the basket back. I grinned. "Besides, didn't you already have something to eat?"

He chose to ignore me and, grabbing me by the wrist, dragged me toward a stall selling spiced nuts. While he tried to charm the old woman running it, I wandered off to look at some lace offered in other stalls. I liked using lace in my own masks; it added softness to a look that was often too severe.

"Hey, Evie!" Aiden's voice broke through my internal designing, and I turned to see him jogging down the boardwalk.

"Hey," I reluctantly said as he stopped to catch his breath, panting slightly. "A little out of shape there," I teased.

He scowled at me. His attempt to express displeasure with me was somewhat lessened in severity when he couldn't stop panting. "You were supposed to wait for me," he accused.

I rolled my eyes. I might have wandered farther than

I'd intended, but I was still perfectly safe. "I'm not going to be attacked in broad daylight, and Hachi will catch any cutpurses before they get too close."

Aiden glared at the dog leaning against my skirts; Hachi simply wagged his brown and white brush of a tail and cocked his head. "Traitor," Aiden muttered, ruffling the patch of hair between Hachi's ears. Hachi closed his eyes and leaned against Aiden's hand, his white face the picture of bliss, and I was struck by how envious I could be of the fur ball.

Not that I wanted Aiden ruffling my black curls. Granted, he was good looking—all tall, dark, and hand-some, with dark curly hair and deep brown eyes peeking out from behind his lavender mask, and with no shortage of girls lusting after him—but I felt like I didn't know him sometimes. He had a peculiar way of disappearing for days at a time. He was like a stray cat that way, appearing for only a hot meal or some company and then disappearing into the night. Who knew when he would simply disappear forever?

Yet somehow he knew me better than anyone else.

I cleared my throat. "I thought you were looking for me, not my dog," I said, trying to shake my mind from that train of thought.

"I don't know. You're being mean to me today. Hachi here always loves me."

I rolled my eyes. "Then I'll just leave you two alone and get on with my day."

He gave Hachi a final scratch before falling into step beside me. "Nope, you can't get rid of me that easily." He crunched his way through a handful of spiced nuts and asked, "Any other errands to run today?"

"I need to go to the palace to visit Iniga," I said, digging around in his hand for a chestnut that wasn't half burnt.

"Is she going to attempt to teach you again?"

I laughed. "Not in the slightest. Her advice on that venture was to stick to my strengths with the ready-made materials and leave the glass-throwing and weaving to those more inclined to the trade."

"Were you really that bad?"

"I burned myself at least twice. I still have a scar on my thumb. Look." I held out my hand for him to inspect, turning it so he could see the pale sliver of a scar at the base of my thumb on my left hand.

"Poor thing," he said. I could tell he was trying not to laugh at me, though, and I jerked my hand out of his.

"She said the maskers in the castle have been working with her on making something new for the harvest balls," I said. "I wanted to see how that was going. I've been hearing rumors of masks made out of glass. Can you imagine?"

"I can imagine the scandal if that were true. No respectable nobleman is going to let his daughter out in a mask that doesn't actually cover anything up!"

"Exactly . . . which is why I'm dying to know what she's working on."

THREE

$\mathcal{D}$ESPITE HACHI'S WHINES AT RIDING THE WATER taxi, Aiden paid for one to take us to the market place by the palace. Once we arrived, it didn't take long to find our friend. Iniga had a nice stall by the entrance, a prized spot of land at the market where the nobles spent their time. The market by the pier might be more famous, and the small stall shops in the canals more accessible, but this was where the expensive luxuries were sold. It also smelled better. If I hadn't known Iniga since before she was a prized glass artisan to the king, I would never have been able to afford anything sold here. Even now I didn't like to take advantage of her generosity, and my purchases from her were few and far between.

Her stall was made of pale bamboo from the north, large enough to comfortably fit maybe ten men inside at once, and three sided with the opening facing the stone street between the canal and the other stall. Covered with a green cloth roof, the stall displayed her family's coat of arms—three plum blossoms inside of a circle— on a flag outside. She'd also painted the walls with elaborate designs, and her skill with a brush was obvious.

When we spotted her, Iniga was chatting with a well-dressed man with gray in his hair and purple in his mask—a nobleman. She laughed at something he said, tossing her sleek black hair over her shoulder. She was still young enough to wear her long hair down and wasn't afraid of using it to her advantage.

Unlike me, though, she genuinely liked mixing flirting with business. Her smile didn't look forced, and she touched the man's arm as she spoke emphatically.

"Now what is all this talk about glass masks I've been hearing?" I heard the man ask as Aiden and I approached. "My daughter speaks of nothing else these days. Is it really true?"

Iniga grinned. "You know that foreigner from Saran? The one that was introduced in court last month? He's an amazing thrower and has been teaching me all these new tricks, and I think we've been putting them to good use. Come and see," she said as she ducked into her stall.

The man followed eagerly, and Aiden and I slipped in behind him, sharing an excited look. Hachi, bored with all the talking, ran off to bark at pigeons that fluttered around the canal's edge.

Inside, Iniga carefully lifted a mask from two pegs on the wall and placed it on a piece of velvet on the wooden counter. Then she announced, "This is what all the talk is about."

"Would you look at that," the man breathed, and I sucked in a breath as well once I got a good look at it.

The mask was pure, clear glass and looked like it was carved out of ice. Even as it sat on the velvet, it looked as if it would melt or shatter by the slightest touch.

"Now, this isn't a finished mask," Iniga was quick to explain. "Obviously we'll add colors to make it opaque or affix some kind of backing so the skin won't be bare. For now we're working on the form and shape of it, and looking to see what interest there is."

"I'm interested," I whispered to Aiden, who chuckled.

"I'm sure you won't have any trouble finding buyers," the man said, his eyes wide. "My girl is sixteen and tells me that this new mask is what all the court is talking about."

"I'm honored." Iniga curtsied, smiling widely with a touch of blush in her flawless dark skin. "You'll have to meet Joch—he's the one responsible for the craze."

"I will indeed. Are you taking requests for the balls?"

"Unfortunately, we've already received more requests than we can handle," she said, her shoulders drooping. "Their majesties have been curious, as well as generous."

The man sighed. "I understand. I hope you'll think of me when the next season starts and you have an opening?" He slipped a silver coin into her palm as he kissed her hand in farewell.

She smiled. "I will do what I can, *signore.*"

As he departed through the stall opening, Iniga cheerfully greeted us. "I assume you're here to learn about these masks as well?"

"Of course! Look at it!" I gushed. "How did you manage to make such a thing?"

She laughed. "I can't go telling you all my secrets."

Aiden and I laughed in return. "As if you could ever keep a secret. How long did it take before the whole island knew you had a new glass master to learn from?"

She blushed. "It's not my fault. I was excited. And it

wasn't really a secret—everyone would have found out eventually."

"I'm just teasing. Even if you did teach me your magic with glass, I wouldn't be able to do anything with the knowledge."

"Ah, I remember all too well," she said with a sparkle in her eye. "How is your hand?"

"Just fine, thank you very much," I snipped and glared at Aiden, who was laughing at me again.

"Any chance we'll get to meet this mysterious foreigner?" I asked as Aiden sobered up.

"I've met him, actually," he said. "Not a talkative fellow."

"He's just serious about his work," Iniga said. "He's also still adjusting to living here, I think. He seems a bit over-whelmed with court life."

"That's understandable," Aiden said. "I've had enough fittings this past month to last me a lifetime."

A trickle of jealousy ran through me. Both Aiden and Iniga were out in court, and I was not. They never seemed to mind the difference in stations between us, but times like this reminded me of my standing. I was just an artisan, even if I was a good one. Aiden was a nobleman's son. Iniga was a nobleman's daughter and a gifted artisan—possibly the best on the island—even though she was only a year older than me.

And she was observant too. She glanced nervously at Aiden as she noticed my silence. "Evie," she said suddenly, "I have just the thing for you. I know you're a lost cause when it comes to glass, but I have a few palace masks you might want to look at."

"Oh?"

"Yes, they were given to me to try to repair or take to pieces if there was no saving them. I don't have to return them for several days. Maybe you'd like to take a look at them?"

She knew I wouldn't be able to resist. "Of course! What's wrong with them?"

"Some maids were clumsy and spilled wine on the silk. I needed to either cover the stains or replace the fabric, and it looks like it'll be the latter. Actually," she said, brightening, "would you like to try your hand at that? I'll pay you for your work, of course."

"You know I'd do it for free for you." I couldn't help but smile. "And don't pay me at all if you just have to do the work all over again."

She waved that comment aside and assured me that I'd be fine. "They're just serving masks, nothing too fancy. Come with me, and I'll go get them right now. Aiden, do you mind watching my stall?"

"Not at all. I'd like to look at what else you've got in here anyway." He'd drifted off to study a mask that looked like it was carved entirely out of mahogany and painted with a glossy finish of some sort.

"And keep an eye on Hachi. Make sure he doesn't fall in the canal," I said, scanning the crowd for my dog. He was still by the water's edge, his tail wagging as he jumped around. He seemed to have attracted the affection of a small boy, who was cheering and clapping at him as his nurse haggled over a fine tunic.

Iniga took me by the wrist and led the way into the palace. The guards at the gate didn't even give her a second glance. They already knew her mask and her business well enough, and her presence was enough to let me through as well. This part of the palace was the servants and artisans' work quarters anyway, and guards were posted along the hallways and at the entrances to workrooms. If we'd gone by the main gate or even the gate that led to nobles' housing, we probably would have been stopped or questioned.

Other maids and servants were milling around us. I had to nearly jog to keep up with Iniga's quick pace. I had never been inside the palace before, and I felt like Iniga might be up to something.

She greeted a handful of maids gossiping outside her workroom and waved at the guard, who nodded in return.

"Here we are," she announced, pushing the heavy door open for me.

Her workroom was clean, though clearly well used. Large containers and bags were everywhere, though I didn't know what was in them. Two large furnaces were also there with piles of coal and stacks of wood nearby. I spied several long wooden tools that I knew were used for throwing glass to make bowls and vases. Some tools I didn't recognize.

"Are those used to make the glass masks?" I asked, pointing them out as Iniga looked for the soiled server masks.

"Hmm? Sort of. We're still trying out a few different methods. Maybe if you're good, I'll let you watch next time," she teased.

"Aren't those supposed to be trade secrets?" I asked wryly.

She giggled. "Oops. You're probably right. Promise not to tell anyone?"

"Of course." I rolled my eyes.

"Here you go." She handed me a small satchel, and I peeked inside. Two masks were inside, and I could see the bright crimson stain on the silver silk of one immediately.

"You weren't kidding," I said. "Any tips before I work myself to the bone for you?"

Laughing, she shook her head. "I'm sure you'll figure something out."

As we started to leave, I noticed that there was only one stool in the room, near the furnaces. "Do you work in here alone? What about that foreigner?"

"I usually have the place to myself. Isn't that nice? Although it can be lonely sometimes, so I'll occasionally get a few others in here to keep me company and do odd jobs. But, yes, Joch has his own workroom as well. He doesn't like distractions when he works."

"Do you work in there or here when he teaches you?"

"He used to come in here, but he's been too busy lately. We've both been working on our own projects and will talk over dinner." She glanced at me sidelong. "You know, you're awfully curious about this guy. He's good looking, if you were wondering. Excellent shoulders."

"Iniga!" I blushed horribly, glad the heat usually stayed high in my cheeks and didn't spread to my neck or chest where she could see.

She sighed dramatically. "It's a shame I'm already betrothed. There are far too many handsome men in this place, let me tell you. Anytime you find yourself looking for a new beau, let me know, and I'll point you in the right direction."

"You—you're being ridiculous," I stammered. "Let's go. We shouldn't leave Aiden for so long."

"Ah," she said knowingly. "Yes, we mustn't keep Aiden waiting." She winked at me.

"Don't look at me like that."

"Why not? I certainly wouldn't fault you if Aiden's your choice of beau."

"I don't have a beau. End of discussion."

She pouted but let it pass as we went out to the hallway. She probably would have continued to hound me about it, but those maids were still hanging around. They weren't gossiping so much as staring at a young man walking away from us. He walked with his shoulders back, proud, and he had shaggy jet-black hair cut just above his ears.

"Speak of the devil and he appears," Iniga remarked as giggles and whispers broke out among the cluster of girls. "That was Joch. You can see how popular he is. If you ever change your mind"—she nudged my shoulder, and I gave her a warning look—"you'll have a bit of competition."

"Let's just go, Signorina Matchmaker."

Thanks to Iniga's words, I had trouble meeting Aiden's eyes for the rest of the night without my face growing warm. To further my embarrassment, he'd even stayed for supper with father and me (with minimal ribbing about my cooking) and then bid me farewell, though not without an extra cautionary warning to keep an eye out. After rolling my eyes at him, I told him I would keep Hachi outside for the night so he could keep watch.

Our dog had only two charges—my father and I—but he was a dear part of my little family. My mother had been of fisherfolk stock and couldn't bear to be stranded ashore for so long. I was so young when she'd left us for the sea that I couldn't remember her anymore. Which was fine by me. You can't miss what you don't remember. I knew Father missed her, though. He threw his heart into his work and nothing else for a long time after she left. He'd pull himself together for brief periods, making sure I was fed and cared for. We were well enough off that I'd even attended school until I was twelve. Then I convinced him to take me as an apprentice by reminding him that even if she were gone, I was still here, and if he didn't take me on, I would have to find someone else who could. He was better after that, almost as if nothing was ever wrong, but I still caught him staring out to sea from time to time.

I quickly got ready for bed and let my mind wander as I tried to fall asleep. It had been a good day, and I fell into bed with a satisfied smile on my lips. All my days with Aiden tended to be good ones.

If I'd known what was coming next, I might have relished that feeling of contentment just a bit more.

FOUR

THAT NIGHT, I WOKE TO THE SOUND OF HACHI whining from the small yard behind our store. He normally slept through the night, so it was unusual for him to make any noise. Then he started outright barking. And I smelled smoke.

I threw off my covers and pulled on my boots under my nightdress. I scrambled to move as quickly as I could in my newly awakened grogginess, still clumsy with sleep. I reached for my mask blindly, strapped it on, and rolled out of bed.

While calling for my father to see if he was simply working through the night and I was in a panic over nothing, I noticed light streaming in from under the door at the bottom of the stairs that led to the workroom of the shop. He didn't respond as I pushed the door open, and my jaw dropped at what I saw.

The entire workroom was in chaos: materials strewn every which way, beads and ribbons littering the floor, shards of glass glittering between the floorboards. But above it all was the overbearing heat of the flames that were beginning to engulf everything.

"Father!" I called again, frantic that I didn't know where he was. I coughed as the thick smoke began to fill my lungs, and I ran upstairs to see if I could find him there.

I threw open the door to his room only to find it in a similar condition to the workroom—things thrown everywhere, and no one in sight.

I stood there, dumbfounded. What was I supposed to do next? The crackling timbers of the house groaned, and I knew the fire was starting to spread. Shaking my head, I gathered my senses about me and realized I needed to get out of the house and fast. My father was probably already out. That was why I couldn't find him. At least, that was what I hoped.

Hachi's cries grew louder and more desperate as I scrambled down the stairs and turned down the hall for the back exit, unable to look at the workroom. Luck kept the way free and I escaped into the backyard, the heat of the flames chasing me out of my home.

Hachi lunged at me, pulling at his leash and whining pitifully. I untied him from his little shed and tried to calm him down, petting him and attempting to speak in an even voice.

I turned to look back at my home. It looked so innocent from outside. The windows were dully lit with what looked like candlelight, and the cool night air dulled the heat of the flames. If I didn't know any better, I'd have thought it was just a bad dream that chased me out here.

As I was staring at the windows and deciding what I should do next, movement caught my eye—a shadow against the firelight. Papa! He was still in there! I must have missed him in my panic.

"Hachi, go get someone—anyone!" I pleaded with him, hoping that whoever found him roaming the streets would bring him back to the store and render some kind of help. Hachi looked up at me with his big dark eyes, licked my hand, and refused to leave me. "Please, I'm going back in! I have to find Papa!"

Gulping a deep breath, I reentered the groaning building. The movement I'd seen came from the farthest window, so that's where I went.

Thick smoke was accumulating, and I wagered that the outside of the building was starting to look less innocent. In the back of my mind, I hoped someone would look in our direction and realize we needed help, but it was the middle of the night. No one would be awake, unless they were drunk and haunting the streets, which wouldn't help me at all.

In my haste to leave the house, the door to the workroom had closed behind me. I pushed against it, flinching at the hot surface and gasping as it opened before me.

Surveying the burning room, I spied a path that would lead me to the other side safely, free of debris and flame. Taking a chance, I sprinted across the room, and called out, "Papa! Papa, where are you?"

I heard no reply and tried to turn the knob that opened the door to the front of the store, but to no avail. Something was blocking it from the other side. I backed up and rammed my shoulder against the door, budging it slightly. I slammed against it twice more, until whatever it was finally gave way and the door flew open.

Although this part of the store was untouched by the fire, it was just as ransacked as every other part of the house.

I wondered why my room had been untouched as I instinctively looked to our inventory of completed masks.

Every last one was gone. They'd been kept in a locked cupboard, which had been broken open and completely emptied.

My mind flashed back to the announcement from the Square. Had the Chameleon struck here? None of our masks were for anyone particularly wealthy or high-ranked, but that didn't matter if one simply wanted to remain unseen. In fact, the lower ranked, the better.

Panic started to rise in my throat again as I remembered the other part of the warning. My father was still nowhere to be found. What if the Chameleon had gotten to him? Killed him for his mask? My father was well respected in his circles, and *his* mask would certainly be worth something if this man were similar enough in build to fool those unfamiliar with my father.

A floorboard creaked behind me, and I spun around. Relief flooded me as I saw my father's mask looking down at me in the pale moonlight. But that feeling was suddenly replaced with terror as I realized that the eyes behind the mask were strange and cruel.

The Chameleon.

"What did you do with the owner of that mask?" my voice rasped out without my permission.

The dark eyes glinted with amusement, the rest of his face obscured in shadows, as the fire danced behind him. "Don't you worry your pretty little head." His voice was smooth, crisp, and low, and he cocked his head to get a better look at me. I backed up instinctively. "He's in a better place," he continued in that mocking tone. "I'm sure he's quite at peace, if you catch my meaning."

"No," I breathed, refusing to believe what he was insinuating.

"I'm afraid so," he continued conversationally, as if he were talking about the price of glass beads going up and not my father's death. "You can go with him if you like. I'm afraid I wouldn't have much use for your mask, though." He watched me, as a cat watches a mouse he's toying with. "Although, it might be fun to try something else . . . ," he murmured.

As he approached me, I shook my head mutely until I collided against the wall.

"Stop trembling, my pretty lady. I'm not going to kill you." He stopped directly in front of me, and I crossed my arms across my body, trying to shield myself from him.

"However," he continued, his hand stroking the smooth surface of my mask just below my right eye, "I would like . . ."

Without another word, he removed his mask and I gasped in shock, turning away at seeing his bare face. He angled his head and caught my chin in his left hand, forcing me to look at him.

His face was twisted in a cruel expression, and once I looked, I couldn't help but stare at him even as my vision blurred from the smoke. I'd never before really looked at a completely bare face of someone outside of my family. I tried not to look at the criminals at the Square, and this was nothing like the simple tattooed foreign faces of the men at the Market. This was a face bare of any paint or ink, almost completely unmarked. It was fascinating in a bizarre and twisted sort of way, and the light from the flames around us threw his features into harsh angles. Everything about him looked sharp—sharp jaw line; straight nose; thin, narrowed eyes filled with hatred.

The most fascinating part, however, was the pink scar on his face, the one stain on an otherwise flawless stretch of skin. Once I saw it, I couldn't look away, and the rest of his face blurred into nothing. I knew he'd been Marked, but seeing it and hearing about it are two very different things. The Mark twisted like a chameleon's tail with another line cutting it sharply in two. I'd never heard of a Mark like that before.

"You see this?" he asked, noticing my stare and pointing a long finger at the scar beneath his right eye. He mocked me; of course I saw it. "This is the scar that marks me, the only constant thing about me. If they know about this Mark and then find someone with this Mark, they will assume *that* someone is the one they are looking for—the Chameleon.

"Now what would they do, I wonder, if they found that Mark scratched into the soot of the fire, or on the wall, and then on you?"

I couldn't help myself; I began tearing up from the smoke and fear. I shook my head in terror as I realized what he was going to do. "Please don't," I begged, struggling to pull away. "Please."

He laughed in my face. "Oh, but this could be fun, framing you. You'd be a great little scapegoat, so defenseless and pretty. And you can still hide behind your mask . . . but for how long? Now there's the question. And an even better question: what would you do with no mask at all?"

I didn't answer him. I couldn't—not anymore. His hand had crept around my neck and was slowly cutting off my air supply, despite how much I struggled. His hand was like a vice, and I could not break free of it.

Hachi's barks—distant, but sharp and growing closer—suddenly cut through the night air. Hope rose in my stomach, but it was short lived. Out of the corner of my eye, I saw the man poke at the fire with a brand.

"Oh, don't worry—this will be quick."

With one fluid motion, he ripped my mask from my face. I cried out in shame and fear, but he held me fast. My muscles were weak from smoke inhalation and I couldn't get my arms or legs to obey my commands.

He held the brand up for me to see, taunting me with the glowing orange tip as he brought it closer and closer. Finally he pressed it against my skin. I cried out in shock and squeezed my eyes shut, incapable of believing what was happening to me. Tears fell from my closed eyes, and I tried to pull back but couldn't move.

"Hold still or it will hurt more," he warned, his free arm still around my neck, his fingers bruising the skin and cutting off my air supply. Tears streamed down my cheeks and mixed with the blood seeping out through the blistering burn, the saltiness stinging as he pulled the brand back.

Hachi's barks grew closer, and the fire in the next room grew louder and hotter. I screwed my eyes shut, willing it to all be just a bad dream, but I could still feel the white-hot burn on my face and smell the burning flesh as the workroom went up in flames around us.

"There," he whispered, "all done." He donned my father's mask once more. "Now run along, pretty one." He laughed again and ran out, leaving me disorientated and blinking, gasping for breath, my vision blurred.

The fire was truly starting to spread now, and I could hear the building groan as it caved in on itself in the gutted-out workroom. I couldn't think straight, but I knew I had to get out of that building. And I couldn't be seen. And I needed to stop bleeding.

Not necessarily in that order.

I saw some scraps of fabric lying around that I could use as a makeshift mask/bandage. I grabbed the cleanest piece I could find and wrapped it around my hand, intending to use it as a bandage when I had more time. I grabbed a couple more lightweight pieces to use as a face cover and stumbled to the door.

The brisk night air shocked me out of my stupor, and I began to run. I ran like the hounds of hell were after me. I didn't know where I was going or whom I needed to find—I just knew that I needed to run away.

I ran until my legs collapsed beneath me and my lungs burned. I was completely lost—without a home, without a family, without a mask, and without a plan.

So I did the only thing I could do: I curled up in a small alleyway between two buildings and cried myself to sleep, allowing myself to mourn and to hurt.

I could be strong tomorrow.

FIVE

I SLEPT FITFULLY, MY CHEEK STILL BURNING AS nightmares and flames plagued my mind. The first time I woke up, I tried to clean the burn as best I could by licking the clean bandages I'd brought and ever so carefully dabbing at the Mark. At least the blood was gone. I couldn't wipe away the feel of his gaze on my bare face, though. I touched my makeshift mask to make sure it was in place, swallowing hard before exhaustion pulled me back to sleep.

When the sun was up and I woke yet again with a groan, I decided it was best to start the day. Even if the sun was just barely up, I had a lot to do. I needed to find something stronger than saliva to clean my wound.

First things first, though. Where was I? That would be a good thing to know. And where could I find some food?

I stood and stretched, fighting to get the uncomfortable crick out of my neck and back so I could think straight. When I looked around, I nearly fell back to the ground.

I was sitting at the foot of the outer wall to the palace.

I'd walked by this place countless times. A thick, stone

wall surrounded the entire property, and there were kilo-meters of gardens and small canals before I could reach the actual building, which was something else entirely. It was a beautiful piece of architecture on the outside, with mul-tiple wings and hundreds of windows, stained glass, and intricate sills. The inside too was a work of art from what I'd heard, with thousands of paintings and sculptures. I'd always known the Royal Family were great patrons of the arts, as demonstrated by the fact that the prince had a dif-ferent mask with every public appearance. I'd always been awed by this place.

But now, to be standing here, staring at the great build-ing, I couldn't help feeling anything but intimidation. Why did my delirious subconscious lead me here of all places?

It was still early morning, and the roads and canals around the palace were beginning to fill with workers, trav-elers, and guards. I didn't know how they generally reacted to maskless vagabonds hanging about the gates, but I could wager a guess that they would ignore me at best, and taunt or harass me at worst. They wouldn't dare do anything more violent than that so close to the courts.

I looked down at myself and realized I was still in my nightdress and boots. I frowned, which proved to be a bad idea when the movement pulled at the raw skin on my face. I really needed to find a better way to treat the wound, as well as find some clean clothes. A more appropriate mask would be nice too. What I wore now was no better than a head scarf with eyes cut out. *And food*, my stomach reminded me with a growl. I couldn't forget food.

I could find all of these things back at my home, pro-vided that there was anything left, and that what little remained hadn't been looted. Thinking back, if Hachi was making that much noise, he'd probably been found by someone and they'd hopefully been able to salvage the rest of the house.

Was it worth the risk of being seen like this, though? I weighed the options in my head. In my current state, I wouldn't be recognized, and no one would likely believe my story. Since the prince's announcement, it was likely that neighbors would be more suspicious of each other—and I had always kept to myself. They would say I had all the means to burn my home, never mind the fact that I had absolutely no motive.

But if I kept this makeshift fabric mask, maybe no one would really look at me.

If I did go back, I could get the things I needed and gather some information. And I craved information more than clothes or food.

I knew my father had to be dead. I hadn't seen him, but I knew he wouldn't have left me alone, and the Chameleon wouldn't have let him live. Despite the Chameleon's cruel words, though, my father *was* in a better place if he was resting at peace with my mother. And he knew I would be a fighter, that I'd be able to take care of myself.

Squaring my shoulders, I made my decision. I would go back.

I didn't run. The distance seemed unbelievably far, unlike the night before. I was amazed how far I'd travelled last night, but I supposed there was truly something to be said for adrenaline and fear.

The canals seemed so quiet this time of day, deep in the city and away from the shouts and labor of the dock workers sorting the early-morning catches. The soft lapping of the water against the walls was soothing and, combined with the soft pit-pat of my footsteps on the cobble street, created a relaxing rhythm that was a welcome change from the frantic dash of the night before.

I wasn't completely familiar with this part of my district, but I knew that the canal would eventually lead me back to my neighborhood, and to Dr. Vito, my doctor since childhood. I figured he'd seen me since before I was masked, and if anyone would help me, it would be him.

His red door greeted me when I turned down a street that led me to familiar territory. I took a deep breath before knocking on the door, bracing myself for whatever reaction might be in store for me.

The door swung open and the doctor peered out from behind it, frowning. "Yes? Can I help you?"

My shoulders slumped; he didn't recognize me. "I need your help," I said hesitantly as he regarded me suspiciously.

"I'm not taking new patients now," he said brusquely. "And as I can see you're not in any immediate danger, I'm sure you'll understand when I say I can't help you."

"But I'm already one of your patients," I protested, cursing my hastily made mask. A mask maker with any pride at all should never wear such a thing. "I'm Evelina diPietro."

With a gasp, he pulled me inside with an arm around my shoulders and shut the door behind us, leading the way to a familiar curtained-off room, speaking rapidly. "Beg pardon, miss, I did not recognize you. Of course you would come to me after that horrible fire. Of course, I understand now. And what of your father? Were you separated? And in your night things, no less! What *happened*? Sit here and tell me what's wrong."

He didn't give me any chance to answer, swiftly examining the minor cuts on my hands and arms. He flitted about the room before finally sitting on a stool, his pudgy hands rubbing salve on the minor burns on my arms.

"Wait, wait," I said, trying to explain as I pulled my hands away. "I'm mostly unhurt, save for one thing." I took another breath as he looked up at my face. "It's under my mask," I began, nervous both to remove my mask and for his reaction at my marked skin.

"Ah," he said compassionately. "I understand, miss. Would you prefer just to show me?"

I exhaled in relief, glad he wasn't going to make me tell the whole story. While he hadn't seen my bare face since I was a young girl, surely he'd still recognize me. I slowly lifted the makeshift mask up, wincing, until it rested on my forehead. Then I peeled back the bandage and—

Dr. Vito stood abruptly, knocking his stool over. He spoke in a cold voice, all compassion gone from his face, "Get out of here. This is a cruel game you play, imitating a missing girl. Never mind one I've known since birth. I don't treat criminals."

"But—" The shame burned in my face, and I struggled to explain, but when the doctor looked at my face, all he could see was a Mark. Just the same as how I'd looked at the Chameleon's face.

"Out!" he shouted, dragging my arm roughly. "And cover yourself, you filthy thing. I want nothing to do with a Marked girl."

I had no choice but to run again.

In a flurry of confusion and blurred vision, I covered my face again and let my feet lead the way as I struggled to keep my pain in check. Was I so scarred that even my doctor didn't recognize me? Or did he see only the Mark and nothing else? I hoped the latter, which gave me some sliver of hope. My Mark could be covered, once it was healed, but there was no saving a scarred and ugly face.

These thoughts spun around in my head as I ran until I finally reached my block. Once there, I was shocked. A small crowd had gathered around my house, and I could hear the gossip from where I stood. No one went in or came out of the building, and I could see that the fire had long been extinguished. I edged closer, trying to hear what was being said by the loudest gossip hens.

"—that dog of theirs, he was tearing up and the down the street in the middle of the night, barking up a storm. I was contemplating shooting him on the spot!" I never liked this particular neighbor. "Thank goodness he finally took off on his own. Thing wouldn't stop yelping."

At least I knew Hachi was safe and alive somewhere. He'd be able to take care of himself; he was a good dog.

"—the fire brigade got there just in time. The building should be salvageable; it just needs some support beams built back in and the flooring redone. The glass in the back windows was blown out too. I have half a mind to convince Abe to buy the place and move in there ourselves. I bet someone's going to get a steal on that place."

I added another thing on my mental list of things to accomplish: inform *someone* that I was still alive, so I could reclaim my home eventually. Though I didn't know how I could convince anyone of my identity at this point.

"Sad thing about Pietro, though." My ears perked up when I heard my father's name. "I heard from one of the guards that they found his body floating in the canal. Stripped of his mask and anything else of value. They say it's likely the Chameleon's work."

I breathed heavily, anxious for more and stubbornly ignoring the pain that throbbed in my chest. It was one thing to accept his death as a logical conclusion. It was another thing entirely to hear it as a topic of gossip.

"I haven't heard anything about the girl, though."

"You think she's still alive?" another woman asked.

"Who knows, with that one," my neighbor responded, shrugging. "She's always been hardy. And they haven't found any remains, so there's still some hope."

"My money is on her being at the bottom of the canal. They just got lucky finding Pietro."

"That's the truth, I won't deny it. But I think she's tougher than that. She'll turn up."

While my neighbor had faith in me, she seemed to be the only one. I'd be hearing more rumors of my own death by afternoon, no doubt about it.

I bided my time, waiting until the crowd thinned before even attempting to get back inside. I thought about going to the house of the neighbor who'd defended me for help, but I didn't think I could handle being thrown out again.

Instead, I used the respite to sit by the canal, lying low. I washed the back of my neck and arms in the water, even though that water was far from clean. It was better than being covered in soot and dirt.

Finally, dusk came, and interest in my empty home

had waned thin. I crept through the shadows as quietly as I could—which was admittedly not very—and pushed the back door open. It creaked noisily, but the sound was swallowed by the waves of the canal and the foot traffic on the street.

I had wanted to go to my room to wash up and change into clean clothes—or even day clothes—but the blackened stairs looked too unstable to hold my weight.

Dejected, I tried to think of other options for getting some proper clothes. I glanced out the window to where Hachi had been tied up. There was still laundry on the line, far enough from the house to have escaped the flames. What a stroke of luck! I gratefully snatched up a clean shift and shirt and returned to the house to inspect the state of the kitchen.

I hadn't eaten all day. My stomach felt completely hollow, and I was growing weak. Thankfully, the fire hadn't made it past the brick of the kitchen entryway and the room looked more or less intact, if somewhat eerie from the shiftings and creaks of the rest of the building. I found some rolls and jam and fruit, and quickly filled my stomach before heading to the workroom, anxious to find a real mask. I would've worn one of my old ones, but I couldn't access my room where I kept them, and I didn't want to be recognized.

I found one mostly completed mask hiding beneath an overturned, charred cabinet. It had neither lining nor a finished setting glaze, but it would suit my needs just fine. It was even a comforting green. It had been intended to be the base for a formal Ball Mask, but it would do for an everyday one for now. Better yet, it sat low over my cheekbones, and if I could manage it, it should cover my Mark while it healed.

Mask in hand, I found the medical salve we kept with the herbs in the kitchen and carried both up to the table where I could work comfortably. Under the dark cover of night, I could use the pump in the yard. I prepared a bowl of clean water, fetched the soap, and sat down.

I unwound my wrap and then peeled the covering from my skin, wincing slightly. I dampened my wash-cloth and dabbed at the wound, cleaning it until no blood came away on the cloth and praying that it wouldn't get infected. I had no way of knowing how sterile the brand had been, but the Mark seemed to be clean enough to avoid infection.

I dabbed at the raised skin with some of the salve and taped a white cloth over it, using as little material as pos-sible to hopefully keep it concealed under my mask.

Walking over to a window to see my reflection, I cov-ered my face with the new mask. A small bit of the fabric still stuck out from the bottom. I would have to wind another veil of sheer fabric across the bottom half of my face until I could remove the dressing, or until I could make another mask.

I sighed as I glared at the offending mask in the glass. Another mask required materials and time that I didn't have. I could redo the one I was currently wearing by adding more fabric or mâché to the bottom. I'd have to see what was left in the workroom.

Before hunting materials down, though, I allowed myself to shed a few bitter tears one last time as I stared at my marred reflection—my face would never be the same.

It wasn't as bad as I feared initially, but I'd never be able to remove my mask for anyone without fear of condemnation.

After this, I swore to myself I would never cry for myself again. I would be strong. I would not let the Chameleon define me.

Taking a deep breath, I reentered the workroom, this time really taking the time to survey the damage.

The fire had destroyed the walls and one of the support beams that held up the opposite end of the building where my father's room had been. In the workroom, material littered the floor in varying degrees of charred debris. Many of the ribbons and lace were surprisingly untouched, though anything of real value was gone.

I collected some ribbons and thread to take to the kitchen to alter my mask as best I could and left the rest of the room untouched, exhausted and unable to look at it any longer. The moon was bright, but the night was too dark for me to really do much, and I didn't dare light a lantern.

Instead, I slumped over the table and let sleep and exhaustion claim me.

* * *

When morning came, I woke with the sun. I redressed my new Mark and went about my morning with such regularity that it once again felt like the past two days had been nothing more than a bad dream. But then I'd see the workroom and its gutted starkness or try to go up the stairs to my room, and that provided a vivid reminder that I was not dreaming.

Today would be the last day in my home. I didn't know

where I was going yet, but I knew I couldn't stay. There were too many unanswered questions and uncertainties.

Once I had cleaned up and looked like a respectable citizen again, I prepared to leave by packing a knapsack with as much food as I dared and tucking money into hidden pockets in my skirts and sash. The only personal effect I allowed was that locket Aiden found for me so long ago. It would serve as a good enough proof of identity for those I knew. I wore it under my clothing, though, so no one could identify me before I wanted them to. I also took the masks I'd received from Iniga, which had thankfully been unharmed. I didn't know what I was going to do with them yet, but they would undoubtedly come in handy.

Then, with one last look around the place, I left my childhood home behind me.

SIX

I FOLLOWED MY FEET TO THE PIER. IT WAS already bustling with activity—the market was still going on after all. *One more crime from the Chameleon, but the world still carries on*, I thought bitterly.

A gaggle of children burst into my path, their faces painted in shades of bright blues—the sign of children from fishing families. From cheekbone to hairline, their skin was coated in a thin layer of blue paint, even their eyelids. The whites of their eyes shone with excitement and one girl who couldn't have been older than twelve smudged a streak of blue across the back of her hand. She must have recently reached twelve, the age when children started wearing paint.

She giggled and pointed at a pair of young men eating on a ship's deck. The other children gathered around her, giddy and slightly scandalized. The two men wore no masks. Instead they had a cluster of tattoos inked directly into their skin around their eyes. They were from Saran, after all, a country to the north of us where the strange people lived almost bare-faced.

The young men noticed their audience and stood to get a better look at the little blue faces. One of the men winked, sending the youngsters into a fit of giggles before they ran off to tell their friends and families.

I used to be one of those children who came to stare at the strangers; every adult of my country used to be one of those children. No child could resist a scandal, and these foreigners were as good as nearly naked. Only the uncivilized and poorest of people went without a face covering, and Saranians were barely a step above them with their inked faces.

I didn't know what I was doing there.

My stomach growled.

At least there was something I could do for that.

I dug out some of the cheese I'd managed to rescue. My fingers brushed against the palace masks, and I took those out as well, making sure there wasn't anyone around who'd recognize them for what they were. Both were formal masks that covered the top of the forehead to the chin, with a thin beaded veil falling an inch or so below the jaw line. The masks were easily recognizable as belonging in the palace. They were dark silver, clearly low on the totem pole, but still in the color spectrum of public service to the government since whoever wore it worked in the palace. A simple silver ribbon lined the edges and crushed glass sparkled attractively over part of the surface. There were also some small engraved curls along the right side.

The first was stained beyond repair. The fabric needed replacing, as well as some of the beading, and even if I'd had fine enough material, it was burned at the workshop. I placed it back in my bag.

The second, though, was promising.

The ties were nearly torn clean off, and the lining was all but gone. Otherwise, it looked pretty good. I could work with that. The ribbons were still in good shape; they just needed to be resewn into the lining. Thankfully there was enough of that along the edges that I could rig it to work. And while a palace servant would want the most comfortable mask available, I could not afford to be so picky, so the current lining would have to do.

After studying the mask for a long moment, I shoved it back in my bag. I would have to be crazy to even think of wearing the mask myself. I would be no better than the Chameleon.

And yet . . .

It wasn't like I'd stolen it. Iniga gave it to me, and it had been given to her. She wouldn't be in any trouble.

And I wasn't stealing anyone's identity in particular . . . just an anonymous scullery maid or laundress or something.

It could work.

It was insane, but it could work.

Finishing my scanty meal, I pulled myself to my feet, brushing off my skirts. I frowned—I would need better clothes if I were to pass as a palace servant.

Maybe if I could just get in there, I could grab some clothes as well.

A twinge of remorse pricked in my gut. It was so easy to fall back on theft when I had nothing else.

But I couldn't ask anyone for help. Iniga would be risking her position if she snuck me in, and I didn't want to rely on her charity when I could fend for myself.

As for Aiden, I had hoped to see him when I'd gone

back to my home, but he was nowhere to be found, and I didn't know where to look for him. Besides, he wouldn't be able to do anything for me that I couldn't do myself.

And it would kill me if he looked at me the way Dr. Vito did.

As the doctor's face flashed across my memory, I made my decision.

I would hide, and I would fend for myself, and I would do it on my own.

* * *

I took a deep breath, steeling myself as I gazed up at the imposing gates of the palace. Great stone kaku-dōrō lanterns stood on either side, flanked with statues of lions growling at those who dared to pass by. They were much more intimidating when I didn't have Iniga to lead the way through them.

The trick was to look like I belonged. The problem was I clearly did not.

I picked at my skirt, trying to concoct an excuse for my dress. The servant's silver mask was on my face, and it felt suffocating being unable to breathe deeply beneath the veil. At least my wound was completely covered.

"Hey, you there!" one of the guards called out. He muttered something to his companion and then took a few steps toward me. "What are you doing out here dressed like that?"

I looked down at my clothes once more, my head spinning. "I, uh, fell in the canal." That might have been convincing if I had been wet. "And so I borrowed clothes from a friend of mine who works in the artisan district where

I was running errands," I added quickly when the guard frowned.

His expression softened, and he looked me up and down. I struggled to keep from fidgeting under his scrutiny, trying to look annoyed at being stopped. When he finally shrugged, I wanted to sigh in relief.

"All right. Go on through," he said, waving back at the gate. "I'm sure you need time to make yourself presentable before dinner."

"Yes. Thank you, sir!"

He chuckled. "You're lucky you're a pretty one. And you can thank me by bringing me my dinner! Name's Matteo—I'll be looking for you."

I gave him a confused look but didn't bother waiting around for an explanation. I didn't understand all the comments about my being pretty, seeing as he couldn't see me at all. And if he could, he would certainly be singing a different tune. My mask was lovely, but it was a servant's and nothing extraordinary, which was my usual rule of defining beauty.

I'd learn later that beauty is measured in a different fashion in the palace.

I hurried inside, pausing when there was no one around to see me. I was completely lost in a matter of minutes. Even if I could go to Iniga's workroom, I didn't have the slightest idea of how to get there.

Walking around somewhat aimlessly, I searched for someone with a mask similar to the one I wore, or a sign of a laundry.

"What are you doing, looking like that?" a scandalized voice asked from behind me.

I spun around, my hand instantly checking to be sure my mask was secure. "What?"

A girl approximately my age, with stick-straight, dark-brown hair and narrow gray-green eyes glared at me. Her uniform black mask seemed to be a size too small. It had large eyeholes so as to cover as little of her face as possible while still being proper. A sure sign of a flirt. "You're a mess," she announced.

"I fell in the canal," I said, narrowing my eyes back at her, daring her to challenge my alibi. I might be intimidated by the palace guards, but I wasn't about to let some silly girl scare me away.

"And you thought you could still serve in that?" She motioned dramatically at my soot-stained clothing.

"I was going to the laundry, but I got turned around. I haven't been here very long," I said defensively.

She rolled her eyes. "I'll say. You're in the wrong wing entirely. You're heading toward the boys' rooms." A grin curved her lips. "Or was that really where you're coming from?"

I didn't bother to dignify that with an answer. "Just show me where to go," I asked, sounding tired.

"Only because Mistress Vera will have my head if you show up like that. Hurry up—I have things to do, you know." I nearly had to jog to keep up with the girl's long legs, and she wasn't joking about going quickly. I lost track of the turns again, but we stopped in front of a door marked with waves carved into the wood.

The girl didn't bother knocking and pushed the door open, calling, "Leo? I've got a girl for you!" Then, without waiting for Leo to appear, she gave me a dirty look and said, "Don't be late for dinner," and flounced back out the door.

Left alone for the moment, I took a deep breath to steady my nerves and looked around.

Cloth was everywhere. Now this was my kind of place—I knew my dressings and trappings. I drifted over to the ribbons and silks and fingered them longingly. I missed them already.

"Can I help you?" a low voice asked, startling me, and I spun around.

An elderly man was standing by the wall that I'd passed by on my way to admire the ribbons. He looked more friendly than the rest of my welcoming committee, but I'd been wrong on every other first impression, so I wasn't going to make any judgments.

"I need a new dress . . ." I said, though it sounded more like a question.

"I can see that. I should have a uniform for you here." He began rummaging through several piles of clothes. The skirt and blouse were so loose and billowy that it didn't matter what size he gave me. "Put these on, and I'll see if I need to hem anything. Can't have you tripping, now."

I pulled the skirt over what I was already wearing and discovered it was too short, hitting my leg awkwardly above my boot top with several inches of skirt showing underneath. Same with the sleeves—they fell just short of my wrists.

"Hmm, let me see if I have anything longer. You might be out of luck, though."

Great.

About five skirt and shirt combinations later, we finally

found articles of clothing that didn't look horribly awkward on me. The material was actually nicer than I expected, but then again, we were supposed to be representing the royal services. We needed to look respectable.

"Thank you," I said. He had actually been helpful, and while not overtly friendly, he wasn't hostile either. He was just . . . uninterested. And I could live with that.

I studied myself in the large mirror propped against the wall, curious to see the new me.

The look suited me, oddly enough. My mask comfortably covered enough of my face that I wouldn't have to worry about things showing that shouldn't be, even if I would have to get used to breathing more shallow breaths. Even better, I barely recognized myself. Ill-fitting clothes and a full mask and in a position of servitude? No one would ever recognize me.

I pulled distastefully at my skirt and resigned myself to my job. Just for a few weeks—that's as long as I'd need to stay here, surely. The Chameleon would be caught, and I could return to my old life, somehow. This too would pass.

* * *

Next, I needed to find where I would be sleeping. I could hardly say I couldn't remember which room was mine and ask for a new one. Luckily an idea struck me as I passed a girl with a mask similar to mine. "Do you know where an empty girls' room is? I'm supposed to get it ready for a newcomer."

She looked at me oddly, her head tilting slightly to the right. "You? Don't they have other servants for that?"

I winced inwardly. Of course the palace would have

different servants for tasks like that, and I clearly worked in the kitchens. "Yes, but I know her and volunteered."

The girl still looked skeptical, but shrugged it off. "Do you know where she'll be working?"

"Kitchens?"

"Wouldn't that just be near your own room?"

Why did this girl have to be smart? "I suppose," I began slowly, "but I don't think there are any more rooms there."

"She'd probably just be roomed with the general servers then. Come on, I'll show you. They're downstairs."

This time I carefully memorized the turns and corridors as she quickly showed me the way. "Most of these are empty," she said, sounding somewhat apologetic, "and much smaller than the ones the other serving girls like you get, but if you're full up there, then there's not much more you can do."

"I'm sure it'll be just fine. She had to share a room before, so she'll be happy to have some privacy for once."

For the first time, I saw a smile in the girl's eyes. "Then this one should be okay," she said, opening the first door on the right.

The room was small, occupied by a single set of shelves and a bedroll directly on the floor. There were no blankets or decorations, and it felt dismal. I'd have to do something to brighten up the place—I'd lose my mind if I had to spend any extended amount of time in that room. I'd also have to see about getting a blanket. And a lantern—the solitary window facing the east would be all but useless in the evenings.

But it would serve its purpose. It would certainly hide me well. Hiding in the basement of the palace itself? Perfect.

"You can get some blankets and things from the laundry, if your friend isn't bringing her own," the girl supplied helpfully. "Anything else you need?"

"Can you help me back to the kitchen?" I asked. "I'm still new myself and keep getting lost."

She laughed. "I remember that feeling all too well. Sure, follow me. I need to get up there soon, anyway."

SEVEN

I COULD SMELL AND HEAR THE KITCHEN AREA well before I could see any of it, and as soon as I walked in the door, a shrill voice called out, "Carese! Who've you got there?"

The girl shrugged and said, "She's new. They must have been keeping her in Etiquette before sending her to you."

"We'll see if this one sticks around long enough to be worth the effort." A woman appeared, and I assumed this to be the Vera that the rude flirt had mentioned. She didn't have the plump motherly qualities I expected from a Kitchen Mistress. Instead, she was fairly tall and slim. As she moved, I spied toned, muscular arms encased in the tight fabric of her dress, signaling she was probably much stronger than she appeared. She had dark brown hair, tied back in a neat plait, and her mask was actually quite pretty. It was pale blue, signaling a high-ranking background in fishing or farming. This made sense, seeing as how she needed an extensive knowledge of different crops and how to prepare and cook them, especially for a palace position. The mask looked to be made of a light material, with intricate cutouts, allowing her skin to breathe in the hot kitchens. Behind her mask, dark eyes studied me as carefully as I'd been studying her, and I wondered what conclusions she'd drawn.

"She's a shapely thing. She'll make a nice Serving Miss with those eyes, provided she can carry those pitchers without spilling." She spoke as if I wasn't there and circled me like a cat waiting to pounce.

"I'm not a mute or a simpleton," I spoke up, unable to keep quiet under her scrutiny, but careful to keep my tone polite enough so she wouldn't send me right back out the door. "And I'm strong. And I'd appreciate being addressed directly."

Her eyes widened ever so slightly at my directness, and she pursed her lips. "Indeed. What is your name, sweetheart?" When she used the pet name on me, it no longer sounded like a term of endearment.

"Evelina," I said, giving my full name.

"Well, Miss Evelina," she said, stretching my name out, "if you are no simpleton, as you say, I assume you already know my name to be Vera. However, only those of equal or better station may address me as such, and you are neither. To you, I am to be addressed as Kitchen Mistress Vera or ma'am, at all times."

I scowled behind my mask at her degrading tone and decided I did not like her very much after all. Of course she would be sweet to the guards. They were her superiors, even if their masks were black.

She began to walk away, and I followed her at a brisk pace as she barked out orders. "As you should have learned in Etiquette, your job is to keep the goblets full and to remain unnoticed at all other times. Keep your head down, don't make eye contact, and do not speak. You do not exist.

"You will eat with the rest of the servers before serving the guests to prevent you from picking off the plates we serve. I don't want a hungry staff. You will be compensated with clean clothes and a bed in the servants' quarters below the kitchen, along with three silver pieces a day, paid every two weeks." The wages weren't bad, but much less than what I'd earned before. A single silver piece bought one good meal.

Curious eyes stole glances at me as we continued our brisk walk around preparation areas and other servants already preparing for dinner. Vera pointed out where I would take my meals: a long table pushed against the farthest wall with at least fifteen seats.

She showed me to the cavernous main dining hall and then directed me to a corner. "This will be your station. When you are not needed, you will stand here to monitor the level of each glass. Never allow a glass to become empty, even if they have completed their meal. If your pitcher runs low, do not leave. Another server will bring a fresh pitcher.

"You will remain here until all the dinner guests have left. Then you will assist in clearing the tables and washing the dishes. Jeza!" she called out in that imperious tone I knew I would grow to hate.

The flirt appeared at her side. "Yes, Mistress?"

Vera looked at me. "You report to Jeza, and treat her as you would treat me. She has the authority to make any corrections she deems fit."

Jeza looked smug, her chin held high and her hands on

her hips. Her lips were painted a bright red, and at a second glance, I noticed the other girls had done the same to their lips. I bit mine self-consciously.

"Now, get busy. You've missed dining with the other serving girls, but I won't have you filching food off the other plates, so eat quickly."

She left then with Jeza at her heels, yelling about smelling something burnt, and I took the chance to finally breathe.

The kitchen was a flurry of skirts, pots, and steam. It was much busier than I expected. Dozens of girls were preparing the food and polishing the silver while more settled around the wooden tables that acted as our dining area.

I found a seat and watched the organized chaos around me. Nearly everyone had a mask similar to mine; color separation of rank barely existed among the servants. Some of the cooks had a little embellishment or hint of color in their masks, but nothing to draw much attention. I could identify the other serving girls—for that was clearly what I was supposed to be—by their matching voluminous skirts. I realized with a start that they all had green eyes like me as well. Some had more gray or more brown, but all were undeniably green.

I didn't have time to ponder that, though, as I quickly stuffed down the food given to me. I was starving. No one bothered me or tried to stir up any conversation, which suited me just fine. I didn't want to form any attachments, or worse, make any more enemies. I was sure Jeza would be enough of a thorn in my side.

Before I knew it, it was time to get to work. I felt a little lost in the throng of crowding servants, with no idea of what exactly I was supposed to do. I scanned the room quickly and spotted other servers filling up large jugs and going into the dining room. I jogged over to them and asked what I was supposed to do.

"No one's here yet," Carese piped up as she came back in from the dining room. Now that I wasn't so distracted with trying to keep from being thrown out of the palace, I had a chance to get a good look at her. She was a petite girl with her hair in a short plait. She turned to me. "Fill up as many of the goblets as you can, starting from where you'll stand. They all need to be filled before the guests arrive, so just keep filling until you reach a cup that's already been filled. Then work on your other side."

She moved quickly and carefully, and if I hadn't been so rushed, I would have liked to just watch her move. No movement was wasted, and I could tell she'd been here a long time.

She pressed a jug into my hands, and I was carried along with the crowd into the great hall that served as the dining area.

The tables were draped with expensive fabrics, floral arrangements, tiny statues, and all sorts of decorations. Even the place settings were beautiful: carefully folded napkins and brightly colored mats that I would be too afraid to eat over. There were no plates—the servants would bring those out with the meal—but at each seat there were cups and more silverware than any one person could ever need. If I thought I'd be bored earlier, just standing and waiting to refill cups, I was mistaken. It would be fascinating to watch this class dine. This wasn't just a meal—it was a performance.

I tried to hurry to fill each glass, but I didn't want to spill on the pretty cloth and, consequently, moved much more slowly than the others. The girl working from the other end filled cups at twice the rate I did. She didn't say anything to me about it, but I couldn't tell if that was out of kindness or distraction.

I was filling the last two cups when trumpets sounded and the doors were flung open. Guests filed in through the entryway, and after some meandering, each person found a seat. I didn't know if there was any sort of order to where they sat, or if it was just according to personal preference. They traveled in small packs, a fascinating thing to watch. In clusters of threes and fours, they circled the tables, searching for something—I didn't know what—until they found their spots. Then the men would pull the chairs out for the women, bow, and take their own seats. But in response to this deference, no woman pulled her chair in before the man.

The tables formed a large rectangle with·the table farthest from me on a dais. It remained empty as the guests filed in and took their seats. I assumed it was for the royal family and their guards.

Fumbling, I filled the last glass and checked my pitcher level. About half full. Was that enough? Did I need to fill up while everyone's glasses were still full and I wouldn't be needed? I glanced around to see what the others were doing, but they were already at their posts. They'd finished before me, and their jugs looked full, judging by the weight and the way their bearers held them.

I stumbled back to my post, remembering Vera telling

me not to leave it *ever*, and hoped that someone would bring me more before I ran dry.

While I waited, I watched the others to catch a clue of how exactly I was supposed to flag a server down. I certainly wasn't supposed to shout, wave, or do anything to draw attention to myself.

I kept getting distracted by the dinner guests. I didn't see anyone who went without masks, but that didn't mean there weren't any foreigners. They were easy to pick out because the wearers moved somewhat awkwardly, clearly uncomfortable with wearing masks heavy with trappings, and unused to not quite being able to see out of the corners of their eyes. Native Venesians of this class knew how to keep masks light but still beautifully appropriate for an audience with royalty.

Of course, even the awkward movement of the foreigners was still graceful and, I'm sure, much better looking than mine would have been had the positions been switched. I couldn't help but stare at these people, wondering how much training and how many lessons had been endured to attain such refinement. I wasn't an outer country savage by any means, but these people put me to shame.

I also noticed that no one drank. Why did the blasted glasses have to be full before their arrival if no one was going to drink? I wanted to make a face in annoyance, but I was sure that with my luck, someone would see and take my expression as a personal attack or something. Oh yes, that would turn out well.

Finally, every seat was filled, except for table on the dais. The guests chatted among themselves until another trumpet sounded, and then, as one, they all rose from their seats.

The Royal Family was here.

I didn't know if I was supposed to do anything, since I was already standing, but it seemed rude to *not* do anything. Again, I looked to the other servers for direction. They bowed their heads, so I did the same, hoping I didn't stand out as much as I thought I did.

My eyes were probably supposed to be glued to the floor, but I couldn't help but sneak peeks at the incoming procession.

Two guards led the way, followed by the Speaker and then the princess. The king and queen entered side by side, and the prince followed behind them. Two more guards brought up the tail end.

Do they really have to travel with guards everywhere? I wondered, remembering the Square and the abundance of guards there. *Or is this just for show?*

If it was just for show, it was certainly an *impressive* show. It was easy to see the guard standard: at least a head taller than I, a thin but muscled physique, and sharp eyes that peered out at the crowd through plain, silver, full-faced masks.

The royal family was completely covered, though the king and queen's dark eyes were visible. They were all draped in elegant white fabrics and jewels, and each had a mask that I had never seen before. I wondered if they had a new one every day. That would be exhausting for the makers. Perhaps these were simply their dining masks.

The bottom halves of their faces were still covered, just with opaque veils instead of full masks. The iridescent veils and their white face-masks were covered in swirling patterns of silver. It was like watching a living painting as they paraded by.

They made a complete circle around the perimeter of the room, not speaking to anyone—of course, they didn't ever speak—and when they passed by me, I certainly kept my head *and* eyes down. I felt them pass me, and when I'd thought they'd moved far enough away from me, I lifted my eyes again to watch them.

The prince's head was turned almost completely toward me.

There was no denying he was looking at me. It wasn't like there was anything behind or near me to catch his attention. My eyes shot back down to the ground, and I started to panic. Had I done something wrong? Was there something wrong with my uniform? I knew my mask was secure—I'd checked it at least a dozen times before leaving my room—and my bandage was completely hidden.

I chanced another glance. By then he had walked past me, so in order to see me he would have to turn around and walk back, and I knew he wouldn't do that.

He'd fallen back into line, as if nothing had happened, but I couldn't help but notice how tense his shoulders looked. As I stared, they shook once, as if he were laughing—or crying—to himself, then they completely relaxed.

I narrowed my eyes.

I didn't have time to process what had happened before the kitchen doors burst open and the servers filed out with the first course: a small salad with some fruit. The royal procession took their seats on the dais, and a fine, silvery curtain was drawn around them.

"Of course," I whispered to myself. "They can't eat with their faces covered like that. The veils on their masks must allow them to eat." I wondered if the veils were removable, or if they could somehow eat with them still on. The guards stood on the outside of the curtain, though, which led me to think the veils came off. Only royalty could see royalty, after all.

I didn't have much time to contemplate the eating routine of royalty, though. Apparently the drawn curtain was a sign to start eating—and drinking.

Still unsure of how to refill my jug, I tried to watch the other servers to see if they used some kind of signal to call for a refill. Thankfully, no excessively heavy drinkers were sitting in my area, and as I refilled the few glasses that required it, attention stayed away from me, as it should be.

At least, that's what it looked like. It still felt like someone was watching me, and the hair on the back of my neck pricked, but I couldn't find the culprit.

By the time my jug emptied, I still hadn't found a way to signal without drawing unwanted attention. We were well into the main course, and servers filed back and forth like lines of worker ants.

"Pstt," I tried to hiss at one, but she either ignored me or didn't hear me and skittered away, and I didn't dare speak louder. A gentleman's cup was getting low, and I was starting to worry. Would they dismiss me after something like this? Such a simple thing as not keeping a glass filled? It seemed ridiculous, yet not beyond the realm of possibility.

"Here."

I jumped as Carese appeared behind me. She whispered

to me and pressed a full jug into my hands. She took the empty one, and I looked at her, incredibly grateful.

"Hey," I risked a whisper, since we were a bit further back from the tables and those in front of me were heavily involved in conversation. "What do I do when I need a refill? No one told me."

She looked at me oddly. "You don't do anything. It's our job to watch you. Usually there's one server assigned to each Serving Miss, but since you're so new, you were overlooked."

Of course I was.

"I'll try to keep an eye out on you," she promised, her eyes gentle, and then she hurried back to the kitchen, empty jug in hand.

That reassured me dramatically. I refilled the dangerously low glass and was able to work throughout the rest of the meal worrying more about keeping cups full than about being banished from the palace before my first day was up.

EIGHT

*D*INNER WASN'T OVER ONCE THE FOOD WAS GONE. Even after the last dessert plate was cleared (some still half full with crispy little pastries filled with vanilla cream), the guests continued to drain their goblets, and the entertainment portion of the night began.

The curtain that had been shielding the royal family from view was pulled back, revealing only three of the members in their finery, their veiled masks replaced with a new mask with veiled eyes for the princess and regular full masks for the king and queen.

The prince was gone.

Before I could puzzle together why and how he'd disappeared, the Speaker announced the musicians for the evening: a foreign man and woman whose names I could never pronounce, with stranger sounding names for instruments. Even listening to their introduction felt like listening to a foreign language. All I knew was that the instrument the man held looked like a fat, squat sort of flute and that the woman bowed over what looked like the inside of a piano sitting on the floor.

Once they began to play, though, the language was universal. Again, I had to remind myself not to get lost in my surroundings, and I stepped forward to fill goblets when needed.

It was indescribably refreshing to hear music again, and I instantly lost the resentment that came with the feeling of a never-ending meal. It was a small joy when it felt like my life had none.

Rudely, though, the guests continued to talk through the performance, and judging by the expressions on any given face, this was routine. The serving girls' faces looked perfectly neutral, and the guests laughed and talked among themselves without a care in the world.

In fact, some of them weren't paying any attention to the couple performing before them. More than a few men's attentions had turned to those supplying the meal.

Unfortunately, that included me.

"Look at the eyes on this one!" an old man with a plum-colored mask said, waving his fat arm in my direction. "So green you can almost see apples spilling out!"

I frowned slightly, not understanding the connection between my eyes and fruit, and the man somehow picked up on my confusion through his drunken excitement. "Oh, she doesn't know! Pretty girl doesn't know! Look how her pretty mouth pouts behind her veil!"

His shouts of glee caught the attention of a few other serving girls walking around with cheese trays; the girls whispered and dashed into the kitchen, though the guests beside him ignored him.

A moment later, Carese appeared beside me, plucked the jug from my arms, and told me I was wanted in the kitchen.

Even more confused, I obeyed, though I heard groans behind me as she explained she would be taking my place for the remainder of the night.

Once behind the kitchen doors, I was immediately confronted by Jeza, who clucked her tongue at me. "Already making a fool of yourself."

"What? I did no such thing. I was just standing there like I was supposed to!" I retorted.

"With your eyes wide open for anyone to see!" she rebuked me. "Don't you know how eyes like yours are seen around here? Why you were chosen to be a Serving Miss?"

When I didn't answer, she laughed. "You really don't know, do you? You act like you're so much better than the rest of us, and yet you know nothing. Green eyes, little Miss Evelina, are a sign of fertility here. I'm sure a smart thing like you can figure out the rest from there. All the serving girls have green eyes. What better to go with a meal than . . ." she trailed off, her voice suggestive, and shrugged.

I shook my head, disbelieving. How had I never heard this before?

"Of course the girls are forbidden from interacting with the guests so above their station in *that* way, but some of the men are . . . playful. They like the . . . potential." She laughed. "And if that's not what you want, you're to keep your eyes *down*."

"Girls!" Kitchen Mistress Vera's voice made me jump, and both Jeza and I turned around guiltily. "What are you doing standing around? I'm sure there is more than enough work to keep you occupied."

"I was just instructing Miss Evelina on some etiquette, Kitchen Mistress," Jeza replied quickly, her voice soft and deferential. "She has much to learn about how things are done here."

"Very well," Vera said, sighing. "Don't let it interfere with your own duties, Miss Jeza."

"Of course, Kitchen Mistress."

"Now back to work. Miss Evelina, I've been informed of your little mishap tonight. Don't let it happen again. For the rest of the evening, I want you back here, cleaning and polishing the silverware. I'm sure you can manage that without making eyes at anyone."

"Yes, ma'am." I was too stunned to do anything but comply.

* * *

When the whole ordeal was over and I was finally dismissed, I collapsed into bed. After I finished with what felt like thousands of salad forks, dinner forks, soup spoons, butter knives, and goodness knew what else, I'd had to pitch in with the dishes. It was a relentless pile of plates, bowls, and trays. My fingers were wrinkled prunes, and my back and feet ached from standing in one place for so long, not to mention the exhaustion I felt from the tension of being watched all night. For someone who was supposed to be invisible, I felt I was as visible as the sun at noonday—especially when the opulent meal loosened the tight discipline of the so-called high-class gentlemen.

It was too late to visit the laundry for blankets, but I was too tired to care. I quickly went through my nightly routine and applied the balm to my burn, which wasn't hurting as badly anymore, though it still ached and was tender to the touch. Almost as soon as I had stripped down to my chemise and fell back on my bed, I heard a loud banging on my door. I stared at it curiously for a moment, wondering who on earth would be visiting *me*, and who would be visiting me at such a late hour. Then my heart started to race—what if I'd been discovered as a thief and a fraud and someone was here to turn me out on the streets?

They knocked again, and as much as I wanted to wait them out with the hope they'd give up and go away, I knew if they didn't confront me now, they'd simply do it in the kitchens in front of everyone.

I picked up my mask from my nightstand and tied it securely before padding my way over to the door. I had no robe, but it was dark, and my chemise was thick enough that it wasn't like they'd be able to see anything. Maybe it was one of the other servers or Vera, coming to tell me how awful I had been today and that I needed to pack my (nonexistent) bags immediately.

Cautiously, I pulled open the door and peeked out. There, standing in the dim, flickering light, was Aiden.

Completely forgetting myself at the joy of seeing a familiar face, I yanked open the door and ran to throw my arms around him, crying his name.

Aiden seemed to have a similar idea and pulled me tightly to his body in a one-armed hug, the other arm carefully holding a lantern.

"I thought you were dead," he whispered. "Everyone was talking about the fire at your place. What happened to you? And why are you *here*, of all places?"

I didn't want to let go of him, even for a moment. To have something familiar after all this upheaval was beyond words. I rubbed my nose against the fabric of his shirt, breathing in his scent.

"We were attacked. There was a fire. I had to hide." I could only speak in short, simple sentences, too distracted by how happy I was to see someone I knew, to see *him*.

"But *why*?" he pressed.

I shook my head against his neck. "I can't tell you everything. Just trust me that I have to hide right now."

Speaking of which . . .

"How on earth did you find me?" I had to pull back to look in his eyes, absolutely astonished that he'd tracked me down here.

His eyes tightened. "I had to find you. Can you just trust me? You know I've always been able to find anyone . . ." he trailed off. "Of course I would find you."

I looked down, suddenly shy with the tension that had built between us. Then I realized how inappropriately dressed I was and flew away from him, hiding behind my door.

"Sorry! I didn't even realize . . . I was just so happy to see you," I babbled incoherently, shutting the door most of the way so I could find something to cover myself with.

"I'm glad to hear that." He chuckled. "I'm just so happy you're alive right now. Please don't send me away."

"What were you thinking, tracking me down in the middle of the night like this?" I scolded as I quickly pulled my dress on so I could invite him in.

"It was all a matter of when I got my information and when I could get away," he said.

"Am I ever going to find out how you're so good at finding people, or are you going to keep that a mystery forever?"

"A man of mystery is far more attractive, don't you think?"

"No. I'd rather know what I was getting myself into, thank you very much." I rolled my eyes and gave myself a once-over. "I'm decent, you can come in."

He pushed the door open and stepped inside, looking at me seriously. "I'm sure you'll know one day," he finally said. "As long as you don't disappear again, okay? You scared me half to death."

"Sorry." I didn't really have a choice in the matter, now did I? And he'd been so far from my mind . . . most of the time.

"I'm glad you found me, though," I confessed. "I was afraid I'd have to resort to having no companions but the stupid girls in the kitchens."

He winced on my behalf. "They're that bad?"

"No," I answered truthfully, "just the ones I've met so far, mostly. Except for maybe one girl, everyone seems to have their own agenda."

"How do you mean?"

I sat on my lumpy bed and motioned for him to sit beside me. I could tell this was going to be a long visit—which was fine by me—and there wasn't really anywhere else for him to sit. I wasn't going to make him sit on the *ground*, though the mattress was really only a small improvement.

"Well, as it was my first day here, you can imagine that I had no idea what was going on. I was afraid I was going to make a fool of myself because no one really explained what to do."

He nodded. "Yeah, I can see that. A noble dining hall is a bit of a circus, isn't it?"

"Which reminds me, on top of all of *that*, someone kept staring at me all through dinner, and I couldn't tell who. And—" As I was about to say something about the prince looking at me, I realized how self-absorbed that sounded. And a bit ridiculous. He was behind a curtain after all. And, you know, a prince.

"And?" he prompted.

"And I don't know. It was just different."

"Yeah. I wish I could've helped you somehow."

"Me too. Though I'm pretty sure you couldn't have. Only girls are allowed as servers, and I think you'd stick out a bit."

He made a face at me, and I couldn't help but laugh. Oh, it felt good to laugh. "You think?"

"Seriously, though," I went back to his original question, "it seems like there's some kind of hierarchy within the servants, and my being here throws it off. I don't know. I'm probably just being paranoid."

"Hey, if anyone has a right to be paranoid right now, I'm sure it's you." He paused. "Any chance I can get more information on what happened the other night?"

I sobered up and stared out my window, picking at loose threads on my skirt. "There was a . . . thief. He set fire to our workshop to cover his tracks. I don't know where my father is, though my neighbors think he was killed, too." My heart constricted painfully at the reminder.

"Oh, Evie," he murmured and wrapped an arm around my shoulders. I let him pull me close and reveled in the warmth. "I'm sorry."

"I'll be okay. I've got this position now, so I won't go hungry or roam the streets or anything like that."

"I don't understand why you couldn't stay in your house and continue your work there. All your talent is going to waste here." His hand began rubbing circles against my shoulder, and it was oddly distracting.

"The thief got away," I said simply. "And he knows I'm on my own and that I could land him in the Square. I'd be an easy target at home."

"But still . . ."

"It's not forever," I said firmly. "I won't slave away as a Serving Miss for the rest of my life. Just until he's caught and I'm safe again."

He sighed. "There's got to be something I can do to help." We sat silently for a long moment, each lost in our own thoughts.

I seriously wondered how he found me here. He had to have one amazing informant, if not *dozens* of amazing informants. It was beginning to make me uneasy, how little I knew about him.

"Aiden," I said hesitantly, wanting to get at least some basic answers to set my mind at ease.

"What if I could find you a job with the mask makers here?" he asked suddenly. "They always need assistants for the more menial skills. I know you're better than that, but it would at least get you out of the kitchen. I don't think I could get you a better job without drawing attention to you."

"What?" I asked, startled and incredulous. "How would you manage to do that?"

"I know people," he said cryptically, smirking slightly.

Those must be some people, I thought. "And what makes you think those people will do you a favor?"

He laughed. "Oh, don't worry about that. I have lots of favors in my pocket. But what do you say?"

I didn't even have to think about it. Away from the madhouse kitchen, Vera, and the others? "Yes, please!"

Laughing again, he said, "Consider it done. I'll try to talk to them tomorrow, and we'll see what happens. Unfortunately, I don't know if I can do much for your room without raising suspicion." He looked at my meager living space—made even more pathetic looking by his lantern—and frowned. "I'll see if I can get you blankets and things, though. Why didn't you just bring some from your house?"

"I couldn't carry anything else," I answered matter-of-factly. "I'm not a packhorse."

"No, that you are not."

We both grew silent again, and I began to feel the effects of my busy day. I tried to choke back a yawn, but it snuck out, betraying me.

Aiden noticed and stood quickly. "I'm sorry—you must be exhausted. I probably should have waited until you got some sleep, but I just had to make sure it was really you."

"No, I'm glad you came by." I smiled at him. "It's always a good thing when I see you."

"And let's keep it that way," he said, grinning. "Hopefully the next time you see me, you'll be in a better position. I can't promise the people will be any nicer, though."

"I'll take my chances. Truly, thank you."

"It is truly my pleasure, my lady."

Smiling at his formality that had always felt more like a term of endearment, I wrapped my arms around him again and bid him farewell. He returned the gesture with both arms this time, then stooped to pick up his light, smiled at me one last time, and disappeared down the dark hallway.

Shedding my clothes and mask for the second time, I crawled into bed, truly exhausted. Naturally, with my body so tired, my mind decided to race, asking unanswered question after unanswered question. I was determined to get some real information out of Aiden the next time I saw him, no matter what it took.

I also needed to work on my cover story. He wasn't one to just let something go; I knew that much about him. I knew he'd drill me about the attack on my house, and any encounter I had with the thief. And if I knew him at all, I'd wager that he'd take it upon himself to help find the scoundrel.

I sat up in bed, my heart beating hard. If I wanted to find someone, the most obvious way was through Aiden. And he'd be more than willing to help me. If anything, I'd have to work to keep him from putting himself in any danger or taking unnecessary risks. He was a little hard-headed that way. He always thought he knew what was best, and I pitied any man that dared to disagree with him. My job then was to enlist his help while still keeping myself hidden. I could do it, somehow. I knew I could.

Filled with a renewed hope, I lay back down and drifted to sleep, dreaming of what my life would be when it was all put back together.

NINE

A HARSH BELL STARTLED ME OUT OF MY BED. I FELL onto the cold stone floor as I floundered around in confusion. I glanced out the window as I reached for my mask; it wasn't even light out yet. I could see the slightest hints of dawn approaching, but it was still far too early for my liking. I was used to getting up early but not before the sun was up. This was unnatural, especially after a late night. I wagered I'd only gotten about five hours of sleep.

When I was properly awake, I wasn't sure if I had been dreaming the night before when Aiden came to my room. His promise to get me into the Masking Workroom sounded too good to be true, so I got ready to work in the kitchens. Mentally and physically, I would be ready to work but hoped that I wouldn't be there for long.

I groaned as I pulled my clothes on and shivered in the chill of the not-quite-morning air. My arms and back ached from the workout they'd gotten yesterday. I'd always thought I was fairly strong, but this duty worked a completely different set of muscles. It was exhausting.

As I wandered into the kitchen, I was taken aback by

the flurry of action and commotion. I thought and hoped things would be more low key in the morning, but the kitchen was just as hectic as it was for dinner, if not even more so because I still felt half asleep. I fell in line to collect my own breakfast—a simple but delicious-smelling warm cinnamon-spiced porridge—and sat at the table to eat. Again, I was left on my own, which was much more desirable than having someone like Jeza accost me.

As if my thoughts summoned her, I heard Jeza's shrill laughter as she walked into the room.

"You know just looking at her she's going to be a disaster," she was saying, "I doubt she'll be here more than a week."

I clenched my teeth. She was clearly talking about me, and it sounded like she didn't like me any more than I liked her. I watched her and the two girls beside her out of the corner of my eye.

"She's not very bright," Jeza continued as she filed through the serving line to pick up her breakfast. "It's a wonder she got in here at all."

I closed my eyes, foolishly hoping that would help me escape her notice.

That didn't quite work out the way I'd hoped as suddenly my hair was drenching in hot cinnamon porridge.

Shrieking, I leapt up and spun around to see Jeza, empty bowl in hand and a smug look on her face.

"Oops," she said, propping the bowl against her hip. "I didn't see you there."

I glared at her and opened my mouth, but before I could say anything, she cut me off. "I wouldn't say anything if I were you." She glanced meaningfully above my left shoulder. Vera had arrived just behind me and was speaking to one of the cooks. "You don't want to draw any more attention to yourself, now do you?"

I hoped she tripped and fell into the canal the next time she left the palace. Or that I would have the chance to push her.

"Sit," she commanded as if I were a dog. When I didn't obey right away, she heaved an exaggerated sigh and gestured toward Vera again. "She's about to give the morning announcements. You can't leave now, and you can't just stand there."

I'd like to tell her what I could or couldn't do, but, unfortunately, she was right.

I sat and combed through my hair with my handkerchief, dumping the clumps of porridge into my abandoned bowl, dreaming of all the ways I'd like to get back at Jeza as Vera made her way to the front of the room.

For some reason, Jeza and her cronies decided to sit next to me, whispering as the kitchen mistress checked on the morning preparations. I tried to ignore them, but it was like trying to ignore a fly constantly buzzing in my ear.

"Have you seen some of the dresses the maids upstairs have turned up?" she asked in that annoying whisper. "They're all in a tizzy getting ready for the ball and some of those creations are just ghastly."

"I heard one lady hated her dress so much she refused to wear it and dared her maid to wear it herself! At the masquerade! Can you imagine?" They all laughed, although I didn't see what was so funny.

"Some people think that just because the prince will be picking his bride there, and just because he has his pick of the women of the kingdom, that anyone has a chance. As if the prince doesn't have better taste than to choose some *nobody*."

They continued to gossip as I fought to make my hair presentable. Then they suddenly fell silent, save for the sounds of their spoons.

"Really, Miss Evelina," Vera chided me, amusement ringing in every word. "Even simpletons know how to bathe. I thought you said you were more intelligent than that."

I bristled at her words but bit my tongue.

She waited, plainly expecting some kind of retort, but I refused to give Jeza the satisfaction. When it become clear I wasn't going to say anything, Vera sighed. "Well, if you have nothing to say for yourself, you best get to your station. And thank your lucky stars that we did not have fish this morning." She wrinkled her nose at the thought and whisked herself off to torment some other poor soul, Jeza and friends in tow.

I scrambled to find something to cover my wet hair, eventually settling for a napkin that looked only crumpled and not actually used. I quickly braided my hair and tucked it under the gold-colored material, all the while marveling they used such fine fabric for napkins here.

The rest of breakfast passed much like dinner the night before. It was a little more low key: the dress wasn't so elaborate, the tables weren't as full of guests, and there was no after-meal entertainment. Despite all of this, it was still clearly a formal affair.

The complete royal family was in attendance again, although there was no repeat of last night's uncomfortable attention from the prince, thank goodness, nor did he vanish partway through the meal. They were again dressed elaborately, with different masks, though the same style.

Maybe that was something I could learn from working in the masking room. Assuming Aiden followed through.

After breakfast was over and cleaned up, we were free to do as we wished. Most of the younger girls went to lessons provided by the palace, which I could attend as well, but it was only basic reading and writing, which I already knew. It seemed the older girls usually went into town to see family or run errands or stayed to do other chores in the palace.

Luckily, I was free to go, but I didn't really have anything I wished to do. I certainly didn't want to go into town; I was too tired from yesterday but not so bored to look for more work.

I decided to familiarize myself with the palace a little more. I knew my room, the kitchens, and the main hall, but that was about it. I'd spied some gardens from the dining hall windows that I'd been itching to explore.

However, I didn't make it much further than the hallway I hoped led to the servants' entrance when I heard a high voice calling.

"Evelina!"

I turned at the sound of my name and saw Carese jogging toward me. "Is something wrong?" I asked, alarmed at her pink face and somewhat disheveled hair.

"No, not at all. I'm just glad I found you." She put a hand to her chest as she caught her breath. "I've been running all over trying to find girls. His highness has called an emergency council meeting, and I need servers, but everyone's already busy with other duties or in town. You're the only other one I've found, but the two of us should be able to make do, I think."

"Of course," I said. "What do you need me to do?"

Carese explained quickly as we walked back to the kitchens. "You'll just need to follow me to the council rooms. During the meeting itself, the two of us will fill drinks in the same manner as dinner, though there are only twelve council members plus the king and prince."

"Both will be there?" I asked, surprised. I didn't think the prince would attend, since he wouldn't speak.

"Yes, along with lords from different parts of the island and some ambassadors, I believe."

"Anyone I need to worry about?"

She winced. "I'm sorry about the other night. You should have had more preparation than you did before going to the floor. I'm not sure how you were missed."

"Probably because Mistress Vera didn't exactly take a liking to me," I said glumly. That was just what I needed. I didn't know what was worse: knowing I should have been more prepared and wasn't, or wondering if there was more I was supposed to know and didn't.

"Mistress Vera is rather . . . singular with those she takes a liking to," she said delicately.

I dropped it, feeling sorry for the girl who couldn't have been much older than me, though it was clear she'd been in the palace a long time. "Just assume I don't know anything when it comes to things like this, all right? Most of the time, you'll probably be correct."

She smiled. "I'll help you when I can."

Carese led the way to the cellar, a surprisingly large room below the kitchens, and showed me how to draw from the barrels. "Not that you'll ever need to do this part," she pointed out. "This is for select kitchen staff . . . too much of a problem with missing bottles in the past. But still, it might be good to know." She shrugged and together we filled two large jugs to take to the council room.

"We need to be in place before anyone else arrives," she instructed, balancing the jug on her hip and handing me a silver tray with empty glasses on it to carry. I tried to copy the way she used her hips to balance. I wobbled a little but didn't drop anything. "And we need to blend into the curtains. Keep your head and eyes down at all times. Only refill glasses during recesses or if addressed directly."

"Why do we need to be in there the whole time?"

"Some of the ambassadors like to take advantage of our hospitality," she said wryly, "and will ask for frequent refills. But we don't want to interfere, so it's best to just stay out of sight until summoned. And it takes too much time to forever be coming and going. You'll see. Recesses are frequent."

I followed her up a narrow staircase that she told me was only for servants; guests came through the main ballroom and the hall with paintings of past rulers. "To remind them of who they are indebted to for their current position," Carese said.

The council room itself was not so intimidating but not entirely welcoming either. Lush curtains hung around the entire room, to muffle the sound, according to Carese.

"Or to hide guards," I ventured a guess.

She looked unamused. "Perhaps." I was quickly learning that she liked to keep things simple and factual, and not waste time on gossip or fantasies.

A horseshoe-shaped table sat in the middle of the

room, the open end facing the door, and the top in front of a raised dais similar to the one from the dining hall. I assumed the prince would sit there, while the king would sit at a particularly plush chair that was also slightly raised above the others.

"You'll stand on this side, here," Carese directed, placing me where she wanted me to stand. "I'll take the other side, where most of the ambassadors should sit. You shouldn't have much to do but stand there. Now, help me fill the cups."

We worked quickly and silently, and before long the voices of the council members announced their imminent arrival.

"Quickly now!" Carese whispered. "Stand there. Don't meet anyone's eyes. Don't make any noise. You'll be fine."

I obeyed, wiping my sweaty palms on my skirt once more while I could still move freely.

The members trickled in more slowly than I would expect for an emergency meeting, talking among themselves. Their masks were a mix of all the main colors, though all were pale—high-ranking, as to be expected. There were more purple of the nobles than I expected, but the fishermen blues, artisan greens, and intellectual reds were also well represented.

After my first glance, though, I looked down at my skirt hem, afraid to repeat my mistake from the night before. Instead, I relied on my ears to teach me.

The members seemed to be predominantly men; I could pick out only two female voices. The others conversed freely about people I didn't know and matters I didn't understand.

A hush fell over the group, and the scraping of chairs

being pushed back sounded as the members rose for the king and prince to enter, or so I assumed.

There was a general rustle as everyone situated themselves, and then one of the women spoke. Instantly, I recognized her as the Speaker, the same regal woman from the Square.

"The situation is thus," she began with no prelude. "A red tide has washed up on our western shores."

I heard a general murmur before she spoke again. Red tides were rare, but not unheard of; algae congealed in the water and poisoned the sea life. Dead fish washed up on shore, and any shellfish collected would paralyze or kill anyone who ingested it. The tide usually washed back out to sea within a few weeks or even days, but it could also last months. "As you know, the red tide presents several problems, and there's no telling how long it will last," the Speaker continued.

"What is the king asking of us?" a deep baritone asked.

"The king asks for assistance for the fishermen in that area." I nearly dropped my jug at the sound of an authoritative male voice instead of the Speaker's and couldn't resist raising my eyes to see the king stand and address the council himself. Expecting some sort of reaction from the members, I scanned the room but found no one in as much shock as I was. A few shifted in their seats, but this was clearly not the first time the king had spoken to them.

He continued, and I dropped my eyes to the floor, listening to his voice. It was smooth and solid, even as he laid out the problems before the council. "The fishermen cannot sell the contaminated shellfish, and if the tide lasts for very long, the men cannot feed their families."

A raspy voice added, "They also have no income for other goods. And they will need to clear the washed-up fish from the shore and dispose of them somehow."

"Yes," the king agreed. "Our immediate concern is the wash-up. We don't want any work animals eating it and falling ill."

"Lord Luca, your villa is on that side of the island, correct? Is there any particular assistance you require or might suggest?"

I couldn't help it—my head shot straight up again. I knew that voice.

As the man I presumed to be Lord Luca listed what needed to be done, I stared at the young man who had posed the question.

Aiden. What on earth was he doing here?

There was no mistake. He was dressed more formally than I was used to seeing, but his mask was the same purple one I knew almost as well as my own green. I couldn't help but meet his eyes, determined to confirm my suspicion, and the spark of recognition was all I needed. He sat on the opposite side of the room, closer to the top of the horse-shoe than I would expect, and he looked comfortable there. *Comfortable,* and not ten feet from the prince and king! It was not an unusual thing for him to be here.

My mind was spinning. Clearly Aiden was from a much more important family than I had assumed. I knew he was noble, but not *this* noble. Did he always attend these meetings, or was he filling in for his father? Who was his father? I should know something like that. I should know so much more about him than I did.

He didn't look at me again, or at least as far as I could

tell. Carese caught me and frowned, reminding me I was supposed to keep my head down.

The council broke for recess often, usually whenever there were signs of an argument brewing, but of course I couldn't talk to Aiden during those times. I held my tongue and acted the perfect serving girl, my impatience building inside. During the first recess, I couldn't help but ask Carese about the king's speaking as we prepared small bowls of nuts in the hallway from a cart another servant brought up from the kitchens.

"It's not the first time," she confirmed. "And he doesn't speak often. But he has been using the Speaker less and less. It makes the members uncomfortable. The first time he spoke he sent the servants out, probably so we wouldn't know how the members reacted." She made a face. "There are rumors that some of the members nearly called for a new king right there and then."

"Just because the current one spoke?"

She shrugged. "People hold tight to tradition. Especially the nobility."

"Even if tradition no longer makes sense?"

"A lot of the things the nobility do don't make sense."

With Aiden in mind, I couldn't argue with that.

Finally, hours later, the Speaker announced the conclusion of the meeting, and I chanced one last peek only to see Aiden slip from the room almost immediately.

Oh, he and I were going to have a long chat the next time I caught him.

TEN

I WASN'T NEEDED FOR ANY LUNCH SERVICES; apparently the palace kept lunch a small affair. Too many things going on during the day, I supposed. Either way, I was grateful for the reprieve. I wanted time to sort things out in my head and to somehow hunt Aiden down and demand some answers.

I went straight to my room, realizing I wouldn't be able to find Aiden and had to wait for him to come to me.

First, I needed to visit the bathing rooms, to tend both to my hair and my Mark. Cleaning the Mark was now a familiar routine. It didn't hurt as much; it mostly just itched horribly and felt hot to the touch, which made me nervous. A clear liquid seeped into the strip of cotton I was using as a bandage, and while I didn't know if that was good or not, the fact that it was clear was somewhat reassuring.

I had been keeping my face as clean as I could, almost obsessively, and I applied the balm I'd salvaged from my house morning, noon, and night. It seemed to help. It was soothing to the heat of my skin at least.

With that taken care of, I left my mask off to let the wound breathe and crawled onto my bedroll. I rolled onto my back to stare at the ceiling while I thought piecing together what I knew of my friend.

He was from a noble, high-ranking family. He'd have to be, to be part of the council. He also had a seemingly free rein in the palace, coming and going as he pleased.

He had a certain amount of power, mostly in the way of favors. How quickly he could get me moved to the Masking Room would be a good indicator of how much power.

My thoughts returned to Aiden's uncanny ability to find missing people and things. He had to have people under his command; it was the only solution I could think of. If he had men to command, they could easily provide him with information he sought, and he was easily charismatic enough to earn the loyalty of anyone in his service.

He was hiding something from me. It felt like some kind of obligation or duty that he was trying to escape. He was always so carefree and eager around me, but whenever I asked him personal questions, he grew quiet and reluctant to share even the tiniest morsel of information.

I sighed, frustrated with this mystery.

A soft knock at my door interrupted my meditation, and I hurried to put my mask back on before answering it.

Not too surprisingly, Aiden greeted me, looking properly like a boy caught doing something he shouldn't have been doing.

"Hello, Evie," he said glumly. "I thought you might be wanting to ask me a few questions. Or, you know, slap me."

I rolled my eyes. "Get in here."

He stepped inside but didn't join me on the bed as he

had before. Instead, he paced in front of me, opening and closing his mouth as he tried to say something, only to change his mind before any sound came out.

"You look like a fish, Aiden. Just talk to me. Who are you, really?"

"No more mystery?"

"No more mystery." My voice was firm.

He sighed. "You know that I will follow after my father when the time comes. He's a member of the council and sends me to speak when he . . . can't." He spoke haltingly, watching my eyes for a reaction. "You've probably guessed by now that my family is, um, near the top of the social ladder."

"Go on," I said dryly.

"I don't know what you want to hear from me," he confessed.

"I just want to hear *about* you. We talk all the time, but you never actually say anything!" I stood up and started pacing restlessly. I spun to face him. "I just want to know who you are."

His shoulders slumped and he scuffed at the ground, no longer meeting my eyes. "It's complicated."

"I don't see what's complicated about it. Tell me about your family. Something from your childhood. Whatever you want, so long as it's *you*. I don't even know if you've been betrothed to some foreign princess or something!"

His gaze snapped back up to mine. "I'm not betrothed. I don't have a secret wife or anything that I'm running away from. Did you really think I could do something like that?"

"I didn't think you could be a member of the king's council, either, and look what happened there."

"I deserved that." He sighed again. "Look, I'll try to be more forthcoming with information in the future."

"You'll actually answer questions when I ask them with something other than another question?"

"Let's not get too carried away," he said, smiling wryly. "Must you take all my charm away in one swoop?"

"Charm?" I laughed, and something in the tension between us broke.

He smiled genuinely now. "I *am* sorry, Evie. If I could have had it any other way . . ."

"Why can't you? Why do you have to keep so many secrets?"

The smile slipped from his face, and he sighed. His voice was sad when he answered, "I wish I didn't have to. Especially from you."

"And yet . . ."

"I'm sorry. They're not . . ." He paused, his face twisting in pain as he searched for the right words. "It's not just about me. I can't tell you things without revealing secrets that belong to other people as well."

"Just tell me what you can, all right? I don't want to be serving again and suddenly see you in the main dining hall announcing your engagement to some beauty from another island or something," I joked, trying to lighten the mood. I was hurt and angry, but he was too dear to lose, especially now.

His laugh sounded forced, but he said nothing more on the subject. "It's still so strange to see you in that mask," he commented. "I don't know which of us was more surprised in that room to see the other. I'm just really glad I saw you last night. If that had been the first time . . . ," he trailed off.

"You would have done more than ignore me and then run away?" I prodded.

He groaned. "Almost definitely. And that would have been bad."

I could feel my face flush and touched my mask absently, making sure it was sitting as it should. "Is it that odd?" I asked to turn the attention from me to my mask.

"Yeah." He stepped forward and fingered it lightly, looking distracted. My breath caught. I wasn't used to him standing so close. And his fingers were dangerously close to my Mark as they brushed my skin. "It's different. And don't take this the wrong way, but the palette suits you."

I gave him a funny look, Mark forgotten. "What's that supposed to mean? I'm suited to work as a palace servant?"

He sighed and backed away. "See, that's taking it the wrong way. I mean the silver suits you. I'd love to see you in a white mask."

"Ha, yeah right! Only the royal family wears white, and the day I stand with them will be the day fish fly and birds swim. Besides, this is more gray than silver."

He shrugged and began walking alongside me. "You never know," he said. "I've heard tell of some birds that can swim."

"You're being ridiculous again." I sighed as I ran a finger through my hair, catching a snag I'd missed earlier. I hadn't been able to completely get rid of the cinnamon smell either, but at least that was pleasant.

I groaned at the memory, and Aiden asked what had happened.

"Nothing," I was quick to answer. "Just remembering

one of the girls was being a nuisance this morning. You know. Making sure the new girl was up to standard."

He frowned again and glanced at the way I was picking at my hair. "By doing what?"

I dropped my hand. "It's not important."

"What did you say her name was?"

"Oh no, I'm not telling you that. You'll go find her and put her out of work. And as much as I might like that idea, I'm not going to be that mean."

"You sure?"

I nodded. As much as I disliked Jeza and would enjoy striking back, she was a gossip, and that was bound to come in handy eventually.

"Well, you have a standing offer, then. Just say the word."

"And you'll pull your strings?" I teased.

"Call me your puppet master," he said, laughing. "Will you at least tell me what she said?"

"Nothing I didn't already know really. Just that the prince can choose from any girl in the country, and this is the year he'll do it. But it would never be me because I'd have to actually meet the prince, and I'm not in any position to do so."

"Oh, really?" The teasing glint was back in his eyes. "Suppose he's riding on a procession through town and his horse shied and took off right toward you and you managed to calm it down—"

"Or get trampled by it," I snorted.

"—and the prince was amazed by your *gentle* nature and whisks you away to be married that night."

"I don't go into town anymore," I pointed out.

"Fine," he continued on undeterred. "You're serving

a meal to their majesties at some royal function or other and—oh no!—spill your whole jug on the prince's least favorite dignitary. He proposes to you on the spot. As soon as the dignitary is gone, of course."

I couldn't help but laugh at him. "Now you're just being ridiculous."

He smiled back at me. "I aim to please."

* * *

The next few days passed much more quietly. I fell into a routine: breakfast service in the morning, picking up various chores during the day, dinner service, then meeting with Aiden for a few moments at night.

Once I'd found my feet, I was determined to find out all I could about the Chameleon. As soon as I had time to explore the palace as only a servant could, it didn't take me long to find where the news runners gathered.

They favored a large parlor near the back of the palace, one with a special entrance just for them; free of the crowds that used the servants' entrance. I wasn't the only non-runner who visited either; it seemed to be a popular spot for many of the maids.

The runners were all quite fit young men, after all.

I didn't have the time or the energy for that sort of thing, but it didn't hurt to have something nice to look at while doing such an unpleasant task as hunting down the Chameleon.

Once I knew where to go to hear the goings-on of the day, it took even less time to find someone willing to tell me all he knew. Unfortunately, all of them knew little. It seemed the Chameleon was keeping a low profile after his latest attack.

I tried not to let it get me down, and Aiden's nightly visits did wonders at keeping my spirits up. When I asked how he managed to see me so late at night, he said he was staying at the palace while the business with the red tide was being sorted, so he didn't have to worry about traveling at night.

Our meetings were short, but they quickly became the highlight of my day. While he still wasn't exactly spilling out childhood secrets, he was a little more willing to tell me a little about his sister, Bianca, or his various exploits as an adventurous teenager.

One particular night about a week after I discovered him in the council room, he greeted me at my door with a wide grin and pulled me into a tight embrace before spinning me once around excitedly. I quickly wiggled out of his grasp and looked behind him, worried that someone would see. Nobility didn't generally go around hugging the help. But it seemed the coast was clear and his expression was too warm to be anything but happy he was there.

"Let me guess. You brought me good news," I said.

That put a great smile on his lips. "That I did, my Lady. That I did indeed."

ELEVEN

*T*HE NEXT DAY, I WAS STILL HUMMING WITH excitement from Aiden's news the night before as I cleaned up after breakfast. When I heard his familiar knock on my door, I wrenched it open, beaming up at him.

"You don't even have to go to lunch. I'm here to take you straight up to the Masking Room," he announced proudly in lieu of a greeting.

"You're joking."

"I wouldn't joke about that," he said, folding his arms across his chest. "I know how much this means to you."

"Yes. I'm going to owe you one huge favor."

"I will certainly keep that in mind," he said, laughing.

"So what do I need to do?"

"Well, like I said, we're going to go to the workroom now. They wanted to send some official notice, but I thought this would be more fun."

"I agree. Am I completely done with the kitchens, then?"

He grimaced. "Unfortunately not. Naturally you'll still have to eat there, at the same times, and you'll still have to assist in the evenings for dinner and for special occasions when they need more servers. I couldn't have you completely transferred without raising some suspicion, and I was pretty sure you didn't want any of that."

"You thought correctly, sir."

"Sorry. I know you don't really like it there."

I shrugged. "It's not that bad. I like watching people at dinner. And it's not a hard job, aside from the constant standing and carrying heavy jugs."

He laughed. "I'm sure people like watching you too. That might be part of why I couldn't get you out. I wouldn't want to deprive anyone of the chance to have you wait on them."

I rolled my eyes, remembering the scene from my first night. "Sure."

"All right, my Lady, let's go. I'm surprised you haven't already tried to drag me up there."

"You're too tall for me to drag. I wouldn't want to stretch you out any further." I stuck my tongue out at him childishly, and he laughed all the way down the hall.

We arrived at the Masking Room, and I stopped in my tracks, stunned. I'd been in many a mask-making workshop, particularly when first learning my trade, but the Masking Room was something else entirely. It was like someone had taken my workroom, enlarged it ten times, and upgraded the materials by twenty.

It was also buzzing with activity, but this kind of activity I understood. I could find the difference between the master workers and the assistants easily, not just by their masks, but also by how they handled the materials and carried themselves.

Mask makers fell under the artisan title and wore masks of green, though that wasn't explicitly the case here. I felt a pain as I missed my old mask, but I shoved that to the back of my mind. The assistants fell under the serving class of the castle, so they were in silvers and grays, like the mask I was already wearing. I would blend in easily, and should I actually rise to a higher level, I could wear my familiar greens. And even if I couldn't wear them, I could see them. That thought alone was comforting. I always thought the greens were more warm and open than the stark grays and blacks of the kitchen's serving class.

In my shop, when I was old enough to work, I was put in charge of making the molds and bases for the masks, as well as any business that took us away from the shop itself. My father preferred to stay with the shop, and always had more than enough work to keep himself busy and his mind distracted.

My beadwork was good enough to sell, but that was the only decorating technique in which I seemed to have any particular skill. And by beadwork, I mean designing the beads into the masks, not the manufacturing of the beads themselves. I'd tried my hand at blowing my own glass beads once, but it ended poorly. I wasn't allowed another attempt. Beads were easy enough to buy, though, and I'd bought whatever I could afford from Iniga and whatever I couldn't from the boats. I'd always preferred the design and to look of the big picture anyway.

I looked back to Aiden, who was standing just outside the door, for reassurance.

He leaned forward to whisper in my ear, "Here is where I have to leave you. Go ask for Milo—he's the master you'll be working under. I'd escort you, but I'm actually supposed to be somewhere else right now."

As he stepped back, I placed one hand on my hip and looked at him, ignoring the sudden racing of my pulse. "I'm not getting you in trouble, am I?"

He waved my concerns aside. "No, not at all. They're used to me being late or not showing up at all. I'll be fine. Don't worry about me at all."

"You're sure?"

"Positive. Now go show them what you can do, my lady." With that farewell, he lightly pressed a kiss to the back of my hand and walked away.

I watched him go, then squared my shoulders and walked into the room, feeling as if I could take on the world. I would be in my element. I would be working in the Royal Masking. Nothing could make me happier, save seeing the Chameleon in the Square.

"Excuse me," I said, using my most polite voice, "can you point me in the direction of Milo?"

The gray-masked, slender girl I had addressed looked me up and down, then pointed over to a surprisingly young man. "That's him there, with the crow's feather on the right."

"Thank you."

"Are you new?" she asked before I walked away. She didn't sound threatening, just curious, which was a nice change. "My name is Emma," she offered, tucking a strand of light brown hair behind her ear.

"Evie."

"Like I said, Milo is over there. I work for him too, so I'm sure we'll see a lot of each other." She gave a tight smile and returned to her task of braiding yellow and blue ribbons together.

"Thanks."

I watched for a moment; her work was good. The braiding was perfectly even and very small. It wasn't difficult work, especially not with what I was used to, but it was something very familiar, and something I'd spent hours upon hours doing as a child. She could be talented someday.

I maneuvered through the packed room, dodging precariously stacked bolts of fabric and tables with loose beads that could fall and roll between the floorboards.

"Milo?"

"Yes, lady?" The man turned around.

Milo was a striking man, broad and muscular, with the look of a former soldier. He wore his dark, gray-streaked hair tied back in a low ponytail and would have been extremely intimidating if not for the errant threads stuck to his sleeve or the ribbons hanging out of his pocket.

The most striking thing was his mask, though not for the reasons I would have expected. Of course a master mask maker would have an elaborate and ornate mask, but most would not have one with the eye holes still blacked in.

Yet his was. The mask was otherwise perfect: green for artisan, silver for royal service, and white for mastery. Simple, given his stature, but intricately beaded and designed with a perfect fit.

Cutting the eyeholes wasn't a matter of difficulty; I spent many hours of my own apprenticeship slaving over them, making sure each was perfectly symmetrical and the precise shape I wanted. Most makers blacked out the unwanted material with paint before cutting, to be sure of exact results. But Milo, for some reason, simply blacked his out and moved on to another part of the mask.

As I watched, his hands continued to work, twisting a tight braid of blue ribbons while he waited for me to speak, and I realized with a shock that Master Milo was blind.

A blind mask maker? I'd never heard of such a thing. How could he design without his sight? How could he construct such perfect creations? I'd seen and admired his work every time I saw the royal family. How did he even come by the position of royal mask maker?

"Lady?" He interrupted the flurry of questions fluttering around in my mind with a gruff voice, and I shook my head, telling myself to pay attention.

"Master Milo, I've been reassigned to work for you. My name is Evelina." Nerves tied my tongue into knots. Where was the ease I had when working with merchants at the Market?

"Hmm. Yes, I heard I was getting another one. Someone must be pleased with me; you're the second one this month." A quick glance around the workroom showed that each station was occupied, sometimes by two young people.

I didn't know how to respond to that. My mind was still distracted and transfixed by how deftly his hands worked even while he spoke with me. I suddenly felt extremely inadequate. "I've admired what work of yours I've seen," I said without thinking.

"I've admired work I haven't seen," he said shortly, and I flinched, rebuking myself for my faux pas.

"Well, lass, tell me what you can do. Why did they send you to me?"

I straightened my shoulders, determined to salvage this meeting somehow. "I've finished my apprenticeship under

Master Pietro in the Green District. I've worked alongside him after my completion."

"How old are you?" He spoke directly, and there was no doubt who he was questioning, though his face turned back to his work.

"Eighteen, sir. As of this last spring."

"Only half a year out of apprenticeship."

My heart clenched. Would he turn me away? Even after whatever Aiden had done to get me here? "Yes, sir."

"I do not know your former master. What are your specialties?"

"He was a carver, sir. He could do beautiful things with a knife. I could not hope to match his skill, so I focused on beadwork, trimmings, and fittings."

"I want you to make a mask for me," he announced, reaching for clear glass beads that he wove into the braids. "I want a measure of exactly what you can and cannot do. It should be a mask fit for a formal occasion, though not so elaborate as a ball. You may use any supplies you find that are not already claimed. And do be sure they are unclaimed. You'll find the makers here are very . . . protective of what has been given to them."

"Yes, sir."

"Don't get too carried away thinking you'll impress me with flashy dyes or crystals." He grinned wryly. "You'll find I'm not persuaded by such things. I want craftsmanship."

My cheeks felt hot. "Of course, sir."

"Any questions?"

"Yes, sir. Whom shall I fit the mask for?"

"Yourself. And I will be checking the fit carefully, so

don't get lazy." He tied his work off with a tight knot, and I was envious to see how clean his work was.

Someday, I vowed to myself, I wouldn't need to see my work to know it was perfect either.

"Emma," he called lazily, turning in his stool. "Show this miss to a station and give her the tour. She'll be making her mask for me. You know what I want."

"Yes, sir." She appeared by my side and, with a rustle of skirt, swept a quick curtsy. I realized that even though Milo couldn't see me, he could of course hear, and I hastily curtsied as well, glad he couldn't see my poor form.

Emma showed me to a small desk nearly in a corner that was to be my workstation. The desks lined the workroom, covered in various odds and ends and masks at various stages of completion. Men and women of varying ages scurried about the room, most close to my age, though some were close to Milo's.

The desk next to mine was occupied by a black-haired young man who appeared to be working on figures and lists, not a mask. He wore a green and silver mask that covered nearly his entire face, save his mouth.

"That's Joch," Emma whispered as we walked back out to where the materials were kept. Looking back, I recognized him—or the back of his head—from when Iniga had led me through the halls a lifetime ago. "He's only just got here. Usually he works in his own workshop, but sometimes he comes in here. He's the famous glassmaker from Saran the palace has been abuzz about lately. Milo has tried to get him to teach a few other people in here, but no one's willing to work with him for very long."

I gave her a sharp look. "Why not?"

She snorted. "He's extremely anti-social. He may be good looking and skilled, but he's a terror to work with. So I've heard. I haven't had a go at him yet. From what I've seen when he's in here, he keeps to himself and doesn't bother anyone, and he gives the nobles shiny new toys to fawn over." She shook her head disapprovingly. "I swear, they're letting anyone in here nowadays."

"How long have you been here?" I asked curiously.

"I was born and raised here," she said proudly. "My parents work here too. My ma's in the laundry and my pa's in the stables. My grandparents lived here too, and their grandparents. Used to be you lived and died here, but so many servants are sent to other households lately that hardly no one's left. So you get kids like Joch with no history," she scoffed.

I listened warily. Her age was difficult to guess; her way of speaking was at odds with what she was saying and how she acted. Her mannerisms showed youth, roughly the same age as me, but she sounded like an old woman obsessed with tradition and what was proper.

After she showed me everything, she left me alone at my desk to work. Joch nodded sullenly in my direction when I greeted him, not bothering to raise his almond-shaped eyes to meet mine, and said nothing.

Fine then. If he wasn't going to pay any mind to me, I wouldn't bother with him.

I wanted to start working on my mask immediately. Since color wouldn't be a factor for Milo, I was going back to my green, with as little palace silver as I could manage. My stomach flipped in anticipation.

First, I needed to draft my design. After our tour of

the workroom, I had a good idea of what was available and drew some sketches. It felt like a lifetime ago I last designed something for myself, though it was only at the last new year as I was close to finishing my apprenticeship.

I knew I should be practical, but with goods like these at my disposal, I might have gotten a little carried away. The jewels reserved for commissioned masks were of course not available, but I had fine silks; glass beads of varying sizes, shapes, and colors; and feathers from any bird I could ask for.

Before I knew it, the bells for dinner were ringing, and I realized I'd spent most of my afternoon drafting with nothing much to show for it. I didn't know when Milo expected my mask to be complete, but I'm sure sooner would be better than later.

I resolved to be more disciplined in my work tomorrow and straightened up my papers before bidding Milo a good evening and reluctantly dashing to the kitchens.

* * *

That night, I wasn't at all surprised to see Aiden waiting for me at my door. "You know, you could just wait inside," I said as I wearily opened the door for him, tired from all the excitement of the day. "It's not as if I have anything for you to snoop through."

"I would never invade a lady's privacy," he claimed, feigning insult.

"I'm sure," I said dryly.

"So?" he prompted, obviously eager to hear about what I'd done in the masking room.

"So?" I responded, intentionally misunderstanding with

a teasing glance. "So you need extra lessons on how to treat a lady? Something that touches on the finer points of the secrets a lady is entitled to both keep and know?"

He snorted. "You have more than your fair share of secrets, my lady. Both of your own and of others. Come on, tell me what I want to hear before I regret my astounding act of generosity."

I nudged his shoulder with mine. "So modest."

"When you're as stunning as I am, I'm as modest as is to be expected."

Groaning and fighting back laughter, I said, "All right, I surrender. Where shall I start?" And so I told him about my first assignment and the possible designs I was considering. I think I saw his eyes glaze over a little with boredom when I began to wax verbose about my designs, but my excitement seemed contagious.

"Will you get to keep the mask when you're done?" he asked.

"I don't know, actually. I would think so, since it'll be so specifically fitted to me, but when would I use it? It's a formal mask. And how would I pay for it?"

"Considering you're doing all the labor, I think you'll earn it," he said thoughtfully. "Maybe that's why they needed another man for figures. Milo might be getting a little generous." We both laughed at that.

"How about the people in there? Are they any better than the kitchens?"

"They're more likely to keep to themselves, I think. Everyone seems too busy to bother with gossip." Except maybe Emma, though she seemed more concerned about rules and regulations than about who was talking with whom. She'd been very thorough on the processes for cutting ribbon or claiming feathers.

"That must be a nice change."

"Yes." I sighed. "I wish I could stay there all day."

"Ah, but then you'd be deprived of my company. And I doubt you'd be able to bear such a loss."

I laughed again. "You have a mighty high opinion of yourself tonight. Is there any special occasion I'm unaware of?"

He laced his hands together and stretched leisurely. "Well, I was able to make good on an important promise of mine, which was no mean feat—"

"And I do appreciate that, truly," I said earnestly.

"—but I was also particularly brilliant in my council meeting today."

"Oh?"

He shook his head at me. "Can't tell you, of course."

"Of course," I replied flatly, slightly annoyed that he would bring it up and then not tell me about whatever it was.

My tone deflated him slightly, and he stood to leave. "I think I'll take my leave on that note, before I say something to really upset you."

"That's probably a wise decision."

"Just remember tomorrow, when you're lost in a daydream of silk and flowers and who knows what else, that I'm the reason you're there." He grinned at me, his eyes twinkling.

I laughed and shoved him out the door. "Good *night*, Aiden."

TWELVE

"*E*VIE?" AIDEN ASKED LATE ONE NIGHT AS I WORKED on my mask. It felt familiar, just the two of us, him talking while I tried to get some work done. I pressed my lips together to suppress a smile. I was still annoyed with him.

"I'm trying to concentrate."

"It's important."

Sighing heavily, I looked up at him. His face was serious and half shadowed in the flickering candlelight.

"You still haven't told me what really happened that night," he said.

I looked back down. "Yes, I did."

"You gave me approximately ten words. What really happened? Why are you hiding here?"

"I don't want to talk about it."

"I think you need to, though. Evie, you lost your home and your father and your masks all in one night. I know you're not okay."

I stared at him, unused to this serious side of him. There was something about being in the palace with him, I realized. I was no longer taking care of him. Somehow, he was taking care of *me*. I don't know if it was thanks to the fear of losing me in the fire that did it or something else, but he was different here.

I exhaled and slumped in my chair, crossing my arms. "I'm not letting one night ruin my life."

"I'm not suggesting that you do. In fact, that's the opposite of what I want you to do. That's why I'm asking."

I didn't say anything. I knew the moment I'd let myself start talking, I'd start crying as well. I'd start thinking about everything I'd lost, about how my life was irrevocably changed forever in that one night. Before, I'd known where my life was going. I'd known I'd be a mask maker and I'd work alongside my father making beautiful things. My life would be simple but content.

Now nothing was simple. I didn't know where my life was taking me. And that terrified me.

But I did know I was not going to cry in front of Aiden. That much, at least, was in my control.

"Please tell me." His gray eyes held mine, and I couldn't look away.

I took a deep breath. "You know about the fire. And I'm sure you've heard the rumors. It was the Chameleon."

He inhaled sharply and grabbed me by the shoulders. "Evie, what did he do to you? Why didn't you tell me?"

"I didn't want to upset you," I mumbled. "And I didn't know what to do. I was still trying to make sense of everything when you found me, and it never really came up since then." I trailed off, unnerved by the ferocity in his eyes.

He released me and ran a hand through his messy curls,

cursing under his breath. "Did he hurt you? Did he even *touch* you?"

Dr. Vito's rejection and repulsion flashed in my memory. I couldn't tell Aiden the truth. I couldn't. "No. I just . . . saw him leave."

"How did you know it was him?"

"He had Papa's mask, but it was clear that man wasn't my father." His taunting laughter echoed through my mind. "It couldn't have been anyone else."

Aiden began pacing across the workroom. "I can't believe you didn't tell me."

"And I can't believe you didn't tell me you had a position on the Council," I snapped.

He paused mid-step, then resumed and said, "Fine. We both have secrets."

I frowned. "You're not allowed to be mad at me about this."

He sighed and his face softened. "I'm sorry. I'm just . . . I don't like not being able to do anything."

"I don't like it either."

We sat in silence for so long that I considered picking my work back up.

"Did you even get to hold a memorial for your father?" he finally asked.

"No." I didn't have anything of him left.

He seemed to remember that fact a moment too late and winced. "I know we can't hold a traditional one, but I think even a makeshift one would help. Give you closure, you know?"

I bit my lip. "What are you suggesting?"

"Do you have anything of his at all? Or could you get anything from your house?"

Traditionally, we burned our deceased and scattered the ashes in the ocean, then displayed their mask in the home.

"I don't think the Chameleon left any of his masks behind."

"It doesn't have to be a mask," he said, growing insistent. "It could be anything of his. I could go back with you to look."

I didn't want to go back to my burnt husk of a home. But he was looking at me with so much conviction that this was what I needed that I couldn't tell him no.

"No, I want to go by myself. I think I have enough free time the day after tomorrow to go back and look."

"Are you sure you don't want me to come along?"

"I'll be fine."

I would be fine if it killed me.

* * *

"You're leaving early today," Emma remarked with a frown as she watched me clean up my station. I'd wanted to leave without being noticed, but thanks to her, everyone near me turned to look. Joch included. Not that he actually deigned to say anything, but his posture spoke volumes.

"I have some family business to take care of," I said, hoping she'd leave me alone.

Unfortunately, she was never satisfied with only a crumb where there was a cookie. "Oh? Everything well?"

"No. Memorial." I shot her a dirty look. She snapped her mouth shut but frowned.

"Well, you didn't have to be rude about it," she muttered as she walked to the other side of the room and inspected another girl's work.

"You didn't have to be nosy about it," I mumbled back for no one but myself to hear, and I quickly finished putting my things away. Joch was still frowning at me as I pushed my hair back and gave my station one last check. "What?" I glared at him.

His frown deepened, and he just shook his head.

I decided to ignore him. I had bigger things to worry about, and I pushed both him and Emma from my mind as I slipped from the palace and returned to the streets. The sounds and smells washed over me with a surprising strength. I'd been in the palace for only a few days; I didn't expect to miss things like the dank smell of the canal water or the shrill calls of the seagulls.

But this wasn't my life anymore.

My former home appeared too soon, its scorched walls glaring at me. I felt accusation in its shadow, its gaping windows cold and hostile despite the bright light of day.

This wasn't my home anymore.

Glancing around, I snuck around back and stepped inside. The streets were crowded enough that no one noticed me, and I wanted to get in and out as quickly as possible. Every muscle in my body was alert, the memory of that fiery night burning steadily in the corners of my vision.

I moved silently through the hall to Papa's room, scanning it quickly for any personal belongings. His room was a mess. Clearly the Chameleon had been searching in here for something. My eyes settled on the leather-bound journal peeking out from under his bed, and I was confused. It seemed like something the thief would have wanted.

I picked it up and flipped through the pages, my papa's familiar handwriting making my heart clench.

It was his work notes. It held nothing of his personal life, which must have been why it wasn't stolen. Instead it held notes about the masks he'd made, about our clients, and about our work. There were diagrams detailed enough that I'd be able to pick up where he'd left off, even if some-one's mask had been completely destroyed and I had to start from scratch.

This was as much a part of him as his mask.

I tucked it into my sash and scanned the room once more, looking for something I could burn and scatter. I sat on the bed and realized with a start that his pillow still smelled like him—like paint, and the sea, and Papa. I could almost hear his voice, and my eyes watered.

I gathered the pillow up in my arms and fled the building.

Aiden was waiting for me outside.

"Aiden!" I skidded to a stop and hastily brushed my cheeks to get rid of any tears that lingered. "I told you not to come."

"I know." He pulled me into a warm hug and didn't say anything more for a long time.

That night, after darkness fell and most of the palace was asleep, Aiden snuck down to my room and led me out to the cliff behind the palace overlooking the sea. We didn't say anything as the pillow burned and the wind scattered the ashes. I held the journal over my heart and listened to the waves, letting them carry me away.

THIRTEEN

*T*ALKING THINGS OVER WITH AIDEN AND GET-
ting back out into the city renewed my desire to
find out more about the Chameleon. Although I felt safe
in the palace, I recognized that it could be taken away
from me at a moment's notice as long as the Chameleon
walked free. I rarely had enough time to leave the palace
on my own for more than an hour or so at a time, and
never after dark.

But I wasn't going to find anything out during the day.

I didn't really have a plan, but the palace walls suddenly felt suffocating, and I needed to get out. I needed to
walk the streets and listen to the stories that weren't important enough to reach the runners' ears. I visited their parlor
daily now, and I'm sure they were annoyed with my single-
mindedness. I'd grown tired of pretending to flirt and so
they'd grown tired of me, but still I asked each day if there
was any news of the Chameleon. Actually, I didn't even
have to ask anymore, I just stopped by and someone would
report the lack of news immediately.

But that wasn't enough anymore.

The runners' entrance was technically the least guarded, because no one was actually posted there, but the room was always buzzing with activity no matter the time of day or night, making it difficult for someone to use it for nefarious means.

Fortunately for me, though, I was a familiar mask and could move about the room freely. I'd tested my luck using the door itself during the day, claiming I just needed a quick turn of fresh air, and no one stopped me.

So, one night after dinner, it was easy to drop by for a visit and slip outside with no one so much as batting an eyelash.

"Going somewhere?"

I jumped, then whirled around to see Aiden lounging against the palace wall, watching me, comfortable as you please.

It was too easy, apparently.

"What are you doing here?" I whispered, glaring at him. "How did you even know I would be out here?"

He shrugged, then pushed himself off the wall with an easy grace. "You don't give the runners enough credit. You think you're the first one to try sneaking out of here? The boys place bets on who will try it and how far they'll get. You gave yourself away when you gave it a test run this afternoon."

I scoffed at him and crossed my arms.

"Just what did you think you were going to do?"

"Nothing dangerous," I said quickly. "Just listen to the talk."

His eyes flashed. "Walking the streets at night *alone* is nothing dangerous? Are you crazy?"

"No," I retorted. "Just desperate for information."

His expression softened for a brief moment. Then he said, "Come inside, Evie. You'll find nothing out there tonight."

"I might have."

"Or you might have been ambushed, robbed, and thrown into the canal at knifepoint. Or worse." He stepped close to me, his gaze never leaving my eyes. I could smell the faint scent of mint on his breath from the dessert I'd served only hours before. "Is that really what you wanted?"

I looked away first and sighed. "No."

"I'm trying to help you, you know," he said, gesturing for me to enter ahead of him.

"I know."

He was the only one trying to help.

* * *

"We need to teach you how to fight," Aiden announced the next night as we sat in my room. He had yet to miss a night of meeting me there after my work in the kitchens was done, even after several weeks.

"What?" I was slightly offended. I knew going out at night on my own had been a bad idea, but I knew enough to defend myself during the day. I wouldn't be winning any contests or fighting any battles, but I wouldn't be involved in any street brawls, either.

"Teach you how to fight," he repeated. "I don't like the idea of you being on your own and you not being able to fight. Especially after you tried to sneak out of here with no one to protect you."

"I can defend myself just fine. I survived the first time, didn't I?" I was getting more offended.

"That was a lucky break," he insisted. "You might not be so lucky next time."

I snorted. "You sound like a bad storyteller."

"Hush. I'm just worried about you, okay?"

I softened a little. "You don't have any reason to be worried. I'm living in the basement of the palace. I work in the Masking workroom, surrounded by dozens of people. No one's going to attack me there, and no one's going to find me here. I'm still amazed that *you* found me." I paused. "Are you ever going to tell me how you managed to do that, by the way?"

He shrugged. "I told you I would someday. Today is today, not someday."

"That's a cheap answer."

"Cheap or not, there it is."

I scowled and began planning. "How about this: you actually tell me something I want to know, and you can teach me something you want me to know. A trade of information, so to speak. Don't think I haven't noticed how you've stopped telling me things. Or how when you do tell me something, it only gives me more questions."

He thought for a moment, looking a bit guilty. "Do I have to answer every question you ask me? Some questions I simply can't answer."

"No, I don't want you to feel like I'm interrogating you," I tried to explain. "I'm not going to ask you any questions. Instead, you volunteer information. You know exactly what I know or don't know about you—all my information comes straight from the source. So you can flesh out each area as little or as much as you prefer."

"And for every area I flesh out, I can teach you a new technique?"

"You're going to be my teacher?" I cocked my head in surprise.

"Of course." Now he sounded insulted. "Did you think I'd try to get you to arm yourself if I didn't know anything myself? I'll never ask you to do anything I wouldn't do myself."

"Fine," I huffed. "That sounds fair." I had to admit that it did. Besides, I was hoping that by showing me what he knew, he might explain exactly *how* he came to know those things. He'd never struck me as a fighter; he was too wiry.

"All right. Lesson one." He stood from his spot on the bed, but I hurried to interrupt him.

"Wait, right now? Here?" I looked around at the small space. It seemed even smaller when I thought about how much I was going to have to move around in it.

"Why not?" He shrugged. "We're not doing anything else, and neither of us is expected anywhere for at least an hour. If anything, you'd have to defend yourself in small spaces like this. Unless you're anticipating joining up with the army after this."

I rolled my eyes. "Obviously. I'm only using you for your free labor and training."

"That's what I thought. Though as good as my labor and training is, you're too girly to join the army. There aren't any ribbons and beads there. Not even feathers," he teased right back, dramatically gesturing with his arms.

"Oh, shush. Teach me something so I can punch you," I grumbled.

He grinned at me. The cheeky grin just made me want to punch him more.

"Okay, first, I want to know exactly what you already know."

"Wait, no! I want you to give me information first," I insisted.

"I'm not going to cheat," he said, exasperated. "I'll talk afterward, while you cool down."

I frowned.

"Oh, come on," he insisted. "Don't you trust me?"

In some weird, twisted way, I *had* come to trust him. And he knew it. Jerk. "That's a low blow," I pouted.

"That's how I fight, m'lady," he said seriously. The atmosphere around us shifted slightly, and I was suddenly uncomfortable with the serious twist his mood had taken.

There was clearly much more I didn't know about him than I realized.

"Now, you have my word that I will talk after." He lightened up a little and pulled me off the bed. He faced me squarely. "Now show me what you've got. Pretend I'm attacking you."

I eyed him dubiously. "I don't want to hurt you."

He laughed. "Seriously? You won't. And if you don't fight back, I'll attack you for real. You wouldn't want that, now would you?"

I sighed, exaggerating my frustration. "All right, but don't say I didn't warn you. You are looking at the only known survivor of a Chameleon attack."

"Yes, well, they are furious little lizards, aren't they?" he mocked.

I scowled and dove at him, still not entirely serious. I knew how to not get hauled away, and I knew to aim for the groin or eyes. Or behind the knee. I still didn't really want to hurt him, but if he was going to make light of the Chameleon's attack on me, well then, I couldn't be held responsible for that sort of thing, now could I?

He dodged me easily and laughed. "Are you sure you know what you're doing?" he asked.

"I didn't say I knew what I was doing," I grunted, circling him. "I said I knew how to defend myself. I'm not usually the one on the offense."

"Fair point," he granted. "Then get on the defense, my lady." He spoke in a deep voice that I could feel in my bones. The vibrations made my body tremble; he had used his predatory voice. I didn't hear it often, but when I did, I knew to watch out.

He lunged toward me, and then it was my turn to dodge him. We played cat and mouse for a mere moment, before he was too quick for me and grabbed my arm. I tugged away, but he had a firm grasp on my wrist that I knew I'd never shake without hurting myself.

Grinning triumphantly, he said, "I've got you."

"But can you keep me?" I shot back, twisting around him so his arm bent at an awkward angle, trying to force him to let go.

But it didn't work. His body mirrored mine—he moved with me and kept my wrist captive.

"That won't be a problem," he growled.

Time for Plan B.

I dropped to the floor, making my body into a dead weight and pulling him forward. He lurched with me, taken a bit by surprise, if I did say so myself, and opened himself up perfectly for a groin kick.

I thrust my heel up, not with all my strength, because I knew it wouldn't take much, but with enough that I knew it would hurt.

It hit with a dull *smack*, and I grinned triumphantly.

But he continued to move so quickly that I wasn't sure how he did, and then we were standing face-to-face and chest-to-chest. His arm wrapped around me like shackles, and all I could do was squirm.

"Evie, really? That's your plan?"

I grunted. "What are you, made of rock?"

He chuckled. "Of course not, my lady. However, my protective gear might as well be."

"You cheater!" I accused, outraged, still struggling to put some distance between us. "You're not allowed to do that!"

He laughed loudly. "And why not, pray tell?"

"Because!" I sputtered. "You . . . no one wears that outside of classes! You knew you were going to work with me before I even agreed to anything! And I can't show you how I work if you're cheating."

"I'm not stupid, either, Evie." He laughed in my face, his breath hot against my cheeks. "I'm not about to let you go crazy at me without some kind of protection."

I sulked. "That doesn't change the fact that you shouldn't have anything right now! I thought this was a spur of the moment thing."

"What makes you think I don't wear it all the time?"

"Um, because that's insane?"

His grin didn't quite reach his eyes this time. "Would you forgive me if I gave you a little information now?"

I became aware of how close we were standing, but he didn't release his hold on me. "If you surrender this round to me, and let me go," I bargained.

"I don't think you can win by any definition if I have to 'let you go,'" he countered, not backing up an inch. If anything, I think he tightened his grip.

"Well, I can't win if you're going to cheat anyway," I argued.

"It's not cheating if this is how'd I be on any random day on the street."

"Okay, that's not true."

He raised an eyebrow. "And how do you know?"

He had me there. I had no way to prove it either way, and he knew it. Jerk.

"Are you not going to let me go, then?"

"Do you really want me to let you go? That'll mean I win, after all."

"You can't win if you cheat."

"Winning is winning."

"Cheating isn't winning."

"I've met my end goal. That's my definition of winning. Do the means of getting there matter?"

"Of course they matter! If anything, they're the most important part!"

"How do you figure that?" His voice was low again.

"If you don't play by the rules, you're missing out on learning how to meet that goal in a way that can be duplicated." I was strangely breathless. "When you cheat, who's to say one cheating method will work again? And in the same way? It's not going to happen."

"Well, who's to say the 'right' way or 'playing by the rules' way would work again?" He was being purposefully difficult, and we both knew it. "Rules change."

"Are you going to let me go or not?" Our faces were inches apart. I could feel his grip tightening.

"Are you going to be okay with losing?" The smirk was back.

I leaned forward until we were cheek to cheek, and I whispered in his ear, "Never." I felt him shiver and his grip loosened just enough.

I dropped to the floor out of his grasp and kicked in the back of his knees, causing his legs to buckle. I slipped around and threw my weight against his chest, knocking him backward in surprise. I straddled his chest. Resting all my weight on Aiden, I grabbed his hands in mine and pinned them above his head.

It happened so quickly that it seemed to be over before it really began. He stared up at me, clearly shocked, and I grinned so big that my cheeks hurt. I leaned over him, so thrilled at my victory that I dropped a light kiss on his mask-covered nose.

"I win."

He stared up at me, eyes wide, for a long moment. Then the spell broke and he sat up, gently shoving me off as I loosened my grip.

"How on earth is that not cheating?" he accused, ruffling his hair.

"I don't know what you mean," I said innocently, grinning cheekily. "Now I believe you owe me some information?"

"You're terrible."

"But I won," I sang, dropping onto my bed and leaning against the wall. "Now tell me a story."

He shot me a dirty look. "Since I know you'll never believe me, I'll tell you why I was wearing protection. I used to get into fights all the time, when I was a bit younger."

"Fights? You?" I looked at him, disbelieving.

"Don't interrupt. And yes. I didn't always start them, but really, how they happened is irrelevant."

"You were a gangly little string bean, weren't you?" I cried happily. "Oh, I bet you were just adorable. You're so tall now." I was getting some wonderful mental images out of this.

"I asked you not to interrupt."

"And when have I ever done anything you asked?" I replied impudently.

He rolled his eyes. "So there I was. Fighting a lot. And I quickly learned that my opponents were not above cheap tricks and lows blows."

"So they cheated?"

He ignored me. "And I found out that if I took measures to block their blows ahead of time, they didn't know how else to attack me. And then it was easy for me to win."

"Did you fight back? Or did you just run away after they wore themselves out?"

"I never ran away," he said seriously. "I've never run away from a fight. I've never backed down, and I never plan on it."

"Yeah, and that's never going to come back to bite you later on," I said sarcastically.

"Have you ever considered that maybe your interruptions

are why you never know anything about me?" he asked snarkily. "Maybe I wanted to tell you something, and you just kept talking so much that you didn't hear anything."

I shut my mouth.

He watched me, waiting for me to say anything more. When I didn't, he sighed and went back to his story. "And I just got into the habit of always wearing something underneath. It's served me well many, many times. You'd be surprised at how many people only know cheap shots and nothing more."

"Probably not. It's all I know, and it's worked for me."

"Until you came up against me, of course."

"Hey, I still won," I pointed out.

"You just used a different cheap trick," he mumbled.

"What was that?"

"Nothing. Is that enough information for me to teach you something now?" He tried changing the subject.

I decided to have pity on him and let it go. "I suppose. Though that was for seeing what I already had. I'll need something else after what you teach me now."

"I know, my lady. I'm going to keep my side of the bargain, trust me."

The air was charged again, and I waited for him to begin.

"First, I'm going to teach you how to punch properly. You know how to hit, or slap, but I want you to punch."

"Okay." I could see the benefits from knowing how to throw a decent punch without him having to spell it out for me. Even if I didn't have a lot of power behind it, the whole idea of a girl like me knowing how to punch would be intimidating. I could fake it.

"Okay. Stand back up." He came to stand behind me. "A lot of your power will come from your legs, even though you're throwing with your arms. So you need to stand in the right position." He put his hands on my hips, shifting me and twisting my torso until I was in the position he wanted. It felt slightly awkward.

"Are you sure this is right? I feel like I'm going to fall over."

"You're putting your weight on your front foot. Split your balance between the two, and when you're winding up, so to speak, you'll shift your balance. Otherwise, yeah, you'll probably fall over."

"Don't tell me, you're a 'learn from your mistakes' type of teacher?" I groaned.

He just chuckled. I had a feeling I was in for a lot of bruising and embarrassing moments.

"All right, so you're in the right position. Now, put your arms up." He reached around me, again moving me like a giant rag doll until my hands and arms were just so.

"This doesn't feel powerful at all," I complained.

"That's because you haven't tried to hit anything yet," he explained patiently. "Now are you going to be this difficult the whole time?"

"I'm always difficult," I muttered. "But I'll try to behave. Sorry." I knew he was just trying to help me. And I was being a bratty student.

"Thank you. Now, as I was saying, you'll feel power when you try to hit something."

He moved around me, and I dropped my stance as he grabbed my pillow from the bed. He wrapped it around his arm and held it up to me. "Now, this is your target." I opened my mouth to protest, but now it was his turn to interrupt. "And don't say anything about not wanting to hurt me. Remember how that turned out last time."

"Yeah, but this time I can see your bare arm. And that pillow is awfully thin."

"Evie, just work with me here."

I put my hands back up.

"Okay, you want to be perpendicular to your target. That keeps your body from being open to any attacks. Now, without me telling you how, I want you to punch my arm with your right hand."

I did so, or tried to. There was little power in it, and my legs felt tangled up. Plus, he pulled back just a moment before I hit, bringing his other hand around to help soften the blow.

"That was pathetic," I moaned.

"That's because you don't know how to do it yet. And you haven't built up any muscle," he added as an afterthought.

"You're not being helpful."

"Sorry. Okay, now this time, bend your knees a little and lean back on your back foot. When you swing forward, push off the ground, using the momentum to add strength to your punch."

I tried to do as he said. The punch still felt weak, but it was stronger than before. "Was that at all what I was supposed to do?"

"Yes, that was just right," he assured me. "But like I said, you still need to build muscle and strength. Someone your size isn't going to knock me out with a straight punch." He grinned.

I was not encouraged by this, funnily enough. And I told him so, asking what the point was then.

"Well, you never know. You might have to go up against someone your size. And you could use this to intimidate someone. And, you know, come off the better side of a fight over materials the next time you go to market."

I groaned. "You are awful."

"I know. Now let's try it with your other arm, and then it'll be story time and you'll have your chance to make fun of me again."

That brightened my outlook considerably. I liked the "making fun of him" part.

We worked on my other side, but not for very long. I was not coordinated enough to transfer what I learned on my right side to use on my left side.

Aiden just laughed at me. "Okay, that'll need a lot more work," he said, snickering.

"Oh, be quiet." I used my newfound punching skills to slug his shoulder. He flinched away, but I think it was just for show. He couldn't have been that much of a wimp that I actually hurt him.

"Okay, story time again?" I asked, situating myself on my bed, stretching my arms across my body and above my head.

"I suppose so. Any requests?"

I shook my head. "That's not how this works, remember? You have to volunteer everything."

"Well then. What don't you know? I don't want to cheat you out of new information."

I laughed. "I won't beat you up for repeat stories, if that's what you're worried about."

"Oh good." He mockingly held his hand over his heart. "You had me worried."

"Just . . . start from the beginning, I guess? I really know ridiculously little about you."

"All right. Well, I guess we could start off with this: growing up I had a sheltered childhood. My parents were—and still are—protective of me."

"I've never met them, you know. Or your sister, for that matter."

"Yeah, sorry about that. They're . . . really busy. So, back to my childhood. I was protected, and my parents didn't like me to leave their sight. Going out was out of the question.

"So I got good at sneaking out," he continued, grinning wickedly. "I used to get caught all the time, and they would be furious with me. But no matter what they did, I would just sneak out again. They hired someone to watch my door, so I snuck out the window. They got new locks, and I learned to pick them. They couldn't keep me locked up, no matter how hard they tried." He looked proud of himself.

"Are you going to teach me some of those tricks too?" Picking locks would be an interesting skill to have.

"Perhaps. How many deep, dark secrets would I have to spill in trade for that one?"

I shoved his shoulder with mine. "I'll let you do that one free of charge."

"Somehow, I feel I'm getting the short end of the stick here."

"I can tell you something about my childhood, if you like," I volunteered. I liked sharing stories.

"I'd like that," he said.

"Well, I didn't have people hired to stand guard at my

door, but I certainly did have a habit of running off whenever my father took me to market."

"All those shiny flags, it's understandable."

"I like shiny things, can you blame me?" I sighed. "I was meant to be a decorator, in one form or another. I'd see someone with a pretty or sparkly mask, and I'd wander away so I could get a better look. Most of the time I could find my way back, since my father was so tall.

"One time, though, I was so distracted, I wasn't looking where I was going. And on the docks, that's not a good idea."

"I can see where this is going. Did you have to get fished out?"

I nodded, laughing. "And by the fishing boats, no less! Some old man with a boring grayish-blue mask had tossed over a net, and I grabbed hold of it. Surprised, he pulled it right back up shouting, 'Lookie here, I caught a mermaid!'"

Aiden laughed so hard that tears formed at the corner of his eyes. "I can just see you, all curls and skirts, floundering around."

"I was terrified! I thought I was going to drown! Have you ever tried swimming in skirts? It's impossible to even move," I exclaimed.

"Now that is something I haven't tried," he confessed. "Your story is better than mine," he said, calming down.

"Of course it's better than yours. It's mine!" I smiled happily. I hadn't been able to laugh this much in a long time.

Unfortunately, our fun ended as the dinner bells chimed.

"Aw," I moaned, "I don't want to go to work."

"I don't want you to go to work either. I like our little world in here."

I liked it too, but I wasn't going to admit that to him.

I reluctantly dragged myself up, checking my mask and hair in the mirror he'd found for me.

"Same time tomorrow?" I asked him.

"I wouldn't miss it for anything."

FOURTEEN

I QUICKLY LEARNED THAT MY POSITION IN THE masking room wasn't going to be easy. Even though Milo was waiting on my mask to see exactly what I could do, he kept me plenty busy in the meantime.

If I wasn't cleaning in the kitchens, I was cleaning in the workroom. Apparently the least desirable chores go to the newest recruit, so it was left to me to scrub the kilns, untangle threads and ribbons, and sweep the floors whenever I wasn't working on my mask. When I had an actual assignment, the chores would be split more evenly, but until then I was the lackey.

I chose to use porcelain clay for my mask, instead of my usual mâché, since it was supposed to be more formal. It was perhaps a little overly ambitious, but I wanted to make a good impression.

The first step was to make the cast of my face, which I could thankfully do behind the privacy of a curtain in the area set aside for client fittings. My Mark was healing well; it itched like mad and had fully scabbed over, but it should be easy enough to work around with privacy.

To make the cast, I used rough strips of mâché dipped in glue. After thoroughly coating my face in jelly—except my Mark, which I bandaged carefully, and my eyelids, which I covered with a thin tissue—I began to systematically form the cast. This was much easier to do on someone else's face, especially once my eyes were covered. But working by touch wasn't as difficult as I'd anticipated, which led my thoughts wandering to Milo as I worked.

I watched him often, mesmerized by the sure way he worked. I'd asked Emma how he came to such a powerful position and if he'd always been sightless.

"No, he wasn't always blind," she said as she helped me sort a shipment of glass beads. "He's been working in the palace nearly all his life. No, those go here."

I corrected myself and asked, "Did he always work in here?"

"Yes, his father was the master before him, and his father before, as far as I know. He pretty much grew up in here, so it was only natural that he developed the skills he has."

"So what happened?"

"It happened not long after his father passed away and he was appointed the new master here. At that time, new recruits were asked to make a mask for him instead of for themselves, like what you're doing. Someone mixed the glue for the cast with something bad—I don't know what— and didn't cover Milo's eyes properly. His sight was completely gone within a week."

"Wow," I breathed. My movements slowed as I tried to imagine how difficult that must have been. "Did that person do it on purpose?"

Emma shrugged. "I don't know. He left the palace on his own, and I've never heard anything more of him."

"And Milo just kept working?"

"He was forced to take time to heal and accustom himself to working without his sight, but as soon as he was able he was back in here again as if nothing had happened." She frowned. "And that's enough gossip for one day. Back to work, please. These need to be sorted before you start your own mask."

I spent the rest of the task lost in thought as I sorted, the repetitive motion lending itself all too easily to distraction. By the time I was finished, it was time for dinner and I'd left with even more respect for Milo.

I was also doubly careful with everything I did in making my cast, paying close attention to the normally routine task. Several days and unsatisfactory casts later, I waited impatiently for the latest one to dry, my skin prickling. I could hear the usual workroom hum—light chatting, the soft brush of fabric and the clicking of beads on desktops—and had to fight to keep from being lulled to sleep. The chair I used was reclined to make the work on my face easier, but it also made sleep so very tempting.

However, the mâché didn't take long to dry, and I carefully removed the mask, scrunching my face in all sorts of awkward ways to dislodge the creation.

That done, I washed off the jelly, cleaned my Mark, and resecured my working mask. I put the cast in the kiln for a few moments to let it harden enough to make the plaster today. I worked quickly, gathering the plaster mix while the cast cooked and mixing while the cast cooled.

I did all of this at my workstation, though if felt like I

was still hidden behind the curtain. I wasn't ignored, exactly, but I wasn't sought out. This isolation made me surprisingly productive. I used to chat to Hachi while I worked, and I'd never realized how distracted that made me.

The thought of my dog made my heart clench, and I tried to push out the memory of what I'd overheard during breakfast. Two girls were chatting loudly about the town gossip, which I'd normally just ignore. But then one of them said, "You remember that shop that burnt down last month? And how they found the man floating in the canals but never found his daughter?"

My ears perked up and my heart started beating faster.

"I heard the same thing happened to another mask maker in the district—my cousin told me. The shop was burned and he washed up in that last storm we had. Isn't that gross? I mean, can you imagine just finding a body like that?"

They gagged and giggled as I felt my heart pound in my ears. I gave up on eating, all taste and hunger gone, a morbid part of me refusing to tune them out for fear of missing any new information.

I hadn't realized how raw my emotions were still. I'd held my memorial for my father and thought I'd moved on, but hearing their news brought the pain back fresh again. And I had a feeling it would keep coming back for as long as the Chameleon walked free. Plus I still didn't know what had become of Hachi. Tears pricked at my eyes, but I shook my head to clear my mind and forced myself to concentrate on the present. It wouldn't do me any good to linger on the past, especially with so much at stake. Besides, I'd promised myself there would be no more crying.

With the cast out of the kiln and cooled, I smeared some more jelly inside and scooped the plaster with maybe a little more force than necessary.

"Easy there," a low voice behind me warned.

I jumped and spun around to see Milo standing with a wry grin on his face.

"I didn't think it was possible to hear plaster splash so," he continued. "You'll break your cast if you keep that up. Or trap air pockets."

My face reddened, the blush peeking out from the edge of my mask. Both warnings were for elementary mistakes. He must think me a fool with no skill at all. "Sorry, sir. My mind wandered a bit farther than it should have. It won't happen again."

"I should hope not. Keep that mind on a short leash, at least while you're handling that which is easily broken."

"Yes, sir." My voice was low, properly chagrined.

He paused before saying, "I've had Emma report to me on your progress. She says your method looks good, though you tend to look a bit lost in your own head when you work. I know we're a quiet lot in here, but talking isn't discouraged. Or you could hum if that helps. Had a girl here once who hummed the same tune every day. Almost missed it when she left."

I didn't know what to say to that. "Sir?"

"Don't be afraid to make a place for yourself here. You need to be comfortable in order to create."

"Yes, sir."

He walked back to his desk, so sure of his own place and route that I never would have guessed he was blind.

FIFTEEN

*I*T WAS REALLY ONLY A MATTER OF TIME BEFORE I crossed paths with Iniga.

Milo was pleased with my work and decided it was my turn to work with Joch, as long as I didn't fall behind in my other work. I was a bit apprehensive after hearing the gossip about him, but I was more eager to learn something new. Even if I had been horrible at my first attempt at glasswork with Iniga, I would get to watch the master at work, and that would be worth any burns I might receive in the process.

My instructions were to meet Joch in his workroom. I was early, and the room was empty, so I decided to look around. It looked nearly identical to the one Iniga showed me, but now I had a chance to inspect the tools more closely.

I was doing just that when I heard the door open behind me. Guiltily I replaced the long wooden tool and turned, clasping my hands behind my back.

"Oh, I'm sorry, I didn't—" Iniga began, stopping short as she looked at me. The door shut behind her with a noisy thump. I pressed my lips together and tried to keep a neutral expression.

I fidgeted as she continued to stare at me. "Is everything okay?" I finally asked, pitching my voice a little higher than usual.

She blinked and drew back. "I'm sorry, you just . . . reminded me of someone. Sorry. How rude of me. You must be Joch's latest victim." She smiled warmly at me, though it didn't reach her eyes. "I'm Iniga."

"Yes, I'm Joch's newest apprentice," I confirmed, not offering my name. It was a common enough name that I doubted she would suspect me, but I didn't want to risk it, especially after she already thought she recognized me. "Do you know where he is?"

She shook her head. "I didn't know he was going to be in here today. He's been in the main workroom a lot lately." I had noticed him in there more than I'd expected; usually he was working out something on paper or reading. "I was just coming in here to borrow a pair of prongs. Mine broke."

I stepped away from the tools I had been looking at, and she selected what she needed. As she pulled the door open again to leave, she turned to look at me once more.

"Are you sure you're okay?" I couldn't help but ask her. She looked so sad.

She managed another weak smile. "I'll survive," she said softly. With one last glance in my direction, she left, closing the door gently behind her.

I exhaled.

Poor Iniga. I felt horrible for not letting her know I was okay, but I didn't see how I could. And I knew she would forgive me. She had an understanding soul.

The door swung open again, startling me, and Joch

strode in. He barely glanced my way as he placed a bag on the worktable and began emptying it.

"You will watch and stay out of my way," he said, his voice clipped. "I don't have time to teach you every little thing. You learn by *doing* in here, if you learn at all."

I frowned, ignoring the goose bumps that rose along my arms and the shiver that slid down my spine. I wasn't going to be frightened off. "I understand."

He turned and folded his arms across his broad chest, studying me. I stared back at him, my chin high. His arrogance marred his looks somewhat, but he was still undeniably good looking. Years of working with glass must have given him those muscular arms and shoulders, though he still wasn't what I'd consider bulky. His black hair was just as messy as the first time I'd seen him, and his mask was deceptively simple, though a bit more concealing than the current fashion. Palace silver with sharp cuts of forest green along the cheekbones gave him an intimidating look, though given his jawline, his face underneath was probably just as sharp.

"Good," he finally said, breaking the tense silence.

And that was the last thing he said to me for the duration of our time together that day. Surprisingly, I still learned a lot, sitting on my stool in the corner and scrutinizing his every move.

He worked quickly, his hands sure and nimble as he coaxed the glass into shape after shape, though he never seemed quite pleased with his results. He got the shape of a mask, but when he tried to embellish it, the glass seemed to refuse to cooperate. Regardless, he was fascinating to watch.

Several hours later, when the clock tower rang, warning me to get downstairs for dinner, I slid off my stool and stretched. "I have to go now, but I'll be back tomorrow," I informed him. He didn't say anything but nodded in acknowledgement. This lesson would have to be good enough for today, unless I wanted to be late and risk a scolding.

Thankfully dinner passed without incident and I could finally return to my room for a much needed break. I hoped Aiden would be there too, so I could tell him about my new assignment.

He was in my room, but he was less than pleased with my news.

"You're alone with him for hours at a time? No chaperone or anything?" he asked sharply, his brow furrowed.

I rolled my eyes. "There's nothing for you to worry about. He barely even notices I'm there. I think he said two sentences to me today. Maybe ten words total."

"I don't like it."

"You're not allowed to use your sources to change anything," I said firmly. "I want to learn how to make those glass masks, and he's the only one that can teach me. And I might be the only one that can put up with him."

His frown deepened. "I can't even suggest a chaperone?"

"No." I crossed my arms. "Definitely not. It'd only draw attention to us."

"Then I'm definitely getting you a knife or something."

"Aiden." I stepped in front of him and uncrossed my arms, placing them firmly on his shoulders. "I'm pretty sure that would make things worse. What if someone found out I was armed? Or if I was attacked and I dropped it? I wouldn't even know what to do with it."

His shoulders sagged.

I continued, "We'll keep up our fighting lessons, though. Will that make you feel better?"

He sighed, lowering his eyes to look directly into mine. "If that's the best I can get from you, I suppose I have no choice."

I suddenly felt too warm. I laughed nervously, pulling my hands back. "You worry too much."

Raising an eyebrow at me, he said pointedly, "Given your history, I think you don't worry enough."

That sobered me somewhat. I'd grown complacent in the palace, surrounded by people and guards and high walls. I bit my lip. "Fine," I surrendered. "I'll let you start to train me in knife fighting too. When I feel like I'm good enough to actually *use* it, I'll carry one."

He relaxed. "That's good enough for me." Then he broke into that boyish smile I knew so well. "Shall we begin?"

* * *

My days fell into an easy routine. Breakfast and lunch were spent in the kitchens with Carese, with the time in between in the masking room. Afternoons were with Joch, followed by serving dinner, and then lessons with Aiden. Every night, I fell gratefully into bed and woke every morning feeling slightly sore but stronger.

Aiden was pleased with my progress and, after a week, he convinced me that I was good enough to keep hold of my weapon. "And if you're really that concerned," he'd conceded, "don't draw it. But it will still make me feel better that you have the option."

Grumbling, I accepted, and he presented me with a fine knife that I kept up my sleeve. It was much easier to hide with the weather growing chillier. I didn't know where I'd hide it during the harsh heat of summer. Under my skirts, maybe, but then how I would get to it?

My progress with Joch was less encouraging. He barely spoke to me and wouldn't let me do anything—it was easy to see why so many had quit before me. Frustrated with the lack of progress, I finally spoke up.

"When do I get to do something?"

He must have forgotten I was in the room, because he dropped the mask he was working on, rod and all, and it shattered on the hard floor into a few pieces. He turned to me with fury boiling in his eyes. "Look what you just did!" he shouted at me, gesturing angrily at the broken mask.

"*I* did? You were the one holding it. It's not my fault you forgot you're supposed to be training me. Besides," I pointed out, "it didn't break into that many pieces. You can just as easily seal it back together as throw it out."

He gave me a dirty, disbelieving look.

"No, really. I remember seeing a glass blower who would use gold or silver as a sort of glue on vases that were broken. They were beautiful when he finished. I don't know if you have such fine material to work with, but surely there's something—"

"I have it," he interrupted. "As a guest to the palace—especially one working on masks for nobles—I have access to anything I need."

"Then you might as well try it," I said, shrugging, unimpressed with his arrogance. "Or let me try it." I hadn't mentioned that Iniga was the one who'd shown me the technique, and that it was one I wasn't horrible at.

Glaring at me, he motioned for me to go ahead, his

expression unchanging the whole time I worked. I picked up the broken pieces with his tongs and placed them in a bowl of water to cool, then went to inspect the jars lining the shelves, selecting one with gold colored sand. I measured it out and placed it in the furnace until it was molten liquid, then went to work on drawing strands of gold and piecing the glass back together.

It was a long and tedious process, but by the end of it, I was pleased with the outcome. Gold lining spider-webbed through the glass, catching the light with the slightest movement. The mask was still clear, though, and needed something to make it opaque before anyone could wear it.

"See?" I asked smugly. "I told you."

He grunted as he continued to work on smoothing the seals. "It's still not perfect," he said.

"Of course not," I said, rolling my eyes. "It's my first one."

Apparently he expected perfection instantly and pursed his lips. "You can start working after the masquerades," he announced. "I have too much work to be done before then."

"Really?" I jumped off my stool in excitement. "I can actually do something? What about until then?"

"You can figure out a way to salvage that mask." He nodded at the one in front of me. "Then it will be yours."

* * *

"So when do I get to see this masterpiece?" Aiden teased as I bragged to him about my achievement.

"Well, it's not done yet," I said, pointing out the obvious. "You can't see it until it's perfect."

"When will that be?"

"It'll be done when it's done," I said patiently. "And it's fancy, so I have to find somewhere to wear it."

"What? Am I not fancy enough for you?"

I shoved his shoulder, laughing. "Sorry, but no."

He pouted but recovered quickly enough to show he wasn't offended and changed the subject. "What about your work in the kitchens? Has that become any more tolerable?"

"It's tolerable," I hedged, and he frowned. "The kitchen mistress hates me, and I don't think there's anything either of us could do about that. But I'm getting used to the way things work and can usually stay out of her way. Besides, I'm in the mask room more often than the kitchen, and that makes up for anything that happens. Did I say thank you for that, by the way?"

He smirked. "You can always say it again."

"I'd better not. Your head might grow too big for your mask."

He laughed. "And on that note, let's get back to your training."

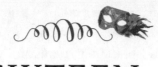

SIXTEEN

AFTER MY FIRST NIGHT AS A SERVER, THERE HADN'T been any repeats of unusual attention from the prince. However, that didn't mean I'd gone completely unnoticed. On one night, one particular guest had received far too much wine, through no fault of mine.

About three quarters through the meal, he raised his cup and loudly asked, "Where's my wine gone?"

As I hurried to refill it, wondering how on earth it was empty already—I'd filled it not five minutes before—he threw an arm around my waist and exclaimed happily, "Here's something finer than wine! Can I drink you up?"

He laughed boisterously, and I politely declined and pulled away.

He wasn't having any of that, though.

"What's that?" he shouted, growing agitated. "You would rather not? No one 'rather not's' me! Now see here, miss—"

I started to panic, memories of flames and smoke flashing across my vision, but before he could even finish his sentence, or threat, or whatever it was going to be, Vera stepped up with a guard.

The guard loosened the man's hold on me, only for my arm to be captured by a barely controlled Vera.

"I think it's time you head up to bed, my lord," the guard suggested gently, looking pointedly at the man's companions. They guiltily ushered their friend out, knowing full well that they could have stopped the show if they'd wanted.

I didn't dare look up, feeling instead the dozens of stares in my direction. I'd gotten so used to being invisible in this room that having this much attention was extremely unnerving. I felt vulnerable and exposed, and my stomach twisted in knots. I was almost grateful when Vera dragged me back into the kitchens, silently commanding another girl to cover my station with a pointed look.

Once safely behind the kitchen doors, she lit into me.

"What were you thinking?" she hissed. I flinched. "Getting so close to a patron, it's disgusting. And letting his cup run dry? Have you learned nothing? You have one simple task, and you can't even complete it?"

I opened my mouth to protest, but she cut me off.

"Don't even think about talking back to me. How dare you! I can't believe it." She paced angrily in front of me, looking like a jungle cat stalking her prey. She had a wild look in her eyes, and I braced myself for whatever way she chose to lash out at me.

Stopping in her tracks and spinning around to point at me, she delivered my unjust punishment. "Since you can't seem to keep a cup full, you'll just have to become more familiar with the dishes. Perhaps after washing every one tonight, you'll remember what a full goblet is supposed to look like."

"All of them?" I cried out, horrified. There would be *hundreds*—I'd be here all night! Which meant I would miss my time with Aiden. And if I wasn't in my room, he'd worry. And who knew what he'd do then?

Vera grinned, clearly pleased that her punishment was causing me such distress. I wanted to slap that stupid grin right off her skinny face.

She all but skipped away, calling back at me, "You'd better get started, little miss. I'd hate for there to be anything left in the morning. Some breakfast dishes might slip into your queue." She cackled and I turned to stare dejectedly at the sinks.

Normally, all the servers took a task in cleaning the dishes. Five would wash, five dry, and five more to put the dishes away.

Tonight, it would just be me.

And I didn't have a choice. If I disobeyed, I could be kicked out at best or submitted to the stocks for a day at worst. In the stocks, my mask would be stripped and my Mark would be discovered.

I sighed and dejectedly stared at the pile that had already started to form. The kitchen hands had heard Vera's declaration and happily abandoned their posts to make room for me. I wanted to finish as soon as possible, so I tied my sleeves back and, with one more sigh, got to work.

* * *

Well after nightfall when I was completely alone in the kitchens, I'd made a small dent in the massive pile, but I still had over half of the dishes to wash and all of them to put away. My theory was to let them dry themselves, which seemed to be working out well enough, but putting them away by lamplight was going to be a chore and a half.

Meanwhile, I was so worried about Aiden worrying about me, I was nearly dropping things. It was just about the time for him to show up at my door, and I listened anxiously for any sound of a ruckus or something.

"Hey there."

I jumped out of my skin and *did* drop the plate I was washing, thankfully back into the soapy water where it landed with a wet splash.

"Aiden! How did you know where I was?"

He gave me a look. "I always know where you are. It's my gift, remember?"

"And that's not creepy." I was so relieved to see him that I didn't have my filter engaged.

He laughed. "I'm not following you everywhere, if that's what you're implying. I am simply aware of you. And I keep my ears open. News travels fast in the palace."

I lobbed a wet dish towel at him, which he caught easily. "If you're going to be here, you're going to work, mister."

He looked vaguely mystified. "Me? Wash dishes?"

"Is there a problem?"

"I've . . . um . . . this is ridiculous," he mumbled. "But I've never washed dishes before."

I dropped the plate I was scrubbing into the sink and turned to stare at him. "Are you kidding me?"

He stared down at his feet. "We've—my family—always had someone else to do them. And it was never something I really wanted to try."

Well, this was something new. He'd always been ridic-ulously curious around me, wanting to know as much as he could about as much as he could. And I'd already known his family was well off—if his position on the King's Council didn't give him away, his nice clothing, having a hired man at his door as a child, and other various clues did. "Really?"

"Yes, really," he said, clearly embarrassed. Normally I'd milk his embarrassment for all it was worth, but this revelation seemed to be a genuine sore spot.

After a moment of pregnant silence (I couldn't help but make him squirm a little), I turned back to my dishes. "All right, come over here. I'll let you off the hook if you talk while I wash."

"I'm not just going to stand here and watch you work," he objected, seemingly offended that I'd even suggest it.

"You want me to teach you how to wash dishes?"

"It can't be that hard, can it? I mean, you just stick it in the water and get the leftover food off."

"Easier said than done. Here, you can take my spot and I'll start putting things away."

He took my position at the sink and rolled up his sleeves, as if preparing for a fight. I had to giggle at the serious expression on his face as he tackled the dirty dishes.

"So," I said conversationally, picking up a stack of salad plates to put in the cupboard, "what do your parents do anyway? They're obviously well off, but I don't even know them."

"You've seen them around, I'm sure." He spoke hesitantly, but I couldn't tell if it was the crusted plate that was baffling him or the subject matter that made him uncomfortable. "They do a little bit of everything."

"And how are you always here, anyway? Wait, let me

guess." I watched his shoulders tense up. "You're not just from a noble family. Are you from a rich old-money noble? Living in the palace? Is that how you manage to get in and out of everywhere and pull all these favors?"

He grimaced. "You caught me. And you make it sound so bad." I laughed triumphantly.

Old money was a funny thing. It was respected only among the elite and noble circles. Among those that made their own livings, those with old money were looked at as lazy, cheating leeches on society. Most of the old-money folks lived up to that stereotype, but in all fairness, some had actually contributed to society. While Aiden seemed to be the latter, he probably couldn't say the same about his parents.

"So that's why you never wanted to tell me about your family," I mused. He grunted his acknowledgement but didn't comment any further. "All right, I'll change the subject. Any news from the outside world?"

He relaxed, but only marginally. "No. Nothing."

SEVENTEEN

*W*E'D FINISHED EARLIER THAN I HAD EXPECTED, thanks to Aiden's surprising knack for getting the dried-on sauces off plates that I'd struggled with. He followed me back to my room, insisting on the escort.

"You never know who could be lurking in the dark hallways," he cautioned.

I just rolled my eyes at him.

When we reached my room, he surprised me when he followed me inside. "You up for more training tonight?" he asked.

"Are you kidding me? I can barely feel my arms," I complained.

"That was actually probably pretty good for you, you know," he commented. "It'll build up arm strength. Make your punches actually do something."

Grinning cheekily, he dodged my halfhearted attempt at slugging him. "You watch out. Don't forget who won that first day."

"'Won' is a very subjective term with you, I've found."

I rolled my eyes at him, and he made a face right back.

"You never know," he said. "There was another Chameleon attack last night—you might find yourself in trouble again someday and then you'd be thanking me."

I tensed. I couldn't believe I hadn't already heard—either through the gossip in the kitchens or through my runners. "I thought you said there wasn't any news! Tell me what happened!"

"I didn't think it was something you'd want to talk about somewhere we could be interrupted at any moment," he said, and I had to admit he was right. He could have at least mentioned the news, though. "It happened not far from your place, actually. They think they caught him, though."

"What?"

He fixed an even gaze on me and explained. "They found a man with the Chameleon's Mark. He was unconscious when a neighbor found him behind the house. He's in Naked Square now. I don't know what the final punishment will be. I don't think it's been decided."

"I want to go see him," I said, clenching my fists.

He hesitated, then asked, "Why? Why would you want to see him again?"

I met his gaze. "You said they think they caught him. I saw his face. I want to make sure."

He watched me for a long moment before sighing. "I thought you didn't want anything more to do with him."

"I want to be sure. It'll make me feel better," I added, flexing my hands and looking away. I could go to the Square without him, but I wanted him to come with me. I couldn't put my finger on why—the Chameleon would be stripped and bound, incapable of physically hurting me.

Perhaps that was what I was afraid of. The nightmares still hadn't stopped. I didn't mention them to anyone, hoping that if I ignored them they would go away.

He must have seen something in my eyes, because he placed a hand on my arm. "Evie," he said with a frown.

I remained silent.

"Evie, what aren't you telling me?"

I didn't want him to think I was weak. Instead, I looked up at him pleadingly. "I want to make sure it is him . . . and if it's not, I want you to help me find him."

"No. Out of the question."

"Please, Aiden!" I begged. "I know you're angry at him too! And you couldn't have expected me to just wait around here in hiding until someone happened to catch him."

"I hoped."

"Are you kidding? When have I ever been the type of person to just wait around for something to fall into my lap?"

"Never," he said in admission.

"And would you really have me any different?"

"No," he admitted. "But that doesn't mean I want you to go hunting for trouble. Have I ever been one to not worry about you? Do you want me to worry even more now?"

"Of course not," I scoffed. "But I don't want to spend the rest of my life worrying he'll come after me again."

His expression softened, and I reddened, clamping my jaw shut. I hadn't meant to say that. I felt vulnerable and exposed. His hold on my arm tightened as he roughly pulled me into a tight hug, tucking me under his chin. I stiffened, then relaxed as his hold showed no sign of pushing me away anytime soon.

"Evie," he said softly, his breath warm as it brushed over me. "I will always protect you. You know that, right?"

"I know," I mumbled softly, my fingers tracing the embroidery on his shirt.

"And you know you can tell me anything, right?"

My Mark burned against my cheek. I didn't want to tell him. I don't know why—it was probably irrational—but I couldn't reveal that part of me to him. It felt too . . . intimate.

Instead, I gently pulled back and said, "I know of a way that you could help me."

"Name it."

"Assuming the man they caught is the wrong one . . . find the real one for me?"

He released me and looked at me in horror. "And what do you plan to do with him once I find him, assuming I can find him at all?"

"I don't know yet," I confessed. "But I know you can find him. You found me when everyone else thought I was dead."

"That was pure dumb luck. Well, part dumb luck, part wishful thinking."

"Regardless, you found me. I know you can find him."

"I have nothing to go on."

"You have me. I'm the only one who's met him and survived. And you know the Mark he bears."

"Yeah, but I can't exactly use that to find him. It'll be covered up."

"I didn't say I knew how you would find him. If I knew that already, I'd just find him myself," I said, growing frustrated.

"It's not that I don't want to help you," he pleaded. "It's just that I don't want to let you down. Also, I'm afraid of what you'll do if I do find him. I'm not going to provide you with a way to get hurt. Besides, why are you so convinced he hasn't already been caught?"

"It seems too convenient, too easy. Do they have any proof aside from the Mark on his face?"

"He was caught at the scene of the crime," he said. "Other than that, I don't know. But isn't that enough?"

"Not for me," I scowled. We stared each other for a long, tense moment, before he finally surrendered.

"Okay." He sighed. "I'm only agreeing to do this because I know you'll go off and do it by yourself if I don't, and probably hurt yourself more."

I rolled my eyes at his insinuations but didn't deny them.

"I do have conditions, though," he began. "You have to keep me up to date on everything. I don't want to hear things through the grapevine. If we're going to do this, I need to know everything. Is there anything else you need to tell me—anything at all—before we go further?"

My stomach in knots, I said, "There's nothing more."

* * *

On Mondays, we got a bit of a reprieve from kitchen duties. Since Saturday and Sunday meals were such a grand affair—to impress visiting dignitaries—Monday meals were simple. Staff was cut in half, and the servers rotated which Monday they got off.

Most servers took the day off to laze about in bed or go into town to visit relatives and just generally spend some time out of the palace. Normally, I would want to spend more time working on my mask for Milo, or I might have tried to get some extra time in with Joch, but he was nowhere to be found, and I didn't trust myself to work alone without burning down the room yet.

Instead, I was spending my day off with Aiden as we headed to the Naked Square. He seemed tense, an odd shift from his usual pleasantness.

"Is everything okay?" I asked him when we'd been walking for a whole five minutes without him saying anything.

He glanced at me. "I hate that I'm taking you to see this rat. I should be doing everything I can to keep you as far away from him as possible."

"Don't think about it like that," I protested. "You're taking me so I can ease my mind. If it's him, you won't have to worry about me anymore."

He snorted. "That'll be the day," he muttered under his breath.

I looked at him with curiosity but didn't push it, and I let him stew as we walked the rest of the way.

The Square was always bustling with activity, but it seemed especially crowded today. "I can't see," I complained as we pushed our way through the crowd. Aiden grabbed my wrist so he wouldn't lose me and weaved through the throng, eventually coming to a stop right in front of the platform where the criminals were held in stocks.

"Can you see now?" Aiden asked through clenched teeth.

The accused man was right in front of me, and I knew immediately it wasn't the Chameleon. He was too young, his face too round, and his eyes too innocent. My memory might have been clouded with smoke and flame, but I knew this man wasn't the thief and murderer. My chest felt tight, as if I couldn't get enough air. The Chameleon was still on the loose, and now no one was looking for him.

"It's not him," I mumbled, and Aiden looked at me sharply.

"Are you sure?"

I nodded, and he quickly led me away from the Square and the noise.

"Where are we going?" I asked, trailing behind him. We wound our way through the streets before stopping at one of the canal boat stops.

Helping me in with one hand, he answered as if we hadn't just been face-to-face with the man accused of my father's murder. Perhaps he didn't believe me. "You're going to get the rare pleasure of meeting one of my informants."

"Really?" I breathed a sigh of relief. Not only did that mean he believed me, but this meant he was going to help me find the real Chameleon. I'd always marveled over his vast knowledge and couldn't wait to meet one of the people that provided it. That person would have to be impressive indeed.

Unless he is actually part of some underground information ring, I thought suddenly. Maybe that was why Aiden was always so reluctant to tell me where his information came from—it came from illegal or unethical means.

As if sensing my sudden trepidation, Aiden chuckled, and the mood between us lightened. I needed that Aiden right now. "And before your pretty little head goes places it shouldn't, don't worry. I'm not involved in any scandals. Yes, I pay for my information, but not like you're probably thinking. It's like trading goods. Only instead of goods, it's word of mouth. Who was seen where, what certain people were seen doing, who met whom . . . that sort of thing. It's simply paying to have an extra set of eyes and ears. Nothing I wouldn't know if I weren't there myself." He grinned. "Well, most of the time."

I groaned. I didn't think I wanted to know what that statement meant. "So where are we going? Or are you going to keep me in suspense until we get there?"

"I'm trying to decide which would be more fun: seeing your reaction when we get there and meet her, or telling you now."

"Her?"

He shrugged. "Why not? A woman can gather information as well as any man. Better, much of the time. You women have your feminine wiles, after all."

I turned my head away to hide the blush that was creeping up my cheeks and down my neck, reminded of the way I'd "won" our brawl. I still refused to let him live that down. "Just tell me so I don't embarrass myself when I get there," I pleaded.

He apparently decided to have pity on me. "We're going to the Lace District."

EIGHTEEN

MY EYES WIDENED. THE LACE DISTRICT WAS where the Ladies in Lace—often nicknamed the Lacies—lived. These women were trained to entertain in every aspect of the arts. Singing, dancing, drawing—you name it, they were masters of it. Every girl admired them for their abilities, but few pursued the lifestyle themselves.

The Lacies also carried a bit of a stigma. Instead of masks of metals or porcelain, they painted their faces white and lips red and wore strips of lace across their eyes—hence their name. The black lace was a clear mark of their profession, advertising the women's expertise. Men were enticed by the sneak peeks of a woman's face that the lace revealed, and many wished they could draw that same attention. In some it turned to awe, and others to envy. You could tell a lot about a person by the way they perceived these women.

I was in awe of the Lacies. From a young age, they were drilled in every aspect of art until they mastered it. Like me and other children who could afford schooling, they were required to study a broad range of subjects until age twelve, and after that, they picked an area or two to specialize in.

Unlike me, that range was much broader—mine included mathematics, history, and reading, while theirs extended to literature, sciences, and things I had no grasp of whatsoever. Then the other areas were pushed to the side while the Lacie focused her attention on her specialty. And by the side, I mean only an hour or two each day instead of the former six.

After age twelve, she also learned other subjects, including combat, public speaking skills, extensive literature, and engineering. Not only could a Lacie entertain you, she could also carry on extremely knowledgeable conversations. It was her job to make her companions completely at ease while also providing amusement.

I'd never been to the Lace District, and I'd only seen one Lacie in all my life. It was at a fair, and she was on the arm of a very well-to-do nobleman. She was breathtakingly beautiful, wore a black lace mask, and had ringlets of chestnut hair. Her gown was elaborate and made of deep green silk. It trailed after her, and all in her wake stared at her. I was only seven or eight, but I have always remembered that moment. She had such poise and such an air about her that I'd played pretend in my room for weeks, imitating her graceful stroll in a childish clumsy way. I'd stopped after my father walked in on me bowing to make-believe courtiers. I'd been so embarrassed that I'd stopped immediately and never played that game of pretend again.

The gentle current rocked the canal boat and I turned to stare at Aiden. "The Lace District?"

He laughed heartily. "Now I'm glad I told you in advance. If I'd just shown up there with you, I'd have to keep a straight face, and I don't think I could. You look as if a fish has just jumped out of the canal into your lap to announce he was your betrothed."

I was tempted to shove Aiden into the canal.

"Oh, Evie," he said, chuckling and calming down, "you certainly keep me entertained."

"Glad to be of service," I muttered, then added as an afterthought, "Jerk!"

"Aww, don't be like that," he said, still grinning. "Imagine how embarrassed you'd be if you went all starstruck like that at her doorstep?"

Begrudgingly, I admitted he had a point. "Just hush up and tell me about her."

"Her name is Arianna. I met her once . . . when my father, um, hired her to accompany me to a palace event," he admitted, ducking his head. Now it was my turn to laugh at him. He shoved me good-naturedly. "Be nice!"

"You laughed at me. Turnabout is fair play and all."

He groaned. "You're so mean to me."

"Hey, it's nothing you can't take. You big, strong man, you."

"Flattery will get you everywhere, my lady." The deep tenor in his voice made the hair on the back of my neck stand on edge.

Nervously, I patted it down and said, "So? Tell me more about this Arianna."

"You'll like her, I think." Thankfully his voice was back to normal. "I've known her for a long time. Like I said, my father requested her to be my escort to a function. He wanted me to look more sociable, I suppose." He shrugged. "She wore a regular mask during the affair and hated it. She doesn't like to blend in."

I laughed. She sounded like someone I would like.

By this time, we'd arrived to the port, and we got out and walked the rest of the way to our destination. Aiden wrapped an arm around my waist after helping me out of the boat.

"Stay close to me," he warned. "I can't have anyone thinking you're a Lacie in disguise and try to steal you from me."

I rolled my eyes at his ridiculous suggestion that anyone would mistake me for a Lacie. "And who says I don't want to be stolen? Or that I'm yours in the first place to be stolen from you?"

He made a sound deep in his throat, not unlike a growl. "Here, in this district, you are mine."

That got my hackles up. Who was he to say that I belonged to anyone, least of all him? I pulled away from him, offended.

He immediately understood what I was doing and pulled me back, by my wrist this time. Much less intimate. Thankfully. Being in such close proximity to him was starting to do strange things to my body.

"I didn't mean it like that and you know it," he said, though not at all remorsefully. We crossed over the ornate stone bridge that marked the entrance to the Lace District. It was littered with carvings of flowers and dancing figures, all done by those who once lived there. The Lacies who chose to specialize in stone carving were that talented.

"You meant it in a way," I insisted stubbornly. "And I don't want you thinking I'm your property."

"Of course I don't," he retorted. "You're too lively and

spirited to ever belong to anyone without having given yourself to them freely."

I wasn't sure if that was a compliment or not, so I said nothing, silently staring at the street below my feet. The streets in my own district weren't nearly so clean.

He sighed heavily. "And now you really are mad at me. Look, I didn't mean to offend you."

I sighed right back. "I know you didn't," I admitted. "I'm just . . . being a girl for once, okay?"

That got a weak laugh from him. "You're always a girl to me."

The air was tense between us again, in that tightly strung way that I didn't know how to respond to. Resorting to my age-old, tried and trusted, natural response, I ignored it and changed the subject.

"So, Arianna?"

"Yes, Arianna. Like I was saying, she didn't like to blend in. Of course, she was a natural Lacie and stood out even without her regular mask, but she didn't like it being chalked up to natural grace. She likes people knowing how hard she's worked to become the woman she is now."

I suspected I knew where this story was going. "What did she do?"

That familiar, cheeky grin was back on Aiden's lips. "She couldn't do anything to reveal who she was at the function, of course. That would have been against my father's orders, and she didn't dare do anything like that. It would have put her position in danger, not to mention my father's reputation.

"So, instead, she found out when the next large function was that had invited as many of the same guests as possible, obtained an invitation, and arrived in her lace mask, making an obvious spectacle of herself while still maintaining her dignity. It was clear she had been the same woman on my arm not weeks before."

"Wouldn't that be an embarrassment to you, though?" I asked, intrigued.

He shook his head. "She's too clever for that. She said she'd had such a good time as my escort before that she couldn't wait to see me again. And that I had proven myself to be so good to her and for her that she couldn't accompany me as only an escort again."

"So you come off as this great ladies' man, and she looks a love-struck fool? That doesn't seem to make sense."

"You might think that, but again, she's clever. It was clear to anyone who spoke to her that she was smart, and everyone came to the conclusion that I really was that amazing. It's common enough to be escorted by Lacies, so there was no shame in that. It was simply the matter of disguising what she was that she didn't like."

"I see." I was eager to meet this lady.

"And here we are," he said, directing me to the door of what looked like a large inn.

The building was lovely from the outside. After all, these women were the epitome of women, and the area they inhabited should display that as well. Pale white and green lanterns were strung up along the water's edge and along the streets, which were all clean and well swept, and waste was disposed of quickly and effectively. The houses from my neighborhood had been coated in light pastels; these buildings were all bold jewel tones edged with silvers and golds. Those that didn't house Lacies or Lacies-in-training were often places of entertainment, such as theaters and music halls, which were also kept in top condition.

Aiden opened the door to the building without knocking and led us into an open lobby. The floors were fine mahogany, covered with intricately woven rugs with colorful designs. No doubt the women of this establishment made the rugs.

Mirrors hung on the walls, an expensive and common decoration for these types of buildings. Lamps were lit around the room, and the mirrors bounced the light around, making the room bright and quite cheery.

"My lord!" a light voice exclaimed, clearly recognizing Aiden.

A tall woman rushed toward him, stopping in front of him and sweeping into the smoothest curtsy I've ever seen, dropping her gloved hand in his, which he kissed in greeting.

"My lovely Arianna, it's always a pleasure," he said, pulling her to stand comfortably. He turned to me and said, "This is Evelina, my good friend."

"It's a pleasure to meet you," I said politely, taking her hand and trying to imitate her curtsy. Mine was not half as graceful as hers.

Her black hair was tightly bound in intricate braids circling the crown of her head and adorned with tiny cream-colored pearls, while her blue eyes glowed like bright sea glass behind her black lace. Her lips were painted a deep red, and her cheeks rouged in pink over the white of the rest of her face. The white paint stopped at the edge of her jaw and hairline as a normal mask would, and her neck was bare save a small silver chain with a jade pendant. I envied her fine dress, a deep blue with silver edging that draped her body in flattering curves and dips. She was all confidence and beauty. I fought to keep my jealousy at bay. I knew I was no sea cow, but it was impossible to not feel just a little insecure next to her.

"The pleasure is mine," she insisted, and though I half expected her to take an unflattering sort of pleasure in my horrible lack of grace, she seemed genuinely pleased to meet me. "Any friend of my lord's is a friend of mine."

I cast a sidelong glance at Aiden, who seemed vaguely uncomfortable with the repeated address of "my lord." I wondered if they'd ever been on a first-name basis. It was odd to hear him be called anything but simply Aiden.

"Would you like to join me for some refreshment?" she asked, gesturing toward what I assumed was a small dining area. "We just received a shipment of lemons that the girls are playing around with in the kitchen. They produced some delicious treats that I'm sure you'd love."

"We'd be delighted," he said, and I trailed behind him as Arianna led the way.

The room was indeed a dining area, with small tables for groups of twos or threes scattered across the floor. It was just as bright in here, though the walls were covered with more paintings than mirrors. One wall was covered exclusively with a bright mural of the oceanside. I was mesmerized by the beautiful strokes that turned into waves of blues and grays crashing along the rocks. I could smell the clean saltiness of the ocean and block out the musk of the canals just by looking at this painting.

"Beautiful, isn't it?" Arianna addressed me, taking me by surprise. I had assumed she would pay attention to only Aiden, because he was her contact.

"Yes, it is. It takes me right back to the shore," I admitted.

"I wish I could say I'd had a hand in creating that"—she gestured at the wall—"but my painting isn't quite that good. Another girl painted it. She's incredibly skilled. As she should be, I suppose. Painting is her specialty. All of the residents here had a part in creating this mural, but she was the main hand and designer. I was relegated to the clouds," she said ruefully.

I looked at the clouds then. They were nothing to draw attention, neither good nor bad. "Clouds are ridiculous," Arianna said. "It's what we practice shading on. It was like having me do the punctuation at the end of a sentence." She laughed. "But that's all right. I best her every time at debate."

I couldn't help but laugh with her. She had that infectious giggle, the kind that drew people in around her and instantly cheered them.

"But that's more than enough about me. Tell me about you!" she insisted, seating us at a circular table near a window before sitting herself. "I've never seen my lord with a girl on his arm of his own free will." She glanced at him slyly. "I thought he left that part up to his father."

Aiden groaned. "Just leave that alone, will you? I think you've given me enough grief over that to last me a lifetime."

She giggled again and consented, again prodding me for information about myself. "Do you live in the palace too? I've never seen you before."

"I do live there," I admitted, though omitted my occupation. Even if it was just a cover, it felt shameful to admit I was a serving mistress in front of this fine lady. "Just recently, though."

She seemed to sense my hesitation and didn't prod me more on the subject. "How did you two meet, then? Did his father try to set you up too?"

Aiden snorted, and said, "Not at all. We met under completely different circumstances."

I smiled at the memory and sat back to let Aiden tell Arianna the story. It was a fond memory for me, and one story I loved to hear Aiden tell—often because it was different every time, and I got to correct him.

"It was a dark and stormy night," he began teasingly.

"It was not," I said, laughing. "It was a perfectly lovely spring evening."

"Are you telling the story, or am I?"

"It depends on if you're going to tell it right," I said.

"I'm insulted that you suggest I'd do anything but!" he said, mockingly aghast.

"Right," I said sarcastically.

"As I was saying," he continued, "it was a perfectly lovely spring evening." He waited for me to interrupt again, but I smiled innocently at him. Shaking his head, he continued as Arianna watched us with an amused expression. "And I was on an errand in the Green District, where Evie here happened to be as well.

"I was in a hurry, because I had a lot of things to do that night and some people my father needed me to meet, so I tried to take what I thought was a shortcut."

"Shortcuts are never short," I interjected, smiling fondly.

"Especially when you're the scenery," he shot back. "But yes, as you can guess, I lost my way."

"Which is really ridiculous, when you think about it," I interrupted again. "All he had to do was find a canal and tell the driver where he needed to go and odds are the driver would know exactly where to take him."

"Which is what I did," he tried to defend himself.

"Only after wandering around until it was dark and you'd followed me home, trying to pluck up the nerve to ask directions!"

Arianna laughed gleefully with me, and Aiden couldn't keep up his affronted façade.

"So Evie had pity on me and gave me proper directions. The next day I returned to thank her, and she became my go-to for any information about that District. And then I just kept coming back," he said, looking at me fondly.

"Like a stray cat," I teased. "I show you a little kindness and then can't get rid of you."

They both laughed, and I belatedly realized something he had said—I was his informant in my district? I'd never thought of myself like that, though it was clearly true. That explained his curiosity.

"How did you come to be knowledgeable about that district?" Arianna asked me.

"I lived there most of my life," I admitted. No shame in admitting my masking heritage to her. And Lacies were renowned for their secret-keeping abilities. I wouldn't have to worry about her blowing my cover. "My family was in the masking business."

"Ohh," she exclaimed. "I envy you that. I've tried my hand at trimming, and it can be tricky work. The material never did what I wanted it to do. And my workstation always became such a mess."

I laughed, proud that I was able to do something she could not. "It takes a long time to learn and even longer to master," I said modestly. "And I'm still very much in the learning process."

"I'd love to see some of your work some time," she said.

I hesitated before saying, "I wish I could show you. A recent fire destroyed most of my current work, and I don't have anything to show."

"Oh, that's awful!" She was also an artisan of sorts, and I was sure she'd felt the pain of losing a piece of work. Artisans put pieces of themselves in everything they did, and to lose a product was to lose a part of themselves.

"I hate to interrupt, but we have some business to take care of," Aiden said, looking truly like he did hate to interrupt. I also think he was getting a kick out of watching me talk with Arianna. He didn't see me socialize or talk with girls pretty much ever, so I'm sure this was a different side of me he was seeing. I was curious to see what he made of it. I made a mental note to ask him about it on the return trip.

"Of course," Arianna said. "Let me fetch the treats and then we can begin. It wouldn't do to simply sit here without any sort of refreshment—they'd kick me out on the streets," she joked. At least, I think she was only joking. These places were infamously strict, so for all I knew, she was serious.

Aiden and I sat in comfortable silence, waiting for her return. I was lost in my thoughts of my life since I'd met Aiden, and he was no doubt lost in his own thoughts. Probably not of me, though.

Arianna returned with a tray filled with bright yellow squares, sprinkled with sugar. The mere sight of them made my taste buds sing. She also carried a silver pitcher of juice and three small cups and matching miniature plates.

Setting everything down, and quickly serving each of us, she made herself comfortable and began to speak.

NINETEEN

*B*EFORE GIVING US ANY INFORMATION, ARIANNA clearly wanted to make sure she wasn't going to reveal more than Aiden wanted me to know. She seemed a little hesitant, and Aiden read her hesitations correctly.

"Anything you think will be useful for me to know, Evie can also know," he said. "And she's caught up on what I know. Mostly. I can fill in any blanks as we talk."

That seemed to put Arianna at ease. "That makes things easier, then. No tiptoeing around what's need to know and what's something I just picked up."

Aiden nodded. "Let's start with the need to know."

"I assume you've already realized the man they think they've caught is a fake?"

I shot Aiden a look. Clearly *someone* had already spoken to her about the purpose of our visit. He held his hands out innocently, then dropped the façade and grinned. I sighed and shook my head, then asked Arianna, "Why do you say that?"

"Well," she said, "it's not really common knowledge yet, but the man had a close friend who knew his face and says she can vouch for him. It seems he was framed."

Aiden looked shocked. "We can't even trust the Marks now?"

She shook her head, then continued. "The newest rumor surrounding this Chameleon is that he might not even actually be a 'he'"—she looked at me pointedly—"if you understand what I mean."

"The Chameleon is a woman?" Aiden sounded incredulous.

"There's no way," I protested. I'd seen him with my own eyes. He was definitely a man. "What on earth started that rumor?"

"Apparently before the fire yesterday, there was a new girl in the market setting up shop the next District over. You know how close knit those people are—any stranger is going to stand out. They said she kept to herself and set up a shop full of mask trimmings, simple things that folks could do themselves.

"Several people tried to talk to her, but she would answer with only a yes or no, or one-word answers."

"What connection is she to the Chameleon, then? It's not that strange to have a newcomer. Uncommon, maybe, but not cause for suspicion."

"True, but when she is gone the very next day without a trace?" Arianna said. "That is definitely more cause for suspicion."

"Why even bother setting up a shop at all?" Aiden asked. "Why not just keep hidden during the day?"

Arianna shrugged her slim shoulders. "Your guess is as good as anyone's. We're thinking that she wanted to get a feel for her targets, so she could imitate them after stealing their masks."

"That could be done just as easily without being so conspicuous." Aiden wasn't convinced, and neither was I.

"No, I think she wanted to be seen. I think the original wanted to confuse anyone who was pursuing him. Now we'll be looking for someone who may be either male or female? He's widening the list of possible suspects," I said.

"Hmm." Aiden drummed his fingers on the table as he thought that over. "I don't think we can rule anything else out right now. And your source is reliable?"

"Extremely," Arianna assured him. Her word seemed to be good enough for him, and it would have to be good enough for me too.

"What else did you find out?"

"That's the only big development. I still don't think I've heard anything useful in my usual circles," she told us sadly. "But no one particularly notable has gone missing or has unaccountable gaps of time where they could be off leading this double life. So I think it's either a foreigner or someone from the lower class."

"I would guess a foreigner," I murmured, trying to recall if I'd detected any sort of accent when he'd attacked me. In the haze of panic, I'd noticed nothing particularly outstanding. "A foreigner wouldn't have any qualms about imitating others by stealing masks."

"True," Aiden agreed thoughtfully.

Our country was unique in its mask system. It wasn't so far fetched to believe that someone from the outerlands, where they went bare-faced, would come in and make a mess of things to stir up controversy in our society. They considered us imposters or proud pretenders, and we considered them naked savages.

"But things have been calm around the borders," Arianna argued. "It would have to be some kind of personal grudge."

"Can you think of anyone who's personally offended outsiders recently? Or rather," I rephrased my question to a better one, "any connection between the victims that would have angered an outsider to the point of acting like this?"

Shaking her head, Arianna replied, "We've thought of that too, looking for some kind of connection. We haven't been able to find one yet, but we're still looking."

I realized she was taking something for granted, something that Aiden already knew. "I know this might seem a stupid question, but who is 'we,' if you don't mind my asking?"

Arianna smiled gently. "Of course, it's an obvious question for you to ask. I should have said earlier. I would have, but Aiden already knows of course, and it's just second nature for me to speak for all of us.

"When I refer to 'we' I mean myself and the other Lacies. Aiden is not the only one who likes information, and he's not the only one who will pay for it." She grinned flirtatiously in his direction. "He is, however, one of my more preferred clients."

Aiden tried to laugh it off, but I caught the way he reddened. Absently, I wondered if there was more of a history between them.

"And so, I get most of my information from other Lacies. We all know what we're personally invested in, of course, but we also like to keep tabs on what others are searching for and help out when we can. It's always beneficial to provide what information you know, since you never know what or who can prove useful. And, again, we're all used to keeping our secrets, so there's no fear of leaking information to the wrong person. The loyalty between us is too strong. No Lacie would ever betray her sisters like that."

She spoke so fiercely that I couldn't doubt her. Added to what I knew about the women, I would have bet my life that any information passed through the Lacies was true and secure.

"What if someone got fed bad information?" I wondered out loud.

"If there's any doubt, it doesn't get passed along. Or if it does, it's passed with the disclaimer that it may or may not be one hundred percent true."

"How can you know if it's good or bad?"

"It depends on the source," she said thoughtfully. "For example, if I see or hear something with my own eyes or ears, then I can trust it, obviously. And there are people that I trust just as much as if I'd heard it myself. If I get information passed on from anyone else, then I'll tack on the disclaimer. I usually don't pass anything on that's more than one or two people removed."

I digested that. "Sorry to ask, or if I insulted you in any way—I don't mean to doubt you. I just want to know."

She waved off my apology. "Not at all. I'd be asking the same questions, if our places were reversed. Which says a lot about the both of us." She smiled at me.

I smiled back. I was definitely looking forward to getting to know her more.

* * *

"So I have a feeling there's more to the story than you originally told me," I said nonchalantly as we left Arianna's place. We'd stayed for a short while longer, talking about nothing in particular. I had a feeling that Aiden had picked up more information from the casual conversation than about I was privy to. I was sure he wanted information other than the Chameleon, but he didn't bring anything else up. I didn't know if it was because I was there and he didn't want me to know, or because he *couldn't* let me know. Either way, it didn't bother me. It wasn't any of my business.

His personal life, on the other hand, was *always* my business.

"What gives you that idea?" He sounded far too casual. I knew I was on to something. If it had been nothing, he'd tease me about how I was either being paranoid or something silly like that.

I shrugged. "Just . . . something in the air, I suppose. Any chance you'll spill?"

"Assuming there is something to spill, of course."

"And I'm pretty positive there is."

"Would you be willing to bet a round of training on that?" he bargained with me.

"In a heartbeat."

"Then I guess you'll see tonight, won't you?"

I groaned. "Come on. Can't you just tell me now? What's a few hours difference going to make?"

"Because I know you. I know that if I tell you now, tonight you'll try to worm something else out of me, claiming that what I tell you now doesn't count as an exchange for something later."

I widened my eyes and gave him my best injured puppy

dog look. "You really think I'd do that to you?" I asked as innocently as I could manage without laughing, because that was exactly my plan.

"Don't give me that look," he said, groaning. "I refuse to look at you until you put that look away. And you know how dangerous that can be if I'm going to be helping you into any boats. I'd hate for you to accidently land in the canal."

I snorted. "Right, and I'd hate for you to come tumbling in after me because I refuse to let go of you when you push me in. You'd ruin your pretty clothes, and I'm still not entirely convinced that you can swim."

"What?! I can swim perfectly well, thank you very much," he cried indignantly. He crossed his arms over his chest and pouted.

"You're such a baby." I laughed, tugging on his arm, trying to loosen his stance.

"I am not." To prove a point, I wasn't sure if it was his or mine, he stuck his tongue out at me childishly.

I dropped my innocent act and dissolved into giggles. He tried to keep up his tough façade, but that didn't last long, and soon he was laughing along with me.

"All right," I said once I'd caught my breath again. "Cross my heart, I won't try to cheat you tonight. I'll make you tell me something else by some other way, like kicking your butt."

I made an elaborate show of drawing an X across my heart and holding out my other hand to show I wasn't crossing my fingers that would negate my promise.

He seemed to accept that. "Fine, fine. You are irresistible, you know that, right?"

"I do my best." I smiled.

"All right. So Arianna and I do have a little more of a history than I'd let on before," he confessed, watching the ground beneath his feet carefully as we continued down the street to the boat docks.

"I never courted her in front of my father. I couldn't give him the pleasure. And there is also the matter of her profession to consider. She's a Lacie through and through, and I don't think she'd ever give that up, not even for me." He laughed at some inside joke. "Perhaps especially not for me."

"How long have you known her?"

"We've known each other for years. We were intimately acquainted for perhaps a month or so before we both realized we weren't fooling anyone and that we'd never amount to anything together. She's far too independent to be with someone like me, and I'm too much of a . . . complication to be with her."

"I thought you liked her independence."

"I do, very much. I admire her extremely. It's just, in our situation, it wouldn't have worked." He struggled to find the right words. "I mean, you of all people should know how I like my girls to have some brains and spitfire in them."

He nudged my shoulder, and I couldn't stop the blush in my cheeks. "I see why you hang around me now," I said, trying to deflect his comments the best way I knew how. "You like to fool yourself into thinking you can conquer my independent streak every once in a while when I let you get the better of me."

"Not at all," he surprised me by saying. "I won't deny that I get a special sort of thrill thrashing you in personal combat training, but you have to know that I like being around you because you're not afraid—of anything, it seems."

"Don't be ridiculous. I'm afraid of plenty of things."

"You never show it. Sometimes I wonder if you're actually real." He looked at me sidewise with an odd look in his eyes.

"Again, don't be ridiculous. Of course I'm real, and of course I'm afraid of plenty of things."

"Name one thing you're afraid of." Before I could even open my mouth to answer, though, he said, "And the Chameleon coming after you doesn't count. I know you're not insane, and he has to scare you a little."

"Actually that wasn't what I was going to say, but yes, that's on my list."

"And what were you going to say?"

"Spiders," I deadpanned.

He stared at me for a silent moment, then cracked up laughing. "Seriously?"

"Don't laugh at me! They're creepy little things with their millions of eyes and legs and the skittering way they walk . . ." I trailed off and shivered. I was creeping myself out.

Aiden, on the other hand, was still laughing. "You're honestly scared of spiders? You live in a basement! How does that even work? And that's so . . ."

"What? Girly?" I said, annoyed. "And I freak out every time I see one. You're just never around when I need you to squish them," I added as an afterthought.

"Well, yeah, it's girly, but I was going to say normal. And it's not my fault that I'm not always around."

"What are you afraid of then, Lord I'm-Too-Dignified–For-Spiders?" I asked, narrowing my eyes at him.

He stopped laughing and looked at me seriously. "Getting lost."

I stared back at him. "You're messing with me," I accused. "You didn't look at all scared when I first met you. If anything, you looked frustrated."

"People deal with fear in different ways," he said, shrugging. "And I didn't really mean physically lost. I meant more in the figurative way. Like, getting lost in the shuffle of life. Losing sight of who I am under the pressures and stress of who people expect me to be."

"That's . . ." I struggled to find the right words. "Really deep. Who knew you could be serious like that?"

He didn't answer, and I worried that I had taken my teasing a little too far that time. "Aiden." I put a hand on his arm and waited for him to look me in the eyes. "I promise, as long as you know me, I won't let you get lost in yourself, okay?"

A small smile tugged at his lips. "And I'll protect you from any and all spiders."

I shoved him away. "Rogue."

He smiled in earnest then. "I feel like I'm cheating you in this deal. But I'll take it, if it means you'll stick around."

"It's a deal, then."

As we walked back to the palace in relative silence, I couldn't help feeling as if we'd passed some sort of milestone in our relationship. He'd become my best friend. And I was starting to feel like I was becoming something more than his best friend.

And I was surprisingly okay with that.

TWENTY

*T*HE QUICKLY APPROACHING MASQUERADES MEANT the mask room was always bursting with activity, and I was more often than not cleaning or working on something other than my own mask.

But today I would put the finishing touches on my mask and present it to Milo. I'd spent hours sanding and smoothing and sewing until I felt it was perfect.

"It looks good," a chipper girl with short brown hair commented. I could never remember her name, but I thanked her. "Don't you think it looks good, Joch?" she asked my neighbor, who was in the workroom today, reading some books of different glass-blowing techniques.

He barely glanced at it before turning back to his paperwork and shrugging, apparently not impressed.

"Oh, ignore him," the girl insisted, adding under her breath, "He's just bitter and jaded."

I raised an eyebrow, surprised. "Oh?"

"You haven't heard?" She lowered her voice conspiratorially. "The reason he came here? He's from one of the Northern Islands and was set up pretty nicely too. Had a girl and everything. But then she ran off with a sea merchant who was quite popular with the palace suppliers. He followed her here but never found her."

"That's so tragic." I looked at him out of the corner of my eyes, seeing him in a new light. No wonder he was always so sullen. "How did he end up here, though? Wouldn't he be reminded of her all the time?"

She shrugged. "I don't know. I just know he showed up in the palace one day as an official guest to the crown."

"I *can* hear you, you know," Joch said suddenly, lurching to his feet and gathering his papers in a huff. "And really, that's none of your business."

He marched out of the room, barely snapping an excuse to Milo before letting the door slam shut behind him.

"Someone has a bit of a temper," Milo remarked calmly as he walked over, as if this happened every day. Although given the lack of confusion in the room, it apparently happened more often than I'd thought. "I hope that means you're ready for my examination, Miss Evelina, if you have the time to chase your desk mate away."

I ducked my head. "Yes, sir. I mean, I'm ready."

He held out his hand, and I gingerly placed my finished product in his palm, feeling as though my racing heart was another ornament on the mask.

He ran his hands over the inner lining, feeling for snags or puckers, but I'd done that as well and knew there were none to be found. Then he felt out the surface, tracing each curve and swirl and bead with his fingertips. He pulled gently on the beaded string that strapped the mask to the wearer. He tested every inch of my creation, his passive face leaving my stomach in knots.

"I'd like to test the fit now, if you please. Would you prefer to go to one of the fitting rooms?"

"Yes, please," I answered immediately, feeling curious eyes on me.

Once securely behind a curtain, Milo asked me to remove the mask I was wearing and put the one I made on. "Now I'm going to feel for the fit, but let me know if you are uncomfortable at any time, all right?"

I nodded, then remembered that he couldn't see and answered aloud.

His nimble fingers felt along the edges, making sure everything was flush against my skin. My whole body tensed as he brushed close to my Mark, but if he noticed, he didn't say anything. Finally, he withdrew his hands.

"Well, Miss Evelina, I think you've done a very fine job."

I beamed with pride.

"I could feel no cracks, and the work is solid. However," he continued, my stomach dropping, "it is very safe. I detected no risks, nothing adventurous. I would wager you've made hundreds of masks like this in the past."

He was right, I realized.

"I'm pleased you have a good grasp of the basics. However, you won't create masterpieces if you are forever playing it safe. When someone asks you to prove yourself, you must also stretch yourself and take risks, otherwise while you might prove something to another, you prove nothing to yourself."

"I understand," I said softly, looking down.

"Don't sound so glum." He lifted my chin up. "I did say I was pleased with your work, and I would be very pleased to have you continue to be in my workroom."

I beamed at him. "Thank you, sir. I would like that very much."

"Good. And how's your work with Signore Joch coming along? He seems to be a bit more testy as of late."

Sighing, I said, "I'm not sure. I thought I was making progress, but he's always so . . . stiff and abrasive. I don't know what he thinks of my work. All he does is grunt at me."

"He hasn't kicked you out yet, which is more than I can say for others that have tried. Give him time, Miss Evelina. I think you'll get through to him eventually."

I doubted it, but I wasn't going to give up just yet.

* * *

"Why are you just standing around?" Vera screeched at me as I floated into the kitchens later that day.

"I—"

She cut me off before I could form a response, not that I'd had any clue how to respond.

"You're supposed to be helping prep for the balls, and the first one is tomorrow! Didn't anyone tell you? You'll be in the first shift of servers and will need to leave an excellent first impression." She rolled her eyes. "I'd keep you serving for both, but I can't have you seen out on the floor for that long. Someone might think you're being over-worked. Instead, you'll be inside the kitchen, working on the dishes. You did so well with them last time."

Grinning happily to herself, she sauntered away, having delivered the bad news. I don't know why she delighted in doing that, but it seemed to just make her day every time she could ruin mine.

"Great," I muttered to myself, my good mood deflated. I'd been hoping to attend at least one of the elaborate masquerade balls, but it looked like that wouldn't be possible this year. Instead of dancing with handsome beaux, I'd be keeping company with the suds and crusty dishes. Fantastic.

"Aw, were you hoping to have a chance at the prince, after all?" Jeza called from her cutting board full of badly sliced tomatoes. "I'm telling you now, sweet lady, you're better off hiding in the kitchens."

"Why would I even think I had 'a chance at the prince,'" I mocked, "at the ball?" I was tired of Jeza's meaningless accusations.

"You haven't heard yet?" she squealed, immediately abandoning her post to come gossip. "The king has decided it's time for the prince to settle down. I think there was some drama in the family or something. I haven't got all the details on that yet." She sounded frustrated about not knowing every minute detail about their royal lives. "But the prince will actually be *dancing* at the ball. I think he might even be in disguise! You know, actually have some inch of his skin visible, so as not to skew the results or something silly like that."

I'd never had my sights set on the prince, but I had to admit I was disappointed that I wouldn't even have a chance to dance with him, if for no other reason than to have a good story to tell. Or something to rub in Jeza's face, should I get the chance and she did not.

Jeza seemed to read the disappointment that caused my shoulders to sag. "It really is a shame that you'll miss out."

I shrugged it off, trying to act like it didn't bother me.

"It's not like I won't be there to see him," I pointed out. "I'll still be serving. I'll be out there. I bet I'll still get to see him."

That stopped her for a moment. "But seeing isn't the same as touching," she finally said. "And as a server, you'll have *no* chance of dancing with him. You'll be all but invisible to him."

She grinned triumphantly. I kept my voice calm as I responded. "I guess it's a good thing I never wanted that 'chance' at him in the first place, isn't it?"

I left her then; I was afraid I probably would have tried to slap her. I don't know how she got under my skin, but she seemed to know exactly how to irritate me.

I couldn't go far because dinner was under an hour away, and I'd be needed back in the kitchens. So I just stalked back and forth in one of the hallways, silently fuming. I shouldn't let her get to me like that, I knew, but I couldn't help it.

I'd even stopped by the runners' parlor again to see if they could distract me, but they were so busy they didn't even have time to flirt. And for the first time they had something to tell me about the Chameleon. They had only rumors, but it was something.

What better time for the Chameleon to use his stolen masks than during a Masquerade? If he'd managed to steal a fine enough mask, he could easily alter it just enough to avoid being suspicious and slip inside. No one would be the wiser that the nobleman in front of them was no nobleman at all.

That's what made the Chameleon so dangerous.

* * *

Later that night as I was waiting for Aiden to come to my room for our nightly combat practice, I was so tightly wound I could barely sit still. On top of the threat of the Chameleon making an appearance, I just couldn't let Jeza's comments go.

"Argh!" I pounded my fist against the stone wall in anger. This action, of course, did nothing to the wall and probably bruised my hand.

"Whoa! What happened to you?" Aiden asked, clearly concerned as he stood at my doorway. I'd taken to just leaving the door open for him. It wasn't as if anyone else came down here.

I spun around to face him and hid my sore fist behind my back, embarrassed. "It's just me thinking I can take on the wall. You know how I can be," I said weakly, trying to make a joke out of it.

He rolled his eyes at my lame attempt and held out his hand. "Give me your hand, my lady."

"Why? I beat that wall down. I totally won that match."

"Evie."

"It doesn't hurt," I protested, but he reached around me and took my hand in his. He massaged the tendons gently, and oddly enough, that helped relax the tension in the rest of my body. So I let him continue for as long as he wished, and when he stopped, I didn't pull my hand away immediately.

I flexed my fingers experimentally. "What did you do? I feel so relaxed now."

He chuckled. "It's something my mother taught me a

long time ago. She'd get stressed, and I'd do the same thing to her hand. It relaxed her almost immediately every time. I don't know why."

"Well, you have my permission to do that whenever you want," I said glibly, "because that felt all sorts of good."

He chuckled. "I'll hold you to that. But back to the original question, why did you feel the urge to take on the stone wall?"

"Would you believe it offended me with its general gray gloominess and I couldn't take it anymore?"

He laughed. "Not a chance."

"I got my duty details for the balls," I said, sighing. "I won't be able to attend as a guest, apparently. I'd known it was too much to hope for. But I'd wanted to sneak in to at least one of them."

His face fell. Apparently he'd been hoping the same thing. "Well, that's certainly a good enough excuse to beat up a poor innocent wall. I'm being forced to go. You'll probably see me all dressed up like a peacock."

I giggled. "And what a fine peacock you'll make."

"It's going to be ridiculous, just you wait. My mask is pretty great, though. At least that'll be one part of my appearance I won't despise."

"Yeah?" I asked, encouraging him to go on.

Masquerade masks were something else altogether. They were much more elaborate than day-to-day apparel, covered with feathers, jewels, and all sorts of detailed carvings and engravings. Much fancier than even the formal mask I was making for Milo. That would be one benefit of being a server—I'd get to see everyone's finery. If I'd been a guest, I'd probably miss the grand majority of it because I'd be forced to stay in the lower levels of the ballrooms. The best ones were in the upper quarters, and I was going to find a way up there if it was the last thing I did that night.

"Yes, I'm told I look very dashing in it," he said with a hint of pride.

"By whom? Your mother?" I teased.

His cheeks tinged pink, and I knew I'd hit the target. "You're just jealous," he retorted.

"I am," I said honestly. "I could never look as dashing as you."

"That's true," he said. "You'd be more of the beautiful type, I suppose."

"You suppose. Thanks," I said flatly, still teasing.

"Okay, I *know* you'd be beautiful. Is that better?" he asked.

I pretended to think it over. "I suppose that will have to do."

"Glad to be of service, my lady."

"What's so bad about the rest of your outfit?" I asked, curious.

He grimaced. "It's . . . really elaborate. I don't know how I'm going to move."

I laughed. "You can hang out with me, then, and just stand in one place."

"Believe me, if I thought I could get away with it, I would."

We both knew what he wasn't saying. If he was seen socializing with a serving girl, he'd get into serious trouble with his father. The purpose of these balls was for match-making. Those with matches enjoyed the general atmosphere and frivolity, but those unmatched were supposed to find a potential desirable candidate. If Aiden were suspected of sabotaging any chances he had at finding a match, oh, he'd pay for it with his parents.

"Do I get to help you find potentials?" I asked.

I was surprised to note that he looked offended. "I'm . . . not really planning on looking that hard," he admitted.

"Ah," I said. "There's already someone you've got your sights set on?"

"I don't have a choice in the matter," he said flatly, then abruptly changed the subject. "Do I get a chance to fight you tonight, or did the wall already take the best out of you?"

"Dream on," I scoffed. "What have you got for me to learn tonight?"

"Well, tonight I thought we'd switch to some leg work for a bit. Give your arms a rest."

"In other words, exhaust me so I can barely stand tomorrow," I said bitterly.

He bit back a grin. "It builds your strength."

"Yeah, right. You just like to see me suffer."

"Guilty as charged. Now, I'm not going to teach you how to kick, because odds are that would open you up to more vulnerable attacks than anything else. Also, kicks are not as effective in a skirt."

I ignored his last comment. "Okay, so no kicks. Sounds boring."

"Please. When have I ever been boring?"

"Would you like me to make a list?" I asked cheekily.

"Yes, please, actually," he shot back, unwilling to back down. "I want to know when I have done such an offensive thing as bore you."

"You're going off on a tangent. I thought you were teaching me something, sire."

He laughed. "Fine, fine. All right, instead of kicks, I'm going to teach you all the cheap tricks."

"I know the cheap tricks already," I said impatiently. "That was how I beat you in the first place, remember?"

He shook his head and held up two fingers. "First, the fact of you beating me is still up for debate, and second"—he lowered one finger so that the one remaining was pointing right in my face—"you hardly know all the cheap tricks."

I glared at his offending finger and reached to grab and shove it out of my direct line of vision, but as I reached, he swung his leg around to tap the back of my left knee, making my leg buckle out of reflex. Then when I grabbed his arm for balance, he managed to somehow knock me on my knees and spin me around so that I was facing away from him and he had me in a headlock.

"W-what was *that?*" I sputtered.

"Another dirty trick. Want me to show you?" He loosened his grip on me and helped me up from the ground.

We spent the next couple of hours knocking each other down, and I was sure I was going to have a few bruises in the morning to show for my efforts. But heaven help the next person who stuck their finger in my face.

TWENTY-ONE

THERE WERE THREE MAIN MASQUERADE BALLS at the end of the tenth month every year, to celebrate the coming of winter and the end of summer. I'd never attended them, but I loved to make the masks for them. I'd never had any client so high ranking that any mask of mine was worn to the palace's masquerade, but the districts held smaller celebrations of their own.

In addition to celebrating the seasons and the matchmaking that took place behind the scenes, it was the biggest opportunity for mask makers to show off their skills. All three nights were extremely elaborate, and each one more so than the previous.

The first night was the least elaborate, though only in comparison to the other two. When pitted against any other celebration from the rest of the year, that first night outshone them in every area.

The theme of the first night was to bid farewell to the hard and hot days of summer and to celebrate the end of the harvest. Growing up near the fishing ports, I'd learned that the fish came in seasons as well. The particular types of fish that our island thrived on migrated to warmer waters during the cold winter months, and most fishermen used the off-season to repair their tools and boats. Some did chase the fish south and sent back their catches, but that was a small percentage. Regardless of which group the men fell in, they had plenty to do during the winter months.

The masquerades also had great feasts, and the first night focused on fish. The palace scouted out the best chefs from every village, and a grand assortment of contests were held for the best use of the various fishes.

And, of course, there were the guests. Traders that used our ports were always extended an invitation, and they always accepted. Some traveled here at this time of year with the express purpose of obtaining an invitation to our masquerades.

Last, and my favorite part, were the masks. Tonight's theme was water, and mask makers from all over designed masks for their patrons to wear, hoping to bring in more customers and to show off their skill. One year, I loitered outside the palace gates, with many other village children, just to watch the carriages arrive and catch a glimpse of the guests' masks. If we were lucky, a woman would peek out the window, so we could admire her. I'd never liked the superficial noblewomen, but I didn't care who wore what, as long as I could see the mask.

This was what I had to look forward to tonight. And this time, I'd be actually in the palace, instead of relegated to the outside perimeter or the small parties in the districts. I didn't even care that I would be all but invisible; in fact, that was more desirable to me. I could probably gawk and stare all I wanted. These people thrived on attention. I would just have to be careful not to spill anything on anyone.

That was my worst fear. If I ruined a guest's dress or costume, I would not only be released from my position, but also likely I'd be put in the stocks and have my mask stripped for public embarrassment, which would of course reveal my Mark. I couldn't even imagine what would happen after that.

So I would take extra care this night. I planned on keeping my jug only three quarters full at best, so there would be no risk of the drink splashing out while I was unaware.

When I entered the kitchens to complete my duties for preparing for the night, it was a whirlwind of activity, as always, but there was also an extra air of excitement and anxiety. It was also a bit unusual to see everyone dressed in their Masquerade uniforms—deep blues and silver instead of the usual black, to match the theme. I hardly recognized some of the girls; the blue brought out some of the spark in them. There was actually some individuality tonight. It was remarkably refreshing.

Before the guests arrived, my job was to simply keep the kitchens clean. Well, it sounded simple enough, but that was extremely misleading.

"What on earth happened in here?" I asked, mouth wide open as I stared at the chaos.

"Where have you *been*?" the normally gentle Carese asked as she dashed over to grab my arm.

"I thought I was clean-up duty. And that things would have to be pretty much over before there was anything to do." I was in absolute shock. How could so few people produce such a mess?

"Definitely not. None of these guest cooks know where anything is, so they just throw everything in the general direction of the sinks. And if one bowl is too small, they just grab another. I don't know why they can't tell it's too small before using it, but there you go." She shoved an apron in my hands before dragging me over to the disastrous washing area. When I just stared, she sighed and took the apron out of my hands, throwing it over my head and tying it around my waist for me.

"I'll see if I can round up some more help. Otherwise you're going to be here all night. And if you don't get some of that junk off before you have to be on the floor, it'll set, and *never* come off."

She was gone in an instant, and I dumbly ran the hot water, filling up the sink and adding soapy bubbles robotically. I began to scrub frantically, knowing how tired I was going to be afterward, and how badly I'd wanted to spend as much time with Aiden as I could. We'd arranged for him to come to me as soon as he could, so I could drill him on what an exciting life he had. He agreed because I'd pulled the puppy dog face and begged him to let me live vicariously through him, just for these three nights.

Carese managed to scrounge up two page boys that weren't needed for another half hour, and managed to persuade them into the kitchens. They worked silently alongside me, but the pile to be conquered didn't shrink. If anything, it continued to grow—as we pulled three dishes out, someone piled ten more on the stack that towered over my head.

I was already starting to feel weary when it was time for the page boys to go and for me to freshen myself up to look presentable to the guests. I only had a minute to pick at my hair and smooth the errant curls back into submission, and then I was out on the floor.

No guests had entered yet and wouldn't until every servant was in place. Most guests tended to be fashionably late anyway, so the timing usually worked itself out. I took my position at the top of the grand staircase that led to the upper ballroom, where I had an excellent vantage point of the lower ballroom and would see everyone as they passed me into the more elite sections of the party. It was also where I'd told Aiden to look for me, since I probably wouldn't be able to spot him in the throng. Not to mention the fact that he'd be all dressed up, and I'd never seen him in anything more fancy than a nice pair of breeches.

Once every server was at attention, the orchestra was settled, and everything was in its proper place, trumpets sounded, announcing the start of the Masquerade. The grand doors were pulled open by two pages, and the Speaker I'd seen before entered first.

She was beautiful, still in purple like before, though this time it was more of an indigo, with the shimmering blues occasionally overpowering the violets. Her skirts ballooned out from her tight bodice, and sheer sky blue material wrapped its way down her body. Her mask also matched the color scheme. It was studded with white pearls and featured gossamer silver threads hanging from each side to frame her strong face. The silver threads were also used to weave intricate patterns into the mask, across her face. It was truly beautiful, but it was only the beginning of what I would see tonight.

She stepped to the side, making way for the king and queen, and announcing them to the room. It seemed a bit silly to me, since there were only servants now, but then they couldn't exactly enter without being announced, even if rank meant less during a masquerade. Social standing could still be seen in the finery of the costumes, and royalty was still royalty, but at least at a masquerade, where society's colors were free to anyone, the division between classes was more lax, and I could look at everything without fear of getting in trouble.

The queen looked simply stunning, and the king was equally impressive. As tradition dictated, they were dressed in white from head to toe, with accents of blues and silvers. I couldn't even begin to describe the elaborate designs or the rich materials of their clothing, but their masks were simply to die for.

I wasn't surprised to discover the queen's mask was lined in nothing but diamonds and sapphires. Blue jay and peacock feathers sprung up from the left side, with one towering white feather that I didn't know the origin of. Silver threads woven into the mask were also threaded through her hair, creating a crisscross pattern that held her hair up in an elegant bun.

The king's mask was more masculine: predominately white in color and only splashed with blue in a striking feather arrangement. His stunning appearance was founded on the extremely intricate carvings and embossings designed into the mask. Impossible knots were his trimming of choice, and the material used to make his mask looked unforgiving. I wished I'd had a chance to watch the person who'd been able to create *that*.

The royal couple took their seats on the opposite side of the staircase from where the Speaker stood, so they could stand and greet their guests.

Then began the parade. Beautiful creation after beautiful creation walked through those doors, and I was glad the party had just begun and my services weren't needed as much as they would be later in the evening, after I'd gotten a good look at most of the guests.

However, I hadn't found Aiden anywhere. And I also hadn't seen anyone that really stood out as someone who could possibly be the Chameleon.

I was keeping an eye out for both. And I didn't really know what to do once I spotted either. With Aiden, that was probably for the better. I didn't know what his father looked like or what kind of mask he wore, so I wouldn't know who to keep my distance from and whom I could relax around.

The Chameleon, though—I was sure it was a good thing I didn't know who he was. It would tear me up to see him and not be able to do anything. I suppose I could pretend he was attacking me and call the guards on him.

That actually wasn't too bad an idea. It'd be worth the attention drawn to me and the commotion it'd cause, if it got the Chameleon caught.

However, I was back at the problem of not being able to recognize him. I could only hope he'd do something foolish to draw attention to himself. Drop his guard somehow, or reveal what he was planning on doing and why he'd stolen those masks.

I had a general description of the stolen masks, but no doubt he'd altered them to make that description worthless. If he still had all the materials he'd stolen from me, and I had no doubt that he did, even someone with zero skills in mask making or trimming could use what I'd already done to change the stolen masks.

An hour or so after the majority of the guests had arrived, the king stood and motioned for everyone's attention. The trumpets sounded a short call, and the Speaker stepped forward, to speak the king's announcement.

"On behalf of their royal majesties," she said in her loud, clear voice, "we welcome you to our festivities tonight."

There was a gentle hum of polite clapping and excited murmurings.

"As you may have noticed, their majesties the prince and princess are not accompanying their parents tonight. Her Majesty, the princess, is away and could not return in time for the masquerades, we are sorry to announce. However, His Majesty, the prince, is in attendance tonight."

This announcement sprouted a burst of furious fast whispers and everyone in the crowd turned to the door, awaiting his arrival.

"I must clarify," the Speaker said with a smile. "He is *already* in attendance. He is already among you, embracing the spirit of the masquerade. He will be in disguise for all three nights, and at the end of the final ball, he will announce his choice for his bride.

"For those of you who are visitors to our land, this is tradition. Once our prince has reached the proper marrying age, he selects his bride from the people of his own country. This is how our current queen was found, and it is how it always has been done and always will be done. We keep this practice to unite our royalty with our gentry and to keep the bloodlines pure within our country.

"For this purpose, the prince has been concealed all his life, save for his family and a few close servants. No one outside of his family is allowed to see him for fear that at this ball, he would be recognized and harmed, physically or otherwise.

"And so tonight, and for the next three nights, we invite you to mingle, dance, and enjoy yourselves. Should any of you lucky women have the fortune to catch our prince's heart, you may find yourself a princess by the end of the week.

"Now, please, enjoy yourselves." She bowed first to the king and queen and then to the guests before exiting a side door, probably to let the prince know that it was all right for him to begin his hunt.

I watched the excitement of the crowd. Girls gathered in little clusters, comparing notes of who could or couldn't possibly spot the prince, and who the possible future brides were.

The men weren't above similar gossip. Fathers tried to use one another in hopes of finding the prince for their own daughters. A daughter married off to royalty would take care of the rest of the family for life and would be an invaluable asset. Should the father decide to continue in trade, his connections would prove very fruitful and make him even richer than the allowance his daughter would grant him.

The young men, however, tried to woo their women away from their gossip circles in pursuit of a dance. Some girls had already given up on the hopes of catching the prince, or simply weren't interested, and happily surrendered to the dance floor.

"Just watch them all," a low voice murmured at my ear, causing me to jump in surprise. I turned my head sharply and recognized Aiden.

It was no wonder I'd been unable to spot him before. If I wasn't so close to him now, close enough to see his eyes and feel his familiar touch on my arm as he steadied me, I probably still would not recognize him.

"You all right there?" he checked with a gentle smirk, and I nodded mutely, staring. It was impossible to look away, and he laughed at me. "I know. I told you it was something else, didn't I?"

Something else didn't even cover it. Something incredible was more like it. I felt like I'd never really looked at him before now, seeing him in this finery.

His mask was a pale silver, painted with small, interlocking blue circles and spirals that faded into the dark blue lining of braided material. The braiding carried over to his tunic, strapped across his chest like a military jacket. I reached out a hand to touch the material on his sleeve, and it was so soft; I don't think I'd ever felt anything like it. It had to be extremely expensive.

"Is that really you?" I breathed, staring at him with wide eyes.

"Yes, it's me," he said, sighing. "Would you believe I had them scale it down a bit?"

"Wow."

"Is it really that ridiculous?" he asked.

I bit my lip. "I'm trying to come up with some smart

comment, but I just can't be that mean to you tonight. You look amazing," I said honestly, squeezing his arm.

That put a large grin on his face. "Thanks." He seemed relieved at my approval. "I wish I could see you all dressed up."

I pulled my hand from his arm, remembering my current station. "I wish that too," I said sadly. "Where are all those favors to call in or strings to pull of yours?"

A sad smile replaced the happy grin on his lips. "I wish I could. And believe me, I've thought about it. I wasn't so sure you'd be up for it though. I mean, you never mention it," he added sarcastically.

"Jerk. If I wasn't afraid of messing up your pretty clothes or embarrassing you in front of everyone, I'd beat you up right now."

That got a good laugh out of him. "As if you ever could."

"Please try to work your magic? If for no other reason than so I don't collapse of exhaustion on the last night?"

"I'll try a few more tricks I've kept hiding up my sleeves," he promised. "But sadly, for tonight, I have to be a lot more social than I want to be. You probably won't be seeing too much of me."

"I think I can handle that. I was getting bored with you anyway."

"Yeah right. You'd never get bored of me."

"That's true. Who else would let me beat them up time after time?"

He rolled his eyes, letting that conversation drop before it started, and picked up a glass from my tray. He bowed slightly, and I didn't see him for the rest of the night.

Instead I amused myself with admiring the costumes

and masks of the other guests. I tried to look for Joch and Iniga as well, since many of their glass creations were on display, but I couldn't find either one of them. Iniga's absence I understood, since she was technically not nobility, but Joch's puzzled me. As a guest of the crown, he should be here.

Eventually, I waved the concern aside, deciding he was probably here after all and I just didn't recognize him. He was, after all, a master mask maker. He could look like anyone tonight.

* * *

"What do you think of this whole Ball for a Bride business?" Aiden asked out of the blue later that night, when we'd reconvened in my room.

He sounded oddly serious, like my answer would be some kind of catalyst, like something was weighing on my opinion. I thought carefully before answering.

"I don't like it," I said finally, too exhausted from my extensive plate scrubbing to be argumentative. "I'd hate to be in his position, to have to pick a bride after three days, even if it is tradition."

"You're thinking from his perspective?" he noted, surprised.

I shrugged. "Well, I guess so. I mean . . . I don't know. I can't even imagine being one of those girls who are trying to be that bride. Maybe if they were being forced into it or something, but to marry for power or money or comfort? I would hate it."

My answer seemed to be the right one, but he relaxed only infinitesimally. "Say it was you and me."

I shot him an incredulous look.

"No, just work with me. Say I was the prince, and you were a courtier."

"In this ridiculous scenario, are you still my best friend, or—" I suddenly blushed, aware that I'd never said those words out loud before. I hurried on to hide my embarrassment. "Or are we keeping with the only three days acquaintance?"

He paused, trying to figure out his story. "Three days. Say you met me tonight, and at the end of these three days, I proposed to you. And in this story, you're actually looking to marry. Would you say yes? Answer me seriously, please."

"I don't know," I said honestly. "I just can't see me pledging myself for life to someone after only knowing them for three days."

"You're not answering my question."

"I don't know! I *can't* answer your question, because it feels loaded. What are you really asking me?"

"Nothing. Never mind. Forget I said anything." He sounded as frustrated as I felt. Well, maybe we both wouldn't be so frustrated if he could just say what he so clearly wanted to.

"I'm sure you're exhausted. I'll let you sleep."

And then he was gone, and I was left alone, entirely confused about what had just happened.

TWENTY-TWO

THE SECOND BALL'S THEME, WITH REDS, GOLDS, and browns, celebrated the earth and the fire that warms us in the winter months.

This time, I went to the kitchens as soon as I was dressed, so I could get a head start on washing dishes. I dressed in my usual work clothes, knowing I'd be sure to get them dirty and wrinkled by the time the ball actually started, and planned to change into my nicer serving dress right before I reported to the floor.

I worked at a steady pace all day, replaying the night before in my mind. I'd not caught any sight or sound of the Chameleon all night. Not even a whiff of someone who *might* be him. He wasn't nicknamed after a creature that could blend in anywhere for nothing, I suppose.

I hoped tonight would be more eventful. There was going to be a large bonfire on the palace grounds; maybe that would spark some kind of activity. Last night, while the masks and costumes were amazing to see, things had been a touch boring after the initial excitement had worn off. All I got to do was stand around and try to catch glimpses of Aiden being social. I liked to think I'd succeeded in the first, but knew I failed horribly at the latter. How was that boy so good at hiding?

I was so lost in my thoughts that my attention started to wander and the pile of dishes I was carrying from one counter to the sink slipped from my hands and landed with a loud clatter on the stone floor.

I gasped. All activity stopped for the briefest of moments while everyone paused to stare at me. Pieces of broken ceramic littered the floor, just waiting to attack and prick the unsuspecting feet of the servers and cooks as they ran to and fro.

Still staring at the mess, thinking things couldn't get much worse for me, the side serving door banged open and Vera burst into the room.

"What was that racket? I could hear it all the way down the hall! What part of 'invisible and unnoticeable' did someone not understand?" Her eyes scanned the crowd, and everyone suddenly found themselves busy with whatever they'd been occupied with before I'd dropped everything.

Her eyes landed on me, like a hawk spotting its prey. "You," she said, sneering. "It would be you, wouldn't it, Miss Everyone-Look-at-Me?"

"It was an accident," I defended myself.

She looked surprised that I'd actually spoken back to her. Usually I just let her insults and comments roll off my back, but not this time. "An accident," she repeated, daring me to defy her further.

"Yes. The plates are slippery from the water and soap, and I dropped them." I spoke clearly, not backing down.

"Well, apparently you need more practice with them. I

would have thought all your quality time with the sinks lately would render you a professional. Apparently, I was wrong." Her eyes narrowed, then scanned the crowd again, calling another girl over. "Rachel, you'll be taking over Evelina's duties tonight. The other servers will help cover your area. Miss Evelina here will be ensuring there will be no more accidents."

Looking down at the mess I made, she sneered, "First you will clean up this mess. Then you will stay in the kitchens the rest of the night until every dish is spotless. Then, to be sure that you've cleaned up after yourself, I want this floor mopped and sparkling by morning."

I opened my mouth to protest. There was no way I'd get all of that done before breakfast tomorrow. Even if I stayed up all night, servers started on breakfast before the sun rose in order to make enough for the vast quantities of guests currently staying within the palace. To top it off, staying up all night would completely drain me for tomorrow, and I'd be sure to drop something again in my near-unconscious state.

"And if you don't," she continued, cutting me off before I could protest, "then you can pack your bags with what measly possessions you have and hit the road. You should consider yourself lucky to be working in the palace, with such fine accommodations and easy living."

She backed away from my face and addressed the rest of the kitchens. "As for the rest of you, if I hear that anyone has assisted her, that person will meet the same fate as Evelina. It is her punishment and her punishment alone to bear."

An uneasy silence fell over the kitchens as Vera swept

out of the doors, and the only sounds were the dull roar of the fires in the ovens and the water boiling in pots. I resolutely kept my gaze away from all of them, hunted down a broom, and began to clean up my mess.

Chatter slowly picked back up as cooks instructed their assistants, and before long I was forgotten, and the gentle roar of controlled chaos reigned again.

I collected the broken china in an old soiled napkin and tied it off to dispose of later. The rest of the night, I stood at my sinks, scrubbing and doing my best to ignore the excited chatter of the girls as they gossiped about the guests and what finery they'd seen out on the floor.

I lost all sense of time, not even noting when the pages came in to light the lamps. I tried to ignore them as they talked excitedly about the bonfire and how it was supposed to be as tall as three horses, and how it took four wagons of lumber to provide enough material to get the fire started.

I could hear the shrieks and giggles from outside, and I doubled my efforts to remove the grime from a particularly large pot. I wouldn't let them get to me. I would be out of here soon enough, and then Vera's threats would do nothing to me. Actually, it would be fun to work her up over something, and when she threatened me with my job again, dare her to actually go through with it, just to see her flounder. I bet she wouldn't know what to do with me. And then, as she'd stand there, good for nothing, I'd tell her I was leaving. I had my own house, my own trade, and I didn't need her anymore.

Reminding myself how that would never happen, I noticed how quiet it had become. It must be very late. Only a few other servers were lingering in the kitchens, cleaning up after their masters and laying their things out for the next morning.

Checking on my pile left to do, I found that I'd actually made good progress. Another hour and I'd probably be done, and then I could start on the floor. Which would, admittedly, also take me another couple of hours, but I guessed I could get it done before sunrise, have time to make it into my bed, and catch a few hours of precious sleep.

A few hours later, I was actually feeling hopeful because I was halfway done with the floor. I was taking a short break to rest my weary arms, when I heard the door creak open again.

In walked Vera, with the muddiest boots I have ever seen. You'd think she'd walked around every mud puddle in the country, then jumped in the manure pile for fun, just to round it out. She surveyed the work I'd done, and then pointedly sauntered across the floor I'd already done, moving a few things from one side of the room to the other, things I knew didn't have to be moved, just so she could walk over the clean floor and give me more work to do.

"Really?" I couldn't help exclaiming. "You really couldn't think of anything better to do with your night than make mine more miserable? And you really couldn't even be more creative in your methods?"

She pursed her lips at me, then shrugged. "I don't know what you're talking about. But I do hope you have a pleasant evening."

She strolled right back out, and I threw a dirty washcloth at the still swinging door, imagining it was her face.

That mess was going to add at least another couple

hours. I didn't know what time it was, but my eyelids were drooping and my arms sagging. It'd take me twice as long as it originally did, thanks to how tired I'd become, and my back and knees ached from scrubbing the floor on al fours. I kissed any hope of getting some sleep tonight goodbye, as well as any chance of seeing Aiden. I'd hoped he'd stop by the kitchen when he didn't find me in my room, but if I hadn't seen him by now, it was unlikely I'd see him at all tonight.

But that was all right. I could survive one night without him. I was actually a little ashamed of how attached I was to him. I needed to stop relying on him to make my days better and start taking better care of myself.

However, I'd also realized that no matter how much I berated myself for wanting to see him again, it did nothing to ease my desire. I couldn't explain it; he just made me happy. He was a bright spot in my dull gray day of kitchens and soapy water.

And worst of all, I trusted him. If he asked me to do something for him, I had no doubt I would do it, no matter what. And if I asked him for something and he said he'd do it, I had zero doubts in my mind that he'd do it.

I wasn't even sure how that had happened. I didn't trust people. And I especially didn't trust people to take care of me. But that little jerk had wormed his way into my heart.

And I kind of adored him for it. How messed up was that?

The door creaked open again, and I picked up another rag, ready to pelt it at Vera if she tried anything funny again.

But to my immense surprise, my visitor was of an entirely different sort.

"Aiden!" I cried, my voice cracking embarrassingly with emotion. He would pick the moment I was having some sort of personal revelation to walk in. "What are you doing here?"

"What am I ever doing here? I'm here to visit you," he answered matter-of-factly. He paused as he looked down at me. "Evie, what are you doing?"

Confused, I looked around me, and realized what a mess I must look. I sat back on my heels and quickly brushed my hair out of my face, trying to smooth it down as best I could with dirty, wrinkled fingers. I was spattered with soap stains, and who knows what sort of food bits still clung to my clothing. Added to the complete mud disaster that surrounded me, I must have looked absolutely pitiful.

The movement of my hands caught his eyes, and he knelt down and grabbed one of my grubby hands in his own finely gloved hand. "You have cuts on your hands, Evie. What happened to you? Why were you on the floor?" There was nothing but concern in his voice.

"I dropped some plates," I said flatly but didn't pull my hand away. "I must have cut myself cleaning up the pieces."

He pulled my hand toward his face and dropped a gentle kiss on my palm. The feel of his lips against my skin sent shivers down my spine, and I pulled my hand away, suddenly self-conscious and uncomfortable.

"Please get up," I said. "You'll ruin your clothes."

"I don't care," he said, determinedly kneeling in a particularly muddy spot of floor to spite me. "I don't care about clothes, you know that."

I winced at the sight of the muddy fabric. "But I can't stand it. Get up, please."

"Stand with me. I won't have you on the floor before me." He pulled me up, and I quickly stepped a more comfortable distance away from him.

"You never answered why you were in here," I said quietly.

"I did. I said I was looking for you."

"At this hour?"

"I was waiting in your room. I didn't want to get you into any trouble here."

I sighed. Yes, his outfit would have caused quite the commotion. "How long?"

"How long what?"

"How long did you wait in my room?"

"Does it matter?"

"A long time, then," I groaned.

"I want to help you. It's always worth the wait."

"Look, I don't want you feeling like I'm some kind of charity case." I backed further away from him.

"I don't feel like that at all. I want to help you. Because you're . . . my friend. I don't have any hidden motives."

I don't know why, but that struck a chord in me, and I was suddenly angry. "What if I don't want your help? What if I don't want you to come to my rescue every night? Maybe I want to rescue myself every once in a while!"

"Calm down, Evie. I didn't mean any harm," he said, clearly startled by my anger.

But his calm voice only made me angrier. All the sleep deprivation, all the injustice served on me by Vera, all my frustrations of being shoved out of my peaceful life—everything just served as fuel to my growing anger.

"No, I will *not* calm down! I don't want you thinking

I'm one of those weak girls that have been fawning over you the past two nights. I don't want you thinking I'm some damsel in distress. Really, I don't want you thinking *anything* about me. You're making me think things that scare me. You're making me want to give everything to you, and I can't do that. I have nothing, and just by looking at you, I can tell you have everything. So just leave me alone."

"You think I have everything?" he shot back, matching my anger, all traces of his calm dissipated. "What if I do? Material things, maybe, I'll grant you that. But what if that isn't what I want? What if *everything* doesn't equal happy?"

"You are nobility! How can you not be happy?"

"Nobility does not equal happiness, and you know it!"

"You know what? Leave," I ordered him. "I don't want to look at you anymore. You and your beautiful clothes and beautiful mask and beautiful *you*, all muddied by me."

"That's not—"

"Leave." My voice was cracked and dead.

His eyes flashed at me, but I think he could see that I was beyond reasoning right now. I just needed him gone, so I could think. And so I could break down without him staring at me, trying to *fix everything* when I just wanted things to stay broken until I could repair them myself.

He opened his mouth one more time but thought better of whatever he was going to say, and stomped out of the room.

And I broke my promise to myself and cried, in the middle of the muddy kitchen, my skin rubbed raw, and all alone.

TWENTY-THREE

*T*HE FLOOR WAS STILL A BIT DAMP WHEN THE SUN began to rise and servers filed sleepily into the kitchen. I didn't care. It was as good as done. I was exhausted and cranky and all I wanted was my bed.

I dragged myself through the halls and collapsed into bed, instantly asleep.

Surprisingly, I wasn't dragged from my dreams against my will. I woke up naturally and glanced out the window; it was nearly evening. I'd completely missed lunch, and I was sure I was running late for dinner. I could hear the carriages rolling along outside as horses whinnied and pages and attendants called directions to one another.

The third and grandest ball was about to begin, and I was still filthy and barely conscious. I shot out of bed, scrambling for my clothes. In my haste as I ran out the door, I nearly tripped over a small parcel with a note pinned over the top. I thought about leaving it until after the ball, but my curiosity and anxiety that it was from Vera got the better of me.

I unfolded the note. It was from Aiden.

My lady,

 I'm sorry for yelling at you last night. I should have kept better control of my temper, and you didn't deserve getting the brunt of it. I hope this will make up for it—I called in my favors and pulled my strings.

Yours,

Aiden

I quickly pulled the lid off the box. Inside was another note on top of a gorgeous dress. I pulled it out of the box carefully, so it wouldn't drag on the floor and so I didn't get it dirty with my own filthiness.

Before even putting it on, I knew it would fit me perfectly. It was the perfect length, and it was a style that I knew flattered my figure. I also knew it was one of Aiden's favorite shades of green.

For a moment, I thought about refusing. I'd yelled at him only last night about how I didn't want him to rescue me like some sort of damsel in distress. And then he pulls this stunt?

Frustrated, I opened the second note.

 PS—I already know what you're thinking. But there's a difference between being rescued and accepting help from a friend. I think the world of you— never doubt that. And I also keep my promises. I promised I would try to get you the chance to dress up and stun everyone who sees you. This is me keeping my promise. Please accept this chance?

 You know where to find me.

I reread the note at least five times. That girly part of me wanted to cry again. That only slightly more reasonable part of me wanted to beat him up for making me feel so much.

The part that finally won was the part that wanted to dress up and feel beautiful again. And not have to work.

I hurried to the bathhouse to clean myself. It was all but deserted, since all the servers and servants were working. I wished I'd had the luxury of time to just lounge around, but I'd wanted as much time scrubbing as possible.

The third ball was the grand finale. There would be dancing, food, and fine drink as there had been every night, but tonight it would be the best of the best, and lots of it. I heard rumors of fireworks once the sun went down.

And, of course, there was the prince's engagement announcement. It was sure to be a story to tell people later on in life. No one would believe I was there, but I'd know it was true and that was all that mattered.

Tonight's color theme was a free-for-all. No one was restricted by their class, occupation, or theme. This resulted in some of the most colorful and brilliant masks and costumes I could imagine.

My costume would not be that outrageous, but it was still beautiful, in a more subdued sort of way. And as for my mask . . .

I'd overlooked it when I first pulled out the gown. I thought I might have to use the one I made for Milo and risk being recognized, or maybe even the glass one, but it might draw too much attention and again, risk my being recognized. But, of course, Aiden provided me with everything I needed.

The mask sat at the bottom of the box next to a pair of

beautiful slippers. It was my familiar green, with emerald green gemstones and crystals at the forehead. Bright white feathers sprouted from the headband, and veins of silver wound their way around the eyes and down the cheek-bones. It was one of the most beautiful things I'd ever seen.

Because, for one night, it was *mine*.

After carefully pinning most of my hair up in what I hoped was an elegant bun, I donned the gown and gloves and shoes, saving the mask for last, to complete the ensemble.

As I turned to admire myself in the mirror, I couldn't be happier with my appearance. I was *me* again. Not some serving miss, but *me*.

I couldn't believe I'd even considered the idea of refusing this gift. To feel like my old self again . . . there wasn't anything anyone could have given me that would have made me happier.

I needed to thank Aiden. I needed to apologize for my behavior the night before. I'd been angry, and he didn't deserve my anger any more than I'd deserved his.

I hurried through the rest of my preparations, eager to see him, and tried to think of the best way to slip in. I couldn't go through my usual route of the kitchens—I'd be extremely suspicious, and even if my luck was good and no one paid me any attention, it was highly likely I'd get something on my dress, what with how ingredients were always flying around.

Just walking through the front door might be an option, though I had no accompanying escort or carriage to climb out of. If it was late enough, I might have been able to slip into the masses unnoticed, but I was impatient and wanted to get in *now*.

With the two most obvious choices out, I ran through the floor plan of the ballroom in my head. Wasn't there another entrance for servants? I racked my brain for a memory of servants hugging the walls and slipping in and out unnoticed. There'd occasionally been a page or messenger that would come in during meals, and they never used the kitchen entrance or the main doors. There had to be another entrance.

Taking one final deep breath and a glance in the mirror, I stepped out of my room. I'd felt safe and comfortable in the private confines of my room, but as soon as I stepped outside, anyone could see me and expose me as a pretender. While it was a little bit terrifying, it was also thrilling. I wasn't a serving girl tonight—tonight I was a lady. Just as Aiden always addressed me.

I hurried through the halls, trying to remember which way might lead me to the right place. My quick footsteps echoed in the empty hallway, and I could hear the music from the ballroom. I knew I was getting closer; I just needed to find the door. Or even another hallway at this point. I'd been going down the same hall for a long time, and I was concerned that I was somewhere I really shouldn't be. Every other hallway I'd been in crisscrossed with half a dozen others before I finally reached my destination.

And then, finally, a door on the left. I might have missed it altogether if I'd been distracted. I put my ear to it, listening to see if anyone was on the other side.

When I couldn't hear anything but the general sounds and noises of the party, I pushed the door open and slipped inside. Closing it carefully, I turned around and leaned against it.

I was in.

And then I realized exactly where I was—the royal quarters. A small room the king and queen used when they needed to confer, or while they were waiting, or for whatever purpose they needed if they wanted some privacy.

It was obvious that it had been recently used. The lights were still lit, and I smelled a lingering scent of perfume. Fabric draped along all four walls to muffle the noise from both outside and inside the room.

I didn't want to stay too long. My luck held—I escaped the room without being seen and maneuvered my way into the main hall.

It was a completely different experience attending a ball as a lady instead of a server. People actually looked at me and saw me. They didn't dismiss me as soon as they looked at me.

And then I saw Aiden, standing at the top of the staircase where I'd been stationed the one day I had actually worked the floor.

He looked amazing, of course; although, he still seemed a little unsure and uncomfortable in his fancy clothes. He was fidgeting with a strand of ribbon that hung from his mask, which today, was a golden yellow with leaves etched in a delicate design.

I was so excited to see him that I walked toward him a little more quickly than I probably should have, pushing my way through the crowd.

I could tell the exact moment Aiden caught sight of me. His shoulders relaxed . . . his whole body loosened up. And his eyes lit up from behind his mask, as if little sunbeams were shooting right into me. The stairs to him took but a moment, and then I stood in front of him, waiting for his judgment.

Not that his opinion of what I looked like mattered to me or anything.

Oh, who was I trying to kid? I wanted to look pretty for him—beautiful, even. I wanted him to feel like I deserved him and his gift.

"You look . . ." His voice was low, and I was unspeakably nervous waiting for him to finish that statement. Nice? Ridiculous? Like I shouldn't have bothered? "Beyond words."

"Good words, I hope," I joked nervously, my throat dry.

"The best words." He smiled and held out his hands to me. "Does this mean apology accepted?"

"Oh!" In my excitement to see him, I'd completely forgotten about that part. "Of course. Although it was just as much my fault, if not more so. I shouldn't have yelled at you like that."

"No, you shouldn't have." His tone was joking, but his eyes were serious.

"I *am* sorry." I looked down at the floor, suddenly uncomfortable. I just wanted to get past this part.

"And I know that. Which is why I forgive you, save you grant me one request."

"And what is that?" I asked, filled with trepidation. The last time I'd granted him a favor, I had ended up with sore muscles that didn't recover for a week.

"Dance with me, please, my lady."

Now that was a request I'd be only too happy to oblige. I couldn't even pretend to think about it and keep him in suspense; I was still too starstruck by how surreal everything felt. I just smiled happily and nodded, squeezing his hand in response.

He led me to the dance floor as a spirited number started to play. He wrapped one arm around my waist, gripping my hand carefully with his other hand.

"Do you know the steps?" he whispered teasingly.

"Oh, I know the steps," I said. "The question is, can you keep up with me?"

He laughed and led me through the twirling number, spinning me around and guiding me across the dance floor. It felt effortless.

For about the first thirty seconds.

After that, the time lapse from when I'd last danced started to kick in, and I stumbled through the steps, stepping on his toes and nearly tripping over my skirts a number of times. He took it all in stride, though, and however ridiculous we might have looked, bumbling around the dance floor, I was having the time of my life.

The way he held me made me feel safe, and even though I was tripping all over myself, I felt like he would catch me before I could really hurt myself—or anyone or anything else for that matter. That funny feeling in my stomach revisited me, and I found myself looking at Aiden in a new light.

He hadn't been a part of my life for most of its duration, but that didn't seem to matter. As soon as he stepped into it, he became a part of it—like a missing puzzle piece to a frustrating jigsaw, or a key spice to a dull and disappointing recipe.

With as much as life twisted and turned, I knew he could be out of my life just as rapidly as he'd been dropped into it, and that caused an inexplicable ache in my heart.

Though perhaps it wasn't so inexplicable. I somehow found myself trusting him. I found myself caring a great deal about him.

I might even have found myself . . . loving him.

The thought didn't shock me as much as perhaps it should have. I think my heart knew it all along; it was just waiting for my mind to catch up. Waiting until I'd unlocked all the locks and loosened all the chains I'd put on it.

And then, having recognized it, a sort of peace settled over me.

"What's got you so cheerful all of a sudden?" Aiden whispered in my ear as the music slowed to a soft waltz.

I didn't want to tell him. Not yet, anyway, and certainly not here, with all these people around us.

"Am I supposed to be feeling something else?" I teased instead. "I'm at the biggest party of the year, I've got beautiful clothes, I have a breathtaking mask, and the company's not so bad either."

He chuckled. "That's true. I suppose you do have a thing or two to celebrate."

"I do, don't I?" I said thoughtfully, meaning it this time. "A lot has changed in the past couple months, hasn't it?"

"That it has," he said somberly. "You haven't really had things easy lately, huh?"

"That's got to be the greatest understatement of the year."

"Believe me, if I could have pulled any strings with fate to make your life easier, I would have done it in a second."

I smiled but shook my head. "You don't play with fate's strings. You never know when she'll just cut them out of spite or boredom."

"Is fate always the only one in charge of our strings, though?"

I got a feeling he wasn't talking about a mythical goddess anymore.

Shaking my head, I said, "No. There are a lot of strings. Sometimes we have to give her a hand. Sometimes we have to force her hand. And sometimes, we have to take things out of her hands."

The music stopped then, though we'd already stopped dancing. The conductor announced the musicians would be taking a short break, but my eyes were solely on Aiden's.

"Evie," he whispered, resting his forehead against mine. I closed my eyes, relishing the feeling of him being so close to me and the brush of his breath as it fluttered across my cheek. Our hands lowered from the dance position to rest at our sides, our fingers intertwined.

When I opened my eyes, Aiden was staring at me with such . . . resolution and determination. We were silent for a long moment as the party continued to swell around us.

"I need to tell you something," he finally said. "Walk with me?"

"Of course," I answered, puzzled, and then followed him out the door.

TWENTY-FOUR

*A*IDEN LED ME OUTSIDE AND INTO THE GARDENS. We passed the place where the bonfire had been the previous night as evidenced by the immense pile of ashes and wet timber. Several other guests were out here, enjoying the crisp autumn night air, but Aiden ignored them all, determinedly leading me by the path to the destination that only he knew.

He walked with such surety, I had to ask him if he knew where he was going or if he was just faking it to impress me.

He laughed dryly, saying, "Yes, I know this place very well. Don't worry, I won't get us lost or in trouble."

I hadn't even thought about us getting in trouble. "Trouble?" I asked, suddenly nervous. "Why would we be getting in trouble? Where are you planning on taking me? Is this the part where you take me out back where no one can hear me scream and kill me?"

I was joking, but the slight stumble in his step really made me anxious.

"Don't be ridiculous. I'm not going to kill you. Or hurt you in any way, before you ask."

"Okay, seriously, though. Where are we going? My feet are starting to hurt."

Really, I was pulling that card? When did I get to be such a weakling? Barely a few hours in these fancy clothes and I was turning into one of those spoiled courtiers.

He cast a sidelong glance at me, probably wondering the same thing. "Sorry, went too far there, huh?" I said weakly. "I'm just impatient."

"We're almost there," was all he said.

I thought he was going to take us to some hidden place in the gardens or back out in the city, but I was wrong. The palace bordered the forest on the north side, and apparently, that was where we were heading. This forest had been around longer than the city itself, and the trees were ancient, easily hundreds of years old. Not too many people ventured into them, because it was extremely easy to get lost amid the giant oaks, especially if you were unfamiliar with the area or the night sky. Not that you could do much navigation by the stars, unless you were to climb up the trees to see beyond the leafy forest rooftop.

"Are you positive you know where you're going?" I asked anxiously.

"One hundred and ten percent," he replied readily. "Relax, Evie. I just want some place private to talk, and the palace doesn't have a place where we'd be comfortable."

"What about my room? That's always worked before."

"Yes, but before, you weren't dressed like the real lady you are. I can slip in and out of certain passageways to make my way down, but I doubt you could in that gown. Besides, I have something to show you."

He had a fair point. And I didn't want to risk using the royal family's room again, especially when I knew it had to be nearing midnight, when the prince made his grand announcement and revelation.

As we marched through the underbrush, I knew we were getting closer when I heard a soft scuffling noise. I turned to him in alarm, but he just grinned at me in that way that said he knew something I didn't. "We're almost there."

Finally, we came to a stop before a large oak tree. I think fifteen men could have encircled it, standing with their arms outstretched. But what really caught my attention was the familiar little brown dog, loosely tied to a stake in the ground.

"Is that . . . ?" I began. "Did you find *Hachi*?"

Aiden beamed at me, looking proud of himself, and my heart felt like it was going to burst. I didn't know what to say or do. I didn't know if I should hug him or the dog first, and I didn't know *how* Aiden had pulled it off.

The little Akita yelped happily and, jumping around, tried to pounce on me, his entire back end wagging so hard I thought he might fall over. I knelt carefully, trying not to muss my beautiful dress, and scratched his ears. He twisted and licked my hands, keening softly.

I turned back to Aiden, still kneeling, and simply asked, "How?"

He shrugged. "I knew he was important to you. You already lost your father. I didn't want you to feel like you'd lost Hachi too, when there was still a chance he was alive. Then, I got lucky."

I stared at him in amazement, absently running my hands through Hachi's thick fur. Aiden stepped forward and, brushing aside some vines, pushed open a small, hidden door.

I gaped at him. He had a hidden retreat out here in the woods? Who managed that? And why?

"A little cloak and dagger, don't you think?" I managed to choke out. "What on earth is this?"

"Just come in and I'll explain. I don't like standing out here longer than necessary. Hachi will be okay. He has food and water, and you know he won't run off."

I hesitated just a moment more but decided that if I was going to trust Aiden, I needed to trust him completely. No going halfway with this sort of thing. If I was going to do something, it had better be worth doing wholeheartedly. And I think that trusting someone fell into that category.

The inside of the tree was carved out to form a small room. It was actually quite comfortable. I was nervous that it would be dark and claustrophobic when Aiden shut the little door, but it was surprisingly light. Looking up, I realized that small slots had been carved all around the trunk, too small to be noticed from the outside, but big enough for moonlight to creep through.

And it wasn't just a hollowed-out tree. There were rugs on the floor, cushions to sit on, and a table with books stacked on top of it. It looked like a home.

"What is this place?" I asked again.

"This is my place," he said simply. "My father helped me make it. Whenever I needed to get away from the . . . life, I could come out here and no one would bother me. No one even knows it exists except my parents. And they know that I want to be alone when I'm here, so they usually leave me to my own devices."

"Wow," was all I could say. A private retreat on palace grounds?

"Yeah. Have a seat." He directed me to the pile of cushions and watched me as I made myself comfortable. He gingerly sat in front of me, fidgeting with the fringe on one of the pillows.

I certainly didn't have anything else to add, and he looked really nervous, so I waited for him to say whatever it was that required him to drag me all the way out here. Not that I didn't appreciate him sharing this place with me, but I wanted to know what was going on.

He didn't speak, and I had to prompt him. "Wasn't there something you wanted to tell me?"

He took a deep breath. "Yes. Yes, I'm just trying to think of the best way to say it."

"Well, you're making me nervous. Just spit it out already," I joked to lessen the tension.

He laughed once. "I guess that would be the best way to say it, wouldn't it? Okay. Here goes. Remember what we talked about the night of the first ball?"

"We talked about a lot of things. What in particular do you mean?"

"The, um, hypothetical situation. If I were the prince."

A beat passed. "Yes?"

Aiden hesitated. "What if that wasn't so hypothetical?"

I stared at him in disbelief. "If this is some kind of joke, I will kill you. And I'm completely serious."

"It's not a joke."

"But . . . but that doesn't make any sense! I've seen you and the prince at the same time!"

He chuckled without amusement. "I have a body double.

When I'm unavailable for public appearances, my father arranges for someone else to take my place. It's not hard, since no one has ever seen or heard me before. Same basic body type, and the prince could be any number of personal servants."

I was completely baffled. "Why would you be unavailable for public appearances?" I asked, putting his words back at him. "Wouldn't your princely duties overrule everything else?"

"According to my father, perhaps," he scoffed. "You have to understand everything, though. I haven't told you the whole story yet."

"Please enlighten me." My voice was flat.

"You know that the prince cannot be seen or heard by anyone outside of the royal family and a few choice servants. One in my case—my nursemaid, who bathed, dressed, and fed me until I was old enough to do so myself. She was also the one to take measurements for clothes, requests for goods I wanted or needed, everything. She was my one link to the outside world.

"And she was good at her job, but that's all it was to her: her job. She distanced herself from me. I didn't need another mother, my own was quite enough. I needed a friend. And she couldn't be that for me.

"I don't know if you can imagine how lonely that is," he whispered. "And then, I couldn't take it anymore. I needed to be seen and heard, but I loved and respected my family too much to do anything to shame or embarrass them or the crown in any way.

"So I began to sneak out and impersonate a normal kid."

"Those stories about you sneaking out of your room," I murmured, remembering.

He nodded. "It was too easy for me to get clothes and an extra mask. I simply had to ask for the first set, and it was given to me, no questions asked. Who would refuse a royal request? And once I had those, I quickly obtained a second set, because I knew once my father realized what I was doing, he would confiscate the first in an attempt to stop me. Which he did, but there was no stopping me.

"It was so liberating to be out on the streets! To have the freedom to move where and how I pleased, and to speak to anyone and everyone . . . it was a dream come true for me."

"Eventually my father realized he couldn't stop me, and I convinced him that I would be a better king if I wasn't so sheltered. So he allowed me a position on the council where I could actually speak, which meant I needed an estate, and to go to all the royal functions as someone who could actually interact with others. That's why he arranged for me to go with Arianna—he didn't trust anyone else but a Lacie to keep my secret. He didn't want to tell her at all, of course, but you can't keep anything from them."

"How can I know this isn't some elaborate hoax?" I asked, reaching for something solid to grab onto.

"That's the thing I want to show you. I want to prove my identity to you, the one way I can prove it with absolute surety. I want you to see me . . . *really* see me. All of me."

And then he did the unthinkable—he reached up and unhooked his mask. He set it gently down beside him and looked at me with such vulnerability that I could not look away.

Right where my own Mark sat was a Mark of his own. Under his right eye was a tattoo of an outstretched wing set inside a crown: the royal seal. I'd heard that each member of the royal family was marked with it when they came of age. The queen received it when she married into the family. Even though no one could see it, it was to represent the pain of ruling, and it helped the royal family to never forget who they were and what they represented.

"Aiden . . . ," I whispered, staring at his face.

He looked exactly as I'd imagined him, but it was so strange to see all of him. And I didn't know what to feel at this revelation. Anger for him lying to me? Betrayal for him gaining my trust when he wasn't who I thought he was? Or understanding for him finding a way through his loneliness? Compassion for someone I called a friend, someone I thought I loved?

"I'm still the same person," he insisted. "I never once pretended to be someone I'm not."

"I think I can understand why you did what you did," I started out slowly, "but this is a lot to take in. I . . . don't know what I'm supposed to make of it all. Or what I'm supposed to do or say." I felt as vulnerable as if it were my mask on the floor beside me.

"You don't have to do or say anything. I just wanted you to know."

Something occurred to me then, the latter half of his story. "Is this the part where you tell me you found your bride and you'll never see me again, and that this was your way of telling me good-bye?" There was no bitterness in my voice. Only sadness. I was losing him. I never really had him, and I was going to lose him.

"Oh, no. I've found my bride, if she'll have me," he said, "but I really hope that doesn't mean I'll never see you again."

"Who is she?" I suddenly had to know.

"Are you truly asking me that?" He looked at me, almost sadly, one eyebrow raised.

"Clearly," I said, indignant. "Am I not allowed to know until the official announcement or something?"

He laughed. "I don't think that would be a good idea. No, it's nothing like that."

"Well, tell me then!" I was growing frustrated again.

"I did."

"You did not!"

"I said that my hypothetical situation wasn't hypothetical," he clarified.

A moment passed. My eyes widened, and my mouth dropped open. "You mean *me?*"

"If you'll have me," he said simply.

"Are you insane?" I asked. "You can't marry *me.*"

"I think the question is if *you* will marry *me.*"

"I couldn't possibly! I can't!" I protested.

His face fell. "Why not?"

"Because!" I thought it should be obvious. "I didn't even know who you were until now. How could I possibly marry you?"

"I'm still the same person," he insisted again. "You know me already. You know me better than anyone else. You're the one I want."

"Why?"

"What?"

"Why do you want me?" I persisted. "Because I know your secret? Is that the only reason?"

"Of course not," he scoffed. "I want you because—you said it yourself—you're my best friend. You make me laugh and you make me work. You make me think about things in a different way, and you make me want to be a better person. You're beautiful and strong, fierce and loyal. I couldn't imagine myself ever being with anyone else."

I gulped, unprepared to deal with his sudden declarations. Those things he said made my heart swell and beat out rapid, syncopated rhythms, but one thing was missing.

"And your veracity is what would make you a wonderful queen. You wouldn't be bossed around or intimidated by anyone. You'd be a wonderful role model for the citizens. Things are changing, Evie. The king and queen are starting to speak for themselves. You heard the king in the council room, and I know there's been gossip among the servants. And you hear me every day. I need a queen who isn't afraid of that—of my voice." He paused, watching my reactions. "And you'd be loved by everyone, I know it."

My breath hitched, and I dared to ask, "Even you?"

"Oh, my lady, *especially* me." He grabbed my hands and held them tight. "Didn't you already know? Evie, I love you so much, I can't put it into words." He hesitated. "You know me better than anyone, and you know that I'm not much for flowery words and pretty declarations. All I can say is that I love you, and I want to be with you for the rest of my life."

I was dumbstruck.

"Can you . . . ?" he ventured to say. "Do you have any feelings for me, Evie? Any hope for me?"

I tried to speak, but my mouth was so dry that I couldn't get the words out.

"If you can't answer me now, that's okay. And we wouldn't have to get married right away. It can be an extended engagement for as long as you like."

"No," I started to say, and his face looked absolutely devastated.

"No?" He sounded so defeated.

"I mean, no, I can't answer you now." I tried to make sense. "I mean, just give me a minute. I'm in shock."

He waited for me to continue, but patience never had been a virtue of Aiden's. He fidgeted and shifted in front of me as I tried to gather my thoughts in some kind of coherent manner.

He wanted me for his queen. Aiden, my silly, lovely friend was the prince, and he wanted me for his queen.

I didn't know anything about being a queen. I didn't even know anything about being a *noble*. I didn't know how to act or what my duties would be. I didn't know any foreign languages, and I couldn't even imagine hosting parties for visiting ambassadors without accidently insulting them somehow.

But despite all of that, all of the reasons I should say no, I couldn't look away from him, and I couldn't forget the way it felt to dance in his arms or the way he looked at me as if I were the only one in the room. I wanted that. I wanted to keep that forever. I wanted to keep *him*. Because, most of all, I couldn't imagine my life without him.

I loved him.

"First, I think . . . I want to say that I think I might love you too," I said haltingly, reaching to touch his bare cheek. He shuddered under my touch, looking at me with bright eyes.

"You think?"

I was so overwhelmed I could barely speak. "I don't know. I don't know what I'm feeling, and I don't know what love is supposed to feel like. But I think that's what it is that I'm feeling right now. All fluttery, and like my heart is about to beat straight out of my chest."

His eyes burned into mine. "That's what I'm feeling."

"And I think . . ." I took a huge breath. I was about to take a tremendous risk. "I think I want you to see me too."

He would believe my story, wouldn't he? He knew me well enough to believe that I could never be the Chameleon.

"Evie . . ."

"Yes. I want you to see me." I was determined now. I gently pulled my hands from his and began to unwind the ribbons that wove into my hair. Finally I undid the clasp that held my mask in place.

I couldn't look at him as I removed it. As I lowered the mask to my lap, there was nothing but silence. A moment passed. Then another.

"Evie." His voice was low and serious. "What is that?"

"It's not what it looks like," I began, then laughed at the turn of phrase. Really? *It's not what it looks like*? But I knew exactly what it looked like—pale and cruel against my skin, still not fully healed. "I mean, it's not a real Mark."

"It looks like the Chameleon's Mark," he said flatly.

"It is. But *he* marked *me.*"

"Who's 'he'?"

"I don't know. He's the one we've been hunting down, remember?"

"Unless he is simply a fabrication to provide a distraction from yourself."

"What?" He couldn't be serious. "You really think that I would do that to you?"

"The Evie I know wouldn't. But now I don't know if that Evie is the real Evie. It could have all been a ruse. There were rumors of the Chameleon being a woman . . ." I could tell he was running through every conversation we'd ever had about the Chameleon. "Marks don't just appear, Evie. Why didn't you tell me when it happened? You said you'd told me everything. Was it all a lie?"

"No!" I cried. "I would never do that. I—" I broke off mid-sentence. I almost told him I *knew* I loved him. I couldn't do that now. Not when he was doubting my every action. He'd laugh in my face.

Instead, I tried a different tactic. "Why would I do that?" I asked in a quiet voice. "What on earth would I have to gain by deceiving you like that?"

"I don't know!" He ran his hands through his hair, frustrated. "Ransom? Conspiracy? It could be anything!"

I gaped at him.

"You know what," he said, grabbing his mask and tying it back on hastily, "forget it. I'm not going to sit here and listen to this."

"Fine then! Run away!" I shouted as he yanked the door open, the wind blowing bitterly in my face. "I look forward to your announcement at midnight!"

He turned around to face me once more, glaring ferociously. "You will never speak to me again. And I hope I never see you again." Momentarily the anger on his face dissolved, replaced by a look of pure pain. My heart burned inside me as I realized that this expression, this devastating pain, was my fault. But all too soon the sadness was gone; his face returned to the steely mask of anger again.

Oh, how much of ourselves we hide behind these masks, I thought.

He stormed off, and I broke my promise again as I broke down in tears.

TWENTY-FIVE

ONCE THE TEARS SUBSIDED, I WAS ANGRY. NO, I was beyond angry—I was *furious.*

I decided I was being stupid, wasting tears over Aiden. I stalked back toward the castle, suddenly wanting nothing more than to be out of these clothes that he'd deigned to give to me. I didn't want anything more to remind me of him—as impossible a task as that was. I even left Hachi by the tree.

When I got back to the palace, I heard the bells chime, declaring the midnight hour had come. The prince— Aiden—was supposed to make his announcement now.

No one would be paying attention to anything else, so I chanced my usual route and tore down the hall to my room. I all but ripped my dress off and pulled on my working dress.

The party was clearly still in full swing, with shouts and hollers echoing all through the palace, but I couldn't stand to hear any more of it. I was too angry.

So I ran. I ran out of the palace with no clear destination in mind. The lamplit streets were filled with the middle classes, celebrating in their own way since they couldn't procure an invitation to the palace's Masquerade.

It was easy to maneuver through the crowds; no one paid any attention to a server this late at night. No one paid any attention to a server ever.

I didn't know where I was going until I got there—my old neighborhood. What if someone saw me? What if Aiden sent someone to arrest me? This would be the first place they'd look.

Scowling and mentally beating myself up, I turned right around, trying to think of a place they wouldn't look for me. Or really, trying to think of any place where someone kind enough would take me in.

Arianna.

It was worth a shot. She might be kind enough to let me in, but even if she didn't, I'd be in the Lace District, a place with all sorts of hidden holes-in-the-wall. It might not be the safest place for a female like me, but thanks to Aiden's defense lessons, I could probably defend myself long enough to get away.

I weaved my way through the crowded streets again until I reached the canals. People lined the edges, but the canal itself was deserted. Too many people in the past had imbibed a little too liberally and drowned while trying to spend their night of frivolity on the boats. I was surprised so many people were even this close to the edge.

Either way, it wasn't good news for me. I needed a water taxi. It was too far for me to walk, and I was already growing tired from the sheer emotional exertion I'd been through.

But it looked like I'd have to walk until I found

something else. I walked a good ten minutes until I spotted an empty boat, tied up and unattended.

Promising myself to take careful note of my location so I could return the boat later, I muttered an apology under my breath, untied the boat, and steered myself down the canal.

By the time I'd reached my destination—after two wrong turns—I was exhausted. I prayed that Arianna would have pity on me and just give me a corner to sleep in. And maybe some food. I had some savings to pay her back later.

I struggled to find the same building Aiden had taken me to. We'd only visited it once, but it wasn't that long ago. The main problem was everything looked so different in the dark. Lamps lined the street, casting eerie shadows in the alleys, and everything just felt so much more claustrophobic.

And then there it was. I wanted to cry with joy for finding it. I doggedly ran up to the door and timidly let myself in. On a night like tonight, odds were she was working, and I didn't want to embarrass her into kicking me out on principle alone.

The building was noisy and bustling with life inside, a complete change from the quiet and refined place Aiden and I had visited. I could smell all sorts of delicious foods cooking in the kitchens, and people of all descriptions were laughing and talking in the interconnected rooms. I scanned the crowds, trying to find Arianna, but I couldn't pick her out. If she was even there.

"Can I help you, miss?"

A young Lacie approached me, smiling politely.

"I'm looking for Arianna," I said bluntly. I was too tired for pleasantries.

"I'm sorry to say that she is out at the moment. Is she expecting you?" Her polite smile remained glued in place.

"Not really. I'm a friend of a friend, though we are acquaintances ourselves. I was just hoping to ask her something." I knew it had been too much to hope for.

"Well, can I assist you in any way, or is it something only Arianna can tend to?"

"I really just need a place to hide for a little bit. Just for a night, if that long. And I needed a kind ear."

Her face turned sympathetic, and I could tell she could see past my vague words and really see how much I was hurting. "I'm sorry to hear you're having troubles. I don't know how late Arianna will be out tonight, but you're welcome to wait here. You look terrible, I'm sorry to tell you, and I don't want you roaming the streets. Any friend of a friend of Arianna's is a friend of a friend of mine," she said with a real grin this time, "and I'm finished for the night, so if you'd like to borrow an ear or two, mine are free."

I was touched by her kindness. "Thank you," I said earnestly. "Truly. But I think this is something only Arianna should hear. It . . . concerns the friend between us."

"I understand. We are all entitled to our own business and secrets, after all. I know that as well as anyone. Can I bring you something to drink at least? You can wait out here. There won't be much traffic through here, believe it or not."

"Some water would be wonderful," I said, feeling my parched throat. "And I'm sorry, but I don't even know your name."

"Oh, how rude of me," she said softly. "My name is Tomoyo. I'll just fetch that water for you. Please have a seat in the meantime."

I sank into one of the plush chairs that adorned the reception area. It was heaven to be off my weary feet. I was sure I'd felt blisters forming all night in the unfamiliar formal shoes, coupled with the mad dash through the city.

Tomoyo returned with a large mug of water. "Here you go, miss. Are you sure there isn't anything else I can do for you?"

From looking at her large eyes, I could tell that she was asking out of sincerity, not politeness. It made me want to cry all over again. And that made me wonder when I'd turned into such a crybaby.

"What you've done for me is already more than I could have hoped for," I told her honestly. "I can't ask for more. I'll just wait."

"If you're sure . . ." She looked hesitant to leave me alone.

I assured her that I was fine, and she took her leave of me. The night's events finally began to catch up with me and an overwhelming sense of drowsiness blanketed my body. Everything felt heavy as lead, from my feet to my eyelids.

I reasoned with myself that Arianna would probably be out late, and that she'd see me when she came in, whether or not I saw her. And I had a feeling Tomoyo would ask her about me regardless, or inform her that I was here if she did miss me. A small catnap wouldn't be such a bad thing right about now, would it?

As soon as I'd curled up and gave myself permission to sleep, sleep came.

It could have been minutes or hours later that a gentle hand shook me awake, calling me back from the heavenly land of slumber. I didn't want to leave—I was happy in my dreams. Nothing could hurt me there.

"My Lady . . . Evelina," a voice called. "Wake up, sweetheart."

I blinked my eyes open until they could focus on the person standing at my side.

"Arianna?"

"Yes, sweetie. I just got here, and I should have known I'd see you here. Please, let's take this up to my room. We have much to talk about."

I tensed, wondering if Aiden had gotten to her first and that she suspected me now too.

Then I realized I was being ridiculous. Hadn't I come here for protection? Or was I really going to start second-guessing everyone I came into contact with? Any hope of me trusting anyone again was completely shattered; did I have to become a paranoid fool as well?

"There will be none of that," she scolded me gently for my hesitation. "I don't know anything of what happened to you. I just know that it had to have involved my lord and that bigger things are going on than you know."

I just blinked at her.

"My room," she prodded.

I was too weary to object. I followed her up the stairs and realized as we ascended to the second floor that the boisterous party had quieted and the sky outside was starting to lighten.

If the night was over, why did I still feel like I was surrounded by darkness?

TWENTY-SIX

"*N*OW BEFORE WE HAVE ANY CONVERSATION," SHE began, pointing me toward a chair and lighting the lamp on the bedside table, "I want to make sure we have all our facts straight. I'm going to assume nothing, and things will go much easier and smoother if you'll do the same."

I nodded my agreement, and she sighed. "Now, I realize that in doing this, I may inadvertently tell some of his secrets, but the risk is worth it, I feel. If everything turns out all right, I feel he'll be thanking me.

"I'm aware of my lord's true identity," she said succinctly. "Are you?"

"As of tonight," I replied glumly.

"And you aren't pleased with the knowledge?" She sounded confused.

"That part didn't bother me so much. It was when the tables were turned that the true displeasure happened," I said.

"I don't understand. Are you something other than you appear to be?"

It was all or nothing. "I'm in hiding. My home was

attacked by the Chameleon a couple months ago. I had nowhere to go, no one to turn to, so I snuck into the palace and worked as a server. I'd known Aiden from before, but only as a boy from a noble family. I thought he was just another noble, one that was my dear friend. After that attack, I couldn't stay where I was. Because he—the Chameleon—marked me. And I needed to find justice somehow."

"When you say marked . . . ?" she trailed off.

I wasn't going to show her. That was far too personal, even for this conversation. But I could tell her. I nodded and held my fingers below my right eye. "He marked me with his own brand."

She gasped, piecing it together. "And my lord . . . *no*."

"Yes," I said grimly. "He believed his eyes rather than his common sense. Rather than me. He told me who he really was, and I spilled my own secrets. But instead of acting like a rational person, he turned on me." I left out the part about the marriage proposal. This situation was already too much of a mess.

"Then this next bit of information may make more sense to you," she said. "He's gone missing. He was supposed to make his announcement at midnight, but he was nowhere to be found."

"He ran away?" I asked, shocked.

"No, that's not it," she corrected me. "The king himself went to fetch him. But in my lord's chambers, instead of the prince himself was a single piece of parchment. Nothing was written on it. Nothing save a Mark."

I gasped. "You don't think—"

"I do think. I almost know," she said, her face tight.

"We both know that the Chameleon was going to infiltrate that Masque somehow. I'm guessing you never saw him?"

I shook my head, my mind still reeling at the possibilities of what could be happening to Aiden right at that moment. "What do they plan to do?"

"We don't know. There have been no demands, no ransom, no threat. It's turned into a waiting game."

I groaned. "Well, what are we supposed to do, then?"

"I'm not sure," she said honestly. "I was hoping you'd have something to add to this equation. We're clearly missing something, but no one knows what."

"Is there any other information about him that you or Aiden might know that I don't?"

She shook her head. "I don't think so. The most we've got is rumors and theories."

"That's better than nothing. And it's all we have right now. Tell me."

She spent the next ten minutes detailing everything she'd ever heard, no matter how ridiculous or absurd it seemed. But nothing seemed absurd enough to be true. Logically, none of the theories made sense.

"Maybe we should go back to the palace," I finally suggested with a heavy heart. I might be infuriated with Aiden, but I didn't want to see him hurt. I just didn't want to see him, period.

"I think that's our only option at this point. The Masque is over now. They kept as many guests as they could for as long as they could in hopes of finding something out that way, but everyone has an alibi. No one's there now except palace workers and guards."

Something struck me. "What if it was a palace worker who did it? Someone who went under disguise, like me?"

"What would be the point of stealing a mask for the ball, then?" she pointed out.

"I don't know, but didn't I essentially do the same thing to move around freely? I snuck into the ballroom. I'm sure anyone with half a brain would have been able to do the same."

"Has there been anyone suspicious that you've seen?"

"Not really, but I work with the girls in the kitchens. The Chameleon is a man, remember? I think he'd have to be somewhere where I wouldn't see him too. He wouldn't risk being recognized by me."

"Did he know you were there?"

"I don't think so. Maybe he did?" I groaned. "I don't know. Let's just head back and keep thinking on our way."

She agreed, and we continued to strategize as we made the trek back to the palace. *Strategize* was perhaps too strong a word, though, because nothing we planned would really work. We had too little information. In order to help Aiden, we needed more.

I'd planned to take Arianna down to my room so she could see how I'd snuck into the ballroom, but when we reached the doors, one of the guards called out to me.

"Hey, you! Evelina, right?" It was Matteo, the guard I had met on my first day at the palace. He looked grim as he beckoned me.

"Yes?" I asked, nervous. Too late I realized that perhaps the smarter action would have been to run, if Aiden had given the order to arrest me on the grounds that *I* was the Chameleon.

I quickly glanced around, looking for an escape, but I had nowhere to go.

"I have orders to take you to his highness, the king." He looked at me seriously.

"To the king?" I asked in horror. No one got taken directly to the monarchs. Had Aiden seriously been that angry?

Matteo nodded. "Didn't tell me what for. My orders were simply to stand guard here until I saw you, and then take you to him."

"I'm not under arrest or anything?"

He managed a laugh. "You? Little lady, what did you do? Aside from forgetting to bring me my dinner?"

I was too tense to even smile at his joke. I was a little offended that he dismissed me so quickly, but I pushed my pride aside and realized it was probably for the better. I looked at Arianna, unsure of what to do.

"Should I accompany her?" Arianna asked the guard.

He shrugged. "Might as well. All I know is things are all in an uproar. If you know anything, go with her and tell all you know. Everything else has been put on hold until we find the prince."

Leaving another guard at the doors, Matteo led us through the winding hallways and staircases to an unfamiliar wing of the palace. We stopped in front a collection of doors in a long, well-lit hallway. My stomach folded itself into all sorts of knots as I anticipated what could possibly be behind these doors.

"These are the prince's chambers," Matteo told us. "The king, queen, and a few advisors are in here waiting for you. I will announce you, so follow me please."

I shot a panicked look at Arianna, whose painted white face was the perfect mask of calm. She gave me a tight, small smile in an attempt to calm me down, but it didn't help. I was about to meet the king and queen. Not only that, but I was about to meet Aiden's parents! And I still didn't know what he'd told about our evening.

But the guard opened the doors before I was ready and announced us anyway. I followed first, with Arianna a step behind me. She came to stand beside me and curtsied deeply. I clumsily tried to do the same.

"Evelina," the Speaker addressed me. I was too frightened to look at her and kept my eyes on the floor. Was this the part where I was sentenced to some horrible fate? "Evelina, please don't be afraid to look up. We need your assistance."

That brought my eyes up as I stared at her in shock. "Pardon?"

"The prince is missing," she said gravely. "Not just missing—stolen away. When he was supposed to be making his engagement announcement, he was nowhere to be found. Guards were sent to retrieve him from his quarters, but they found this note instead." She handed me a small folded piece of parchment. The following words were written in a scrawling script:

As love was stolen from me,
So shall the prince be stolen from his kingdom,
And nothing but love can bring him back.

A seal in the shape of the Mark on my cheek was the only signature, but there was no doubt it was from the Chameleon.

I stared at the paper in my hands, shaking my head in disbelief. "Sire," I said, addressing the king, "I mean no disrespect, but this can't have anything to do with me. He ran away from me after I confessed that I loved him. I don't know what happened to him after that, but I don't think I can help you." His running away wasn't a direct result of my confession, granted, but that didn't change the fact that he'd run away and left me alone.

The king shook his head firmly and looked at the Speaker. "His highness has no doubt that you are the one we need," she said gently. "And if I may be so bold, neither do I. The prince spoke of nothing but you. He was undeniably in love."

My heart suddenly lodged itself in my throat, and I involuntarily took a step back. "That can't be," I repeated, my voice thick.

Then, to my absolute shock, the king spoke. To *me*. It was one thing for him to speak to nobility and councilors, but to a mere serving girl? I was so stunned I nearly missed his next words. "But it *is*," he said, as the queen looked at him in alarm. "Oh, don't look at me like that, my dear," he chided her gently. "Time is precious right now, and I'm not going to let a dying tradition eat it all up."

My eyes couldn't open any wider, nor my thoughts race any faster. The *king* was speaking to me. The situation was so much more than I expected. I struggled to rein my thoughts in, to concentrate on what the king was saying, and to think about how to help.

The king sighed deeply. "My son has told us a great deal about you, Evelina. I know how close you two have become and how important you are to him. I was hoping you could shed some light on what happened last night. All we know is that the last time I saw my son at the ball was right before he said he was going to meet you. I knew what he was going to offer you. I haven't heard from or seen him since. When he didn't reappear to make his announcement, I sent two guards to his room, hoping he'd be there. What they found was this note," he said, gesturing toward the paper still in my hand. "And we haven't found or heard anything else since that discovery. Please, what happened?"

"Sire," I said, my voice shaking. "Of course. I will do whatever I can to help find him again."

Pushing aside any residual anger, I told him what I could. I told him how I'd been the victim of a Chameleon attack and sought refuge in the palace as a server. I told him how Aiden had helped me, but all of this seemed to be old information, as his face betrayed no surprise at anything I told him. Even after I told him how Aiden had provided the mask and dress for me, he remained unshaken.

"You tell me things I already knew or suspected," he said. "Aiden spoke to me often regarding you, I feel I need to remind you. What happened last night?"

"He said he wanted to tell me something important, and we needed to go someplace private. He took me to, um . . ." I shot a glance around the room at all the listening ears and couldn't bring myself to betray Aiden's confidence about his secret room. "To where he goes when he wants to escape."

The king nodded to show he understood and motioned for me to continue.

"I didn't know he was the prince until he told me

then." I couldn't bring myself to tell them of how we'd removed our masks—that seemed too personal to share with a roomful of strangers, not to mention his parents. And it wouldn't help find him. "In turn, I told him some things about me. We fought. He ran off," I finished helplessly. "That was the last I saw of him. I was angry, and I ran back to my old home and then to Arianna's. She told me what happened and we came back here."

The king frowned. "That still doesn't tell us much. When did you last see him?"

"I don't know," I said, but then I remembered hearing the bells toll. "Wait! It was just before midnight."

His eyes lit up. "That gives us a precise timeframe, then. You there." He pointed to two of the guards. "Go search the area from the north gate to the tree line. See if there are any signs of struggle or anything at all that might have been from the prince."

They bowed and hurried to follow his orders.

"I still think he managed to make it all the way back to his room," he murmured. "Why else would the note be here . . ."

I glanced around the room. "Sire, what do you think the note means? What am I supposed to do? And how?"

"I should think it would be obvious what you are meant to do." He sounded surprised that I would ask. "It can only be one thing—you, as the one he loves and who loves him, are meant to bring him back." He paused. "Do you mind my asking what you two fought about? It surprises me you would fight on a night like that. You *do* love him. Why else would you be here?"

I froze.

"I understand that this might be difficult for you," the Speaker said while the queen whispered in her ear. "But this is our son. *Anything* might be a clue."

She was breaking my heart. I had no choice. I turned slowly and kept my eyes glued to the floor. "I told you—and him—that I'd been in a Chameleon attack. I neglected to tell you both, out of pride and shame but nothing more, that I'd been marked during that attack. That man tore off my mask and branded me with his Mark."

There were audible gasps around the room, and I pressed forward.

"When I finally told Aiden this, he thought I'd been lying to him all along—that *I* was the Chameleon. Nothing I could say could persuade him otherwise."

"How can we be assured he wasn't right?" the king asked, frowning. "If our son, who loved you enough to reveal himself, didn't believe you, how can we?"

"Because I have nothing to gain from this!" I shouted in exasperation and hurt. I immediately apologized when I saw their shocked faces. No one shouted at royalty. "I'm sorry, your majesties. But truly, I have nothing to gain here. I never knew he was the prince before tonight—I didn't think anyone did. And before I knew he was missing, I just wanted to be left alone. Aiden is the last person I wanted to see."

The queen placed a hand on her husband's arm, and they exchanged a glance—the kind that said more than words ever could.

"My son is a fool," the queen said firmly, without the aide of the Speaker. My eyes shot up to meet hers. They were glistening with unshed tears. "It is clear to me that you care for him, and I've met you for only five minutes."

"Why didn't he believe me?"

"Because he was vulnerable," she said simply. "He was so vulnerable. And he can be a bit stupid, sometimes. I am so sorry, dear."

TWENTY-SEVEN

A YOUNG PALACE SERVANT DELIVERED ANOTHER note containing instructions on where I should go, and things happened quickly after that. The servant was immediately questioned, but he couldn't provide any useful information. The note had been passed to one of the runners by an ordinary looking boy who was now nowhere to be found. It was only when the runner brought it to his master, thinking it was only another piece of news, that he realized how important it was.

I was to go to an old neglected manor that had been abandoned after it had been flooded a few years ago. I'd heard stories of it being haunted from neighbors that came to the market, but apparently it was being used for some-thing more criminal. Only a handful of guards would be allowed to accompany me for fear of the Chameleon harm-ing Aiden at the sight of an encroaching army. The king and queen would stay at the palace, preparing more men if they needed to attack the manor, and Arianna had been sent away on a mission of her own.

I protested at first, insisting that someone better

suited should retrieve the prince, by force if necessary, but the king wouldn't hear it. The Speaker explained for him, "You're the best way to solve this without any fighting. We're in a time of peace. Our defense force isn't prepared for this sort of attack." It seemed once we were out of Aiden's room, the haze broke and the weight of tradition was too heavy to ignore.

"I still don't know what I should do."

"You won't be entirely alone, and plans are being made in case this one fails," the Speaker unsuccessfully tried to soothe me.

"It's time!" a guard called out, and I was ushered into a carriage, carried down to the canals, transferred to a gondola with four men-at-arms, and rushed down the waterways.

Before I knew it, we were at the manor. The sun was low, and the sky turned an ominous shade of purple in the fading light of dusk. Lights flickered down at us from the windows.

I would have been impressed if I hadn't been so terrified. The manor had clearly been magnificent once, and even then an eerie sort of beauty hung over it. Overlooking the ocean, it was quite large and imposing despite the half-collapsed roof and the bushes and vines claiming the walls. As we stepped ashore, I looked at one of the guards in alarm. "We're not just going to walk up to the front door, are we?"

He shrugged. "The simplest approach is often the best. Besides, he's sure to be expecting you."

I couldn't argue with his logic. The servant girl at the door took one look at me and ran inside without a word.

Baffled, I stared at the closed oak door for a moment before it opened again, revealing another servant, an older boy this time, in a plain black mask.

"You were expected, Miss Evelina, and I am pleased to bid you enter. Your company, however, is not welcome and is asked to please wait outside."

Looking to the guard again for direction, I saw him nod, and he said, "It is as we expected. If there is no other way, then we will wait for her return here."

"Those are my orders."

"Very well."

He had to give me a little push, but soon enough I was through the door. I looked back over my shoulder one last time, hoping the sight of my guards would instill some measure of confidence. Instead, I saw the young servant girl, this time with a heavy veil over her nose and mouth, brush past me with several small bundles in her hands.

Before I could shout a warning, she hurled them at the guards. The bundles exploded in a silver cloud of powder and smoke. The guards shouted in alarm and began coughing violently as the girl slipped back inside and the heavy doors swung shut, blocking them from sight.

I expected them to charge the door, but I only heard a moment's more shouting before all went silent.

"Poison," the boy leading me explained simply. "You were instructed to come alone."

"They were going to wait outside!" I protested, horrified.

"Don't be so naïve. How were we supposed to trust the word of the enemy?" He shrugged and spoke as if the subject bored him. "Besides, this way is easier. Don't worry, it was only a sleeping powder. We'll return them once this is all over, good as new."

Dumbstruck, I wiped my clammy palms against my skirts as I was led down corridor after corridor, fighting to remember which way I'd come. The air was damp and heavy, and stank of decay.

Finally, we came to a large open ballroom, flickering with candlelight. Curtains that had once been fine silks were now nothing more than ratty pieces of cloth draped on the walls. Some were pulled to the side to reveal small alcoves.

The boy led me to one of those alcoves and directed me to sit on a mossy stone bench. "You're to wait here, miss."

I nodded.

"And you're to remain silent. That is vital," he warned me, and I watched a more intimidating man step out from behind a curtain with trepidation. "If we feel you're unable to do so, we will have to take measures to ensure you make no noise. Do you understand?"

I nodded again, feeling as if I'd been struck mute. I might have been expected, but I couldn't have been welcome. Everything felt wrong. My skin itched and the hair on the back of my neck stood up straight.

Another moth-eaten curtain was drawn over the alcove's opening, sheer enough that I could still see through it, though only barely. I knew the light was dim enough that no one would be able to see me. Even without the curtain I was hidden in shadow.

We waited in silence. I don't know for how long. I heard my heart pound in my ears and struggled to keep my imagination under control. Were they going to torture me in some way? Or hurt Aiden in front of me?

The sound of shuffling feet drew my attention, and I peered through the thin fabric. I could just make out the shapes of men, one of which looked all too familiar.

I stifled a gasp, ignoring the dirty look from my guard as Aiden spoke angrily. "What is it you want from me? You don't want me dead or you'd have done it already."

"No, I don't want you dead." The voice that answered was cold, and a chill raced down my spine when I realized how both familiar and unfamiliar it was. "I want you to suffer."

The memory of that terrible night flashed before my eyes and that face expanded to more than just the Mark.

Joch.

It had been Joch all along.

How had I been so blind? How many hours had I spent alone with him, learning from him, *admiring* him? I felt sick, my stomach churning and threatening to empty itself. I swallowed thickly, forcing my body to obey, and the Chameleon continued.

"I have someone I'd like you to meet," he continued conversationally. "A young woman whom I'm sure you're quite familiar with."

I braced my shoulders, sure that he meant me. But the servant shook his head, and the guard held up a strip of fabric, silently questioning if he should gag me.

Instead, I watched as another woman—already gagged and hands bound—was brought before him.

Joch held Aiden back as he called out my name, and I instantly understood.

The other girl could easily pass for me in this dim light and from this distance. Worst of all, I realized with a shock and a surge of anger, she was wearing my glass mask—the one I'd spent hours and days toiling over, the one I was waiting to show Aiden on a special occasion, and the one I'd made with Joch right beside me. This girl wore it with a simple black silk backing to make it opaque, and the gold caught the flickering light of the torches around us. It was beautiful, and it should have been mine.

My heart sank, and I felt cold.

The girl did not speak, but Aiden had enough to say for everyone. "Evie, I'm so sorry," the words burst from him. "I shouldn't have said any of those things, and I know you could never be what I accused you of. I was stupid and scared, and I never should have run from you."

A little bubble of hope started to form inside me. Though I was still hurt, it helped to hear he knew how stupid he was.

"I'll do whatever I can to make it up to you, I swear it. Anything at all—just name it."

"How sweet." Joch's voice dripped with sarcasm. "You know, I was in a situation similar to this one. Fell in love, swore I'd do anything for her. And you know what happened, my prince?" I watched in horror as my double walked over to Joch and wrapped her arms around his waist. "She was taken from me."

"No!" I cried out, but the guard already had his hands over my mouth and was working to gag me before I could make enough noise to be heard across the room.

"I don't understand." Aiden sounded so small and confused. "Evie?"

"What if I told you all your accusations were correct?"

Joch asked patiently. "Or that your timing for your apology was all wrong?"

"I don't believe you. I refuse to believe you. You've done something to her."

"The evidence is right in front of your eyes. Does she look at all afraid to you? Or like she's being forced into something she doesn't want? You were right the first time."

I couldn't take it anymore. I bit down on my captor's hand and let my body go slack, the deadweight pulling him off-balance enough that I could squirm around and kick him twice—hard—where I knew it would do the most damage. He grunted and curled in on himself as I ripped the gag from my mouth and cried out, "No, Aiden! It's a lie!"

The servant rounded on me, trying to silence me, but the damage had been done—and I knew how to deal with unwanted fingers in my face. The boy was smaller than Aiden and was on the floor in no time at all. I whipped the curtain aside and ran out to where I could be seen.

Aiden stared at me in confusion, mouth open, as Joch frowned.

"Why would you do this to him when you've been through the same thing?" I demanded.

"Because breaking him is the only way to bring my love back!"

I stared at him, dumbfounded.

He sneered at me, all traces of the man I thought I knew gone from his hard dark eyes. "I know you heard the gossip about me. About Tatiana. The girl I came to this country for, the girl I've been hunting for all this time. The girl *your prince* stole from me."

"I did no such thing," Aiden interjected, but Joch silenced him with a look.

I almost pitied him for a moment before questioning him again. "But why go through all the trouble of working as a mask maker in the palace? Why teach me glass blowing? Why did you even talk to me?"

His eyes slid to mine in an exasperated expression. "It was easier. You wouldn't give up, and eventually that would draw attention, which was the last thing I wanted. I was sent here with a mission, and if I completed that mission, I would get Tatiana back."

My eyes narrowed. "Who sent you?"

"Someone with connections." He sounded tired of the conversation. "Someone that could help, and that's all I cared about."

"And your mission?"

"To dispose of the prince, of course. And to hurt him the way he hurt me."

"Then why all the others? Why *my father*?" My voice cracked.

A brief flash of recognition and something like remorse flickered in his eyes, but it disappeared so quickly I must have imagined it. "I didn't pick the targets. I just did the work. He was a means to an end."

Aiden had had enough. Joch's callous last words were enough to provoke the sleeping dragon that was his temper.

Until that point, he'd been frozen in place, but then he was burning for some action. He punched Joch squarely in the jaw before he could defend himself, and the action seemed to be a signal for Joch's men to descend upon us.

TWENTY-EIGHT

HE MEN SWARMED FROM OUT OF NOWHERE, rapiers at the ready, as they surrounded us. The girl Joch brought with him—the one who was meant to be me—melted behind the wall of fighters and disappeared. Joch watched with an unreadable expression as Aiden rose to his full height, then crouched into a fighting position I knew well.

"I know you're good, Aiden, but you can't fight all of them," I hissed as I automatically went to protect his back. My knife sheath was cool against my skin but hardly reassuring. I doubted I could even draw it before being cut down. "They have *swords*."

"Watch me," he growled back and then lunged at Joch. The Chameleon laughed and dodged neatly away, a burly guard taking his place and swinging at Aiden.

The guard managed to catch Aiden's side, and he let out a choked cry, glaring at the man. Not to be deterred, Aiden dropped to the floor and knocked the guard's legs out from under him, then quickly seized his arms and relieved him of his sword. Armed, Aiden turned again to glare at Joch while the other men awaited orders.

"Fight me," Aiden whispered, a threatening timbre to his voice that I'd never heard before. It gave me shivers, and I looked around us, my heart pounding in my ears.

Joch met his gaze for a long moment, head tilted to one side as if considering his offer. Then he shook his head, ever so slightly. "With pleasure."

He drew a rapier from the guard standing behind him and shifted easily into a perfect form. Without even a single strike, it was clear he knew how to fight.

Aiden slipped into position as well, his hand coming away red from where the guard had already struck him.

"Aiden," I whispered anxiously.

He didn't take his eyes off his opponent. "Don't worry about me," he said in a clipped voice. "That's my job, remember?"

I choked out a laugh despite the situation.

The two men circled one another, each weighing the other, searching for weaknesses. I couldn't tear my eyes away.

I'd never fought Aiden with any weapon other than my small knife, but it was clear he'd been trained thoroughly. He looked perfectly in control, his body tense with anticipation.

Finally Joch struck, quick as a snake, and the sound of metal on metal rang out as Aiden blocked him. I winced with every blow as Joch attacked again and again, putting Aiden on the defensive.

Joch shouted in triumph as a line of red seeped through Aiden's left sleeve across his bicep. I cried out, and it was all I could do to keep myself in place as Aiden glared at his attacker, ignoring his wound.

Then, suddenly, it was Aiden on the offensive. The room was silent save for the sound of their weapons, their footsteps on the stone floor, and their breathing, all echoing too loudly in the enormous ballroom. Their rapiers moved too fast for my eyes to follow as Aiden began a complicated series of attacks: right, left, and center. Joch's face lost his cocky expression as he concentrated and then contracted in pain as Aiden landed a solid blow to his right shoulder.

It wasn't enough to stop Joch, but it was enough to send him across the room, momentarily out of Aiden's reach. Joch bent over, gasping for air. When I looked back to Aiden, he was covered in a thin sheen of sweat and his mouth was tight with pain, but he clearly wasn't going to stop anytime soon.

Joch seemed to reach the same conclusion as he straightened.

"Well fought, prince," he said in a low, breathy voice. Then he simply turned and slipped outside the ring of guards. As Aiden's eyes flitted to mine, I knew he wanted to chase the Chameleon down, but he couldn't leave me behind. I doubted he would even have the strength to run for very long, let alone continue the fight.

Again, I thought of my knife, feeling as if it suddenly weighed three times its normal weight.

"Things aren't looking so good, Evie," Aiden murmured to me as I ran to his side, the animalistic sound gone from his voice, replaced for the first time with concern.

"Now *really* isn't the time for talking, Aiden," I said through clenched teeth, looking over his injuries. His sleeve was completely drenched in blood, and his clothes were cut from hits I'd missed earlier, each cut rimmed with red.

"It might be the only time."

"I never thought you were so pessimistic."

"Do you have something up your sleeves that I don't know about that's got you so optimistic? Because I would love to hear about it right now."

The doors to the ballroom swung open, and I couldn't have planned the timing better if I'd tried. In poured Arianna and a half dozen Lacies, followed by at least twenty fresh men in royal guard uniforms. As soon as Aiden saw them, he groaned. "Like that. *That* would have been nice to know about."

I flashed him a grin, then glanced in the direction Joch had fled. Aiden followed my gaze then looked at me with a grim expression. "Don't you dare follow him on your own," he threatened me.

"I have to," I replied, just as grim. "You're bleeding, if you haven't noticed. You'd pass out before you caught him."

He looked down, and I honestly think he was surprised to see blood. He gripped my arm. "Don't. Please."

"I have to," I repeated, pleading now. "He killed my father, stole my life, and *betrayed* me. I can't just watch him run away."

Even as the battle swirled around us, he said, "I need to tell you something."

"Is now really the time?"

"I don't care! It needs to be said!"

"I already heard your apology, even if it was to the wrong person." I could see him cringe even as he used his stolen rapier to block and disarm an attacker.

"I meant it, though. Every word. And I understand if you never want to speak to me again. But," he hesitated before finding his way directly in front of me, "there is one more thing I have to do, in case I don't see you after this."

"Of course you'll see me—"

His hand roughly cupped my chin, cutting my words off as his lips pressed against mine in a hurried, desperate breath of a kiss.

I didn't have time to react before he pulled back, looking as sheepish as he could while incapacitating a man who dared to interrupt.

"I just needed to do that once."

I stumbled back out of the reach of a particularly long-limbed guard, my eyes wide, cheeks burning, and lips tingling. Aiden's eyes wouldn't meet mine, but that could have been because they were needed elsewhere. He pressed his lips together as he swung at another oncoming guard with a grunt.

"Q-quit being so dramatic, Aiden," I stammered. "We'll talk once we get you home, all right?"

Either that offer was good enough for him, or he had no more breath to spare on arguing. He was swept back up into the madness of battle while I slipped away, though not without being hit a few times.

Once out of the ballroom, I headed in the direction Joch had gone, trying to think a step ahead of him. Obviously he'd be looking for a way out—it was much too dangerous for him to hide here. I turned my path to the short pier we'd docked by, and sure enough he was there, out of breath and preparing a gondola by lamplight, favoring the shoulder Aiden hit.

I could hardly make him out, but I was burning with the need to fight, and I drew my knife.

The sound of steel on leather caught his attention, and he whirled to face me, the white of his wide eyes bright in the lamplight. He stopped untying the knots of the rope that secured the gondola and faced me, legs wide and braced for an attack.

He surprised me by chuckling first, though. "So. You're going to fight me? Is this how it's going to end? Cut down by one woman while in search of another."

"Don't you dare act the victim," I said, my voice low. "You deserve whatever I do to you."

"You were a casualty of war. You cannot blame the soldier for following orders."

"Can't I?" I narrowed my eyes. "Tell me, Joch, was she worth it? Was she worth killing innocent people?"

"I would do anything to get her back. I have nothing else to give and nothing else for anyone to take."

"You had human decency."

He let out a hard laugh. "What use is decency when you're alone in the world? I don't regret anything I did for her."

"Your note . . . you said love could bring the prince back. Was that just another lie?"

"Of course. For a country that hides behind masks, your people are far too trusting. I simply needed you here in case anything went wrong. Your prince is rather unpredictable." He smirked.

I saw red. Every single one of Aiden's lessons fled from my mind, and I relied on pure reflex and muscle memory to attack. I jumped forward, swinging the knife and barely catching his jaw on the side opposite his Mark. I cut enough to make it bleed, but not enough to really hurt him. It shocked me to land a hit, to draw blood with so little force.

He took me seriously then. He frowned, wiping away the thin droplets of blood. "You're not a target, you know," he said so quietly that I could barely hear him over the water lapping at the shore. "I don't need to fight you."

"Well, I need to fight you," I retorted, adrenaline pumping through me, amplifying every move he made. I sprang forward again, slashing at him and pushing him back toward the edge of the pier.

He didn't try to fight back, and that made me angrier. "Fight!" I shouted at him as he continued to dodge me until he had no room left to retreat.

He looked at me one last time while I caught my breath and steeled myself for another attack. Pity that I didn't understand appeared in his eyes.

And then, before I could do anything more, he jumped off the pier and disappeared into the inky darkness.

"No!" I shouted after him, almost throwing my knife into the water in frustration. I knew that by the time I got a boat ready, he'd be long gone, and I had no chance of catching him by swimming after him. "No," I whispered again, sinking into a crouch and staring into the darkness. His abandoned lantern still flickered behind me, taunting me. I'd been so close, and he'd slipped away.

I'd find him again. I had Aiden by my side, and he could find anyone and anything.

At the thought of Aiden, my heart stuttered and my cheeks warmed, until I remembered the chaos I'd left behind me.

When I returned to the hall, the fighting was over. I drifted over to one of the alcoves where I could rest and attempt to recover, which is where Arianna found me.

I smiled at her, my gratitude outweighing my weariness. "Tell me how you knew the exact moment we needed you."

She laughed. "A Lacie never reveals her secrets. But I will tell you that the king sent me ahead of you to help keep you safe. He thought that if you didn't know about us, it was less likely for the Chameleon to discover us. And he knew that a Lacie is as well-trained in defense as in any other art, and that we'd work more quickly. As soon as we heard of your arrival, we came as swiftly as we could. This place is like a maze, or we would have been here sooner."

"I'm just glad you came at all," I said, my shoulders sagging.

"Let's get you back to the palace and cleaned up. I'm sure your prince will be demanding your attention all too soon."

I grimaced, unsure of how I was even going to handle that. "Let's take this one step at a time. I'll worry about what to say to Aiden when neither of us is bleeding."

TWENTY-NINE

I DIDN'T SEE AIDEN FOR A WEEK. HE WAS confined to his rooms as the royal physician fawned over him, and while I could have sought him out, I was too sore and exhausted both emotionally and physically.

Iniga came to me immediately, emotional and full of apologies. "I can't believe I didn't recognize you," she sobbed as she sat next to my bed, helping me with my breakfast.

"It's not your fault," I reassured her. "That was the point, not to be recognized."

"But still," she protested. "I should have known. And *Joch*," she moaned theatrically. Despite the guilt I felt at letting him escape, I had to fight not to smile. "You should have told me something."

"Iniga," I said firmly. "It wasn't your fault. I didn't tell you because I didn't want to get you in trouble. You and I both know how hard it is for you to keep a secret. And you didn't talk to Joch if you could help it. *He* didn't talk if he could help it. I forbid you to feel bad."

She sniffed and gave me a dirty look, though I could see she was fighting a smile too. "That's cheating."

I shrugged and grinned. "Nothing more can be done. There's no point in moaning over the past when the present is still so messy."

She sobered. "I still can't believe Aiden was the prince. Is there anyone out there who is actually who they say they are anymore?"

Rumors flew around the palace after everything was said and done, and it became widely known that the prince had his own secret identity, though it wasn't really known what that identity was. I'd confided in Iniga when she first came to see me, with permission from the royal family. I was worried that she might be in danger if she didn't know, and it'd been nice to tell someone the whole story. However, it also made everything feel much more real. Before I'd put it all into words, it sounded like a fairy tale, a mad adventure of storybooks.

"It does explain a few things, though," she said thoughtfully. "Like why I never saw his parents at court. Or why I *thought* I never did. The king and queen—I still can't believe it. And did you know they made the announcement of his safe return *themselves*? They said it was time to let the old tradition die. Everyone in court is talking about how they actually spoke with the prince without realizing it." She shook her head in amazement, then chattered on for a moment more, piecing many of Aiden's mysteries together, and I let my mind wander.

Truth be told, I was terrified of seeing Aiden again.

But I couldn't hide forever, and in the end, Aiden came to me.

Thanks to a bruised skull and some minor scrapes still in the process of healing, I was under orders to rest in my room, but I was restless and without supervision, so I often got up and went for long walks on the palace grounds on the pretense of having to walk Hachi. He would have been perfectly content to stay at the foot of my bed after being separated for so long, but I could barely sit still. I was still excused from my duties, or else I would go to the workroom and try to be productive. That didn't stop me from trying, but Milo sent me away immediately.

"Just because you're young doesn't mean you're invincible. Go back to bed and heal properly. I don't want to hear you in here unless there's a healer at your side giving you leave."

I was even so restless as to try to find something to do in the kitchens. I knew Vera would put me to work no matter how bad off I was, but the gossip was too much to handle.

"I heard the prince proposed marriage to someone and was *rejected*."

"No, the girl was a spy from the Northern Islands!"

"My cousin said he hasn't made any public appearances because he's so heartbroken over it."

"Did you hear how he was living a double life? My ma said they do that every generation, but people are forbidden to speak of it. There's no way that can be true, right?"

And so on. I slipped back out into the hallway and refused to go back to the kitchens until some new scandal became the popular gossip. Unfortunately, it seemed that was not going to happen anytime soon.

Instead, I found myself wandering the quiet garden paths in the brisk autumn afternoons. In my defense, I thought the fresh air would do me some good.

Apparently, someone felt the same for Aiden.

I saw him sitting alone—unusual—under an ivy-covered trellis. Frozen and caught unawares, I ordered myself to turn around, but I couldn't walk away from him. Then he looked up and I knew I had no excuse.

His lips quirked up in a small smile, but it was plain to see how uncertain he was around me. "Evie."

"Aiden," I greeted him hesitantly. "You're alone out here?"

"It's hard to believe, isn't it?" he said wryly. "I haven't had a moment to myself since we've returned to the palace or I would have found you sooner."

It dawned on me. "You're waiting out here for me?"

"You're never in your room, and the gardeners mentioned they'd had a visitor the past few days. I put two and two together. Please, come sit by me."

I cautiously stepped forward, my blood pounding in my ears. Surrounded by ivy, it felt like we were completely isolated from the outside world.

"I know you've been avoiding me," he said abruptly. "I can't say I blame you. I still can't believe I said those awful things to you. And you came after me despite it all."

"*I* meant what I said," I replied, then winced at the implications in my voice.

He was quiet for a moment. "I deserved that. I should probably clarify something, though, Evie. I meant what I said, too, when I said I wanted to marry you. I probably shouldn't be saying this now, but I want to marry you now more than ever before. I regretted what I accused you of almost as soon as I left, but the Chameleon attacked and drugged me before I could fix my mistake."

My heart was drumming, my breath coming too quickly.

"I don't dare ask for your hand now. But I'm not giving up on you. I've been granted another year to find a bride before one is chosen for me. Another outdated tradition we're throwing out to sea."

I laughed softly. "I spoke to your parents, you know. When you were taken. They care about you a lot."

"They speak highly of you as well." His eyes searched mine. "Please tell me I'll have a chance to ask you again before that year is up."

My thoughts raced, and while I still felt the sting of his accusations, I also could not forget the way my heart had shattered when I thought he would die and leave me for good. Nor could I forget the warmth that filled me after his brief kiss in the hall. Did his one mistake—granted, a *huge* mistake—undo everything else about us?

"I can't give you a definite answer," I said finally. "But I won't tell you that I'll refuse if you ask me again in a year's time."

He scooped me up in his arms, burying his face against my neck, and I relaxed into his embrace. "That is more than I hoped for, my lady," he whispered.

"Now cheer up," I said wryly. "This somber, woe-be-gone prince does not suit you. I want my charming Aiden back."

He laughed and pulled back, finally smiling. "And who am I to deny my lady-love her wish?"

Just like that, the suffocating tension between us crumbled, and we were simply Aiden and Evie again. A little battered, and a little broken, but all the better for it. At last, nothing more remained hidden.

ACKNOWLEDGMENTS

I WANT TO THANK EVERYONE WHO HAS HELPED raise my book baby: Alissa and the wonderful team at Cedar Fort, for being the fairy godmother to my Cinderella story; Kris, for helping me take that final step; Adair, for being my sounding board and cheerleader; and all my early readers who've stayed with me through the long journey.

Also a huge thank-you to the Internet, particularly my friends and supporters on Tumblr, the hard-working people at NaNoWriMo, the welcoming and helpful writing community, and all the YouTube users who made researching glass throwing so much easier.

And lastly, thank you to my family, for supporting and encouraging me through everything.

DISCUSSION QUESTIONS

1. What masks—literal or metaphorical—do we wear in our lives today?

2. If you lived in their world, what would your mask look like?

3. Imagine you lost everything in one night—home, family, and belongings. Where would you go? What would you do?

4. Evie is forced into many unfamiliar surroundings and must quickly adapt. How do you react to strange or new circumstances?

5. Why do you think Aiden acted the way he did when he saw Evie's face?

6. Do you think the Marking system is fair? Why or why not?

Photo by Stephanie Staples

*L*AUREN SKIDMORE GREW UP IN KANSAS, WITH stints in Ohio and New York, and currently lives in Utah. She attended Brigham Young University where she earned a BA in English teaching and minored in Teaching English as a Second Language and Japanese. She then spent a year in Japan teaching and travelling. She hasn't made it to Europe yet, but it's on the list. She has been to thirty states in the United States so far. When she's not exploring new places, you can probably find her on the Internet with fifteen windows open and looking at just one more thing before actually getting something done.